In the Fields *of* Fatherless Children

ALSO BY PAMELA STEELE

Paper Bird
Greasewood Creek

In the Fields *of* Fatherless Children

A Novel

Pamela Steele

COUNTERPOINT
CALIFORNIA

IN THE FIELDS OF FATHERLESS CHILDREN

This is a work of fiction. All of the characters, organizations, and events portrayed in this novel are either products of the author's imagination or used fictitiously.

First Counterpoint edition: 2026

ISBN: 978-1-64009-760-5

The Library of Congress Cataloging-in-Publication data is available.

Jacket design by Victoria Maxfield
Jacket photograph © Roger May
Book design by Wah-Ming Chang

COUNTERPOINT
Los Angeles and San Francisco, CA
www.counterpointpress.com

Printed in the United States of America

1 3 5 7 9 10 8 6 4 2

For

Beulah Fern
October 1, 1955–April 15, 2015

But love, sooner or later, forces us out of time . . . Of all that we feel and do, all the virtues and all the sins, love alone crowds us at last over the edge of the world.

WENDELL BERRY
Jayber Crow

Part I

Earth

Granny Justice

THEY'S THINGS THAT CAN ONLY BE KNOWED IN THE blood—the Memories, Mommy used to call it—a wordless knowin passed down through the generations. Things experienced in older times and languages that come back to us in dreams like we, ourselfs, had lived them: familiar frozen battlefields, dolls lost and found agin, the way sunlight lays on a wooden floor plank.

If I was yet livin, I'd try to feature what it would've been like for June if things hadn't turned out the way they did. I'd let myself imagine her gone to town, sometimes sensin Grace before she actually seen her—a lectric hum on the back of her neck or the momentary picture of a raw, green leaf turnin and turnin in the coal-black water. When she would look up, she would find the girl, her own child, almost a woman by then, a-standin in a store aisle or a-walkin toward her on a sidewalk, beautiful in the awkwardness of her age, her dark hair a veil over the scar that still yet cuts through her right eyebrow.

June would be certain that Grace won't, cain't remember a particular gray sky, a roar that echoed off the houses and hills, the metal cocoon that pertected her from the angry churnin blackness, or the hands—June's hands—reachin for her, liftin her little body free of that car seat, holdin her to the warmth of June's own. There might would be times she'd come so close June might touch her—so near as to stop June dead for fear Grace might reach through the ether between them, and the girl would look up from whatever had her attention, and then, nerve to nerve, they wouldn't be no way for either to return from the knowin.

That were one way of seein it, I reckon. When you are dead, or *in spirit* as they say now, you're sposed to know why somethin or another happened and what will occur next. That ain't the way it goes. The dead have to wait to find out the future, just like the livin do.

April

IT WAS LATE WHEN JUNE PUT ON THE KETTLE—LATE enough, she hoped, for Isom and Bethel to be asleep. Late enough, for sure, to hear the brittle attic shrinking into its bones, the house beneath it shifting into the steady breath of night. Beyond windows and walls, the soft whir of spring peepers in the snowmelt branch between there and Granny Justice's house, where no lamp had burned in the bedroom window since Granny passed away. Since she was a girl, June had looked for the light that told her Granny was up late reading her Bible or book of the month.

When the water had boiled, she poured most of it into the washtub, then added dipperfuls from the well bucket to cool it enough to tolerate. She stood over the kitchen sink and washed her face with the rest of the kettle water and the Noxzema that Rena gave her last Christmas.

The day had been warm for early April, more summer than spring, and just then, creek-cooled air drifted through the window screen, finding June's skin as she pulled off her shirt and pants, the waistband button already difficult to undo. She reached up and tugged the light string and the room went dark, except for the yard light Isom kept on. She unhooked her bra and stepped out of her panties into the steaming water, sat hugging her knees to her chest.

The water stung her feet and backside, her privates, but she waited it out—remembered those times that Granddaddy took them over to the swimming pool at Twenty-Two Mine, remembered how Rena, Tom, and the cousins dove into the icy, chlorinated water to get the shock over and done, how she'd held back, plodded in a few inches at a time, tried to acclimate to the cramp of cold water against her groin and then the sharp ache of it against her nipples. Truth was, she had always been a little afraid of deep water.

June closed her eyes, let the creek air chill her tender breasts. The hot water still stung her skin below. She shivered, recalled a steaming day last summer when she and Ellis went swimming with her brother Tom and Lena Faye Hall in the holding pond up on the strip mine, how, after Tom had taken Lena Faye to lie on a blanket in the brush, she and Ellis had merely been two heads floating above the oily skin of water, blinded by the glint of minerals that lay on its surface, how their hands and legs sought each other below. She felt safe with him, and that day, she let him kiss her, both of them stunned by the strangeness of kissing in daylight.

She wrung hot water over her shoulders and arms, took the Ivory soap from the seat of a nearby chair, swiped away the sludge it left on the vinyl. She scrubbed herself until the water had gone cool and turned the color of milk.

A car drove past the house, moving up the holler, its headlights catching the undersides of the spring-tender leaves on Granny's sugar maple. It made a metallic scrape as it crossed the bridge to Justice Branch. Probably Roger Dale going home after second shift. The sound of it reminded her of Tom's coming home after late nights with Lena Faye. How she longed to be able to talk to him just then.

A twinge started up in her belly, brought her back to her bath. She wasn't sure whether it was time for the baby to be quickening. It was more like a feeling of absence than presence, a sadness brought on by thinking of Ellis, only weeks before, leaning over the truck seat to push open the door, offering her a chance she would take: a late winter's afternoon ride to Morrison's Drive-In in Myrtle Gap. She went without thinking much of Bethel's disappointment should she be caught in the lie, or of Isom, who might whip her if he found out. She'd gone with Ellis, went skirting the foot of the mountain with the heater blasting and Percy Sledge on the radio. They rode by the green glow of dash light, with the rough heat of Ellis's leg against hers and the scent of British Sterling that would stay on her tongue for hours, her coat collar for days.

Then there was the quiet ride back, the tipple lit up against the bare, hulking mountain and her stepfather somewhere in the tunnels below. Ellis's high beams scything the snow-crusted slate dump. Then, an early turn onto a side road where the startled eyes of night creatures stared from under frozen berry canes. Finally, the shut-off engine and winter stillness, the muffled ribbon of creek water running beneath a skim of ice and snow.

He had turned to her in the darkness and kissed her. And then, again. She heard—felt—his breath and sigh, the roar of his blood in her own body. Her mind ran along behind it, chasing it across startled synapses.

She had let him reach inside her coat and unbutton the

buttons of her shirt, let his hand find her skin. No one had ever touched her there. She shivered.

Are you cold? he'd whispered.

A little, she said. Just then, she'd been picturing her mother at home, opening the stove door, letting orange light into the room as she banked coals for the night. She'd heard Bethel sigh as if she were in the car with them.

Ellis turned the truck key. The sound of the roaring heater, the dash lights shining like a clock face, jarred her back from where she'd gone, reminded her of the hour.

I need to get home, she'd said. But then she had turned her face to his and, just weeks shy of her seventeenth birthday, gave in to the thing they had known was coming since they were kids. And then, just nights later, another parked car—another man—something she couldn't have foreseen. Thinking of it made her ill.

June came back to herself in the kitchen then, stood from the cold bathwater, let it sheet off her body. She ran a hand over the rising hill of her belly, then reached for the towel, buried her face in it, drew a deep breath of sun and outdoor air.

Across the branch, Granny's house was still dark, but there were times that June could swear she saw a light burning from deep in the house. When she pulled down the window to close off the draft, a sudden, soft light struck the glass, then a flood of it on the kitchen floor. June realized that the door had been opened, knew before she turned around who she'd find. Light streamed around her mother, already in her nightgown, standing in the doorway, mouth open, staring at her. Seeing.

Granny Justice

I KNOWED BETHEL'S GIRL WAS IN TROUBLE EVEN AFORE she did, for I could tell it in her eyes. Women get that particular look, like they carry a secret even they don't yet know. I knowed Bethel was pregnant with Corrina, too, before she even knowed. Hit's a story I seen over and over in my livin days, for my mommy was a granny woman, just like cousin Carrie Vance.

By my accounts, the child was made in the wolf moon, the time of year for new beginnings. I do say! I spect that it belongs to that Akers boy, for I seen him drop her off down past my garden a few times. People allus forget that my land goes that far down, with part of it hid by kudzu on the fence and weeds grown up among the willows. I've seen some things from there. Besides, anyone could hear the boy's truck comin for miles. I hope they're in love.

Isom is liable to pitch a walleyed fit after what went on with Rena, Bethel's oldest. He's the touchiest of men, gets riled up over a little bit of nothin, carries a slight forever. He'll try to whup her for share, or worse, put her out, but I don't believe Bethel will tolerate that. They lucked out that Rena and Watt could get married afore she was showin too awful much.

They's a even bigger reason Isom will rage, and that's

because Ellis is not pure white like Isom expects folks to be. He allows for that down in the mine when he's workin alongside folks with darker skin, but he for shore don't aboveground. He's conveniently forgot that Bethel has some Indian in her, but you cain't tell by lookin.

If Isom throws June out, she can go live in my house. Ain't nobody there since I been gone, save me, the roly-poly bugs, and a odd mouse or two. She could have my old bed, and I'd watch over her, wouldn't pester her t'all less I had to.

Sometimes I get to studyin on how life would be different had Bethel's first husband Shag Branham not got hisself killed over on the Yellowjacket Mine road. Honey, he were a corker. He was but twenty-six when he died. Hit tore all of us up when it happened. I loved him like he were one of my own. It like to have killed all of us when we got the news.

Even though this land has been passed down through the generations of women in my family, the old way, I had it in my will that Shag and Bethel would be equal owners after I was gone. Honey, soon as she married Isom Fields, I caught me a ride straight over to Myrtle Gap and had that lawyer, Mr. Fancher, draw up new papers. Hit's Bethel's land now, les Bethel dies first—and I cain't feature she will, for Isom is poorly in his lungs. The scriptures says *Remove not the old landmark; and enter not into the fields of the fatherless.* Isom Fields will not get even a speck of dirt off that land. I'm just liable to scrape it from under the fingernails of his dead hands when the time comes—take it back. He never grew up here, anyways. He's from over to Oceana. No, buddy. When Bethel passes away, this land will go to Rena and June in equal portions if it ain't blasted all to hades by then.

Mostly, though, I just keep to myself and mind my own matters, but I wish I could tell Isom about June's trouble so as to soften the blow—to prepare him and Bethel. I know my situation. They cain't hear me if they ain't listenin for me. They cain't see me if they ain't lookin. Bethel has not welcomed the second sight that the women in our family have. She's awful religious and don't believe in such.

Hit's a sorry thing the way Isom has done them kids. And now he'll punish June for doin somethin he probably did plenty of in his day. It ain't right that women have to carry all the shame. I prayed on it and decided to let it alone. Cain't do nothin about it, no ways.

Fort Campbell, Kentucky

JUNE WATCHED THE BUS PULL AWAY FROM THE STOP. Diesel fumes lingered to mix with the odor of urine that filled the phone booth. She pushed a dime into the slot and dialed the number her brother had scribbled at the bottom of his letter.

Above her, a moth battered the cracked light cover. She grabbed the shelf for the phone book, tried to steady herself, took a deep breath. Stale aftershave on the mouthpiece, layered over the other smells—cigarettes and anxious breath—brought up a small retch. At the other end of the phone line, a pulsing buzz, then the sound of the dime dropping into the change return as she hung up the receiver.

She buckled the folding door, poked out her head into the late-spring evening. Traffic whooshed by on 41-A, sent up fans of rainwater that settled on the storefront parking lot. She surveyed the glittering windows of the dry cleaner, tiny bar, a Chinese restaurant. Across the road, at Gate 4 of the army base, a lighted sign with pictures of a parachute and the head of a bald eagle, the bold black words under them: *101st Airborne.* Beneath the sign, a line of cars waited to drive past the guardhouse. Tom was in there, somewhere among the rows of buildings and columns of lamp-lit trees. She pictured the stark barracks he'd described in his letters and remembered what he'd said when he enlisted on his eighteenth birthday.

I cain't go down in that mine no more, June. It'll kill me for sure.

She'd begged him to stay, to get a job on the state road, to think about his girlfriend Lena Faye, but in the end, he'd said, At least, this way, I'll have a chance of gettin out of here before I kill Isom.

•

June flattened the door against the noise and spray of traffic, pushed the dime back into the slot, dialed again. The phone rang, then a man answered in a peculiar accent—*Somewhere far north of here, farther than Ohio*, she thought—and she asked for Tom. The man told her they'd send a runner for him, and as he said it, his voice cracked some of the words in half. She featured that he probably wasn't yet even eighteen.

Rain tapped an uneven rhythm on the phone booth. June opened the door again and waited. She thought back to an evening last week, when she'd come home from the ball field down in the creek bottom and found her stepfather standing in front of the mirror that hung on the outside wall of the house during warm-weather months. The sun was not yet down, but it skimmed the yard, settled on the diagonal ridges of bone beneath his thin T-shirt.

He'd flattened the creased skin of his face with his fingers, scraped at a pale cheek with the safety razor he kept in a wooden cheese box on the kitchen shelf. He stopped, nodded at June's reflection in the mirror.

June, he said.

Hey, Isom, she'd answered, trying to gauge his mood.

Isom wiped his face with a thin towel, once white but grayed by coal dust, then turned his head from side to side to check his work. He said, Where you been?

Just then, she'd called up a memory of him rubbing his whiskers on her neck when she was a little girl, his stretched-out arms, him laughing and pretending to want a hug. When she went to him, he'd scratch her neck and cheeks with his stubbly face while she squealed—their long-ago game.

She said, Down the road, playing softball in the bottom.

He ran his hand over his face, said, Was hoping you weren't up at Beauty's. Jewel's boarders are drinking this evening and making a racket, and I don't want you walking past there by yourself.

Too late, she thought, as she watched him dip the razor into the soapy water of the wash pan, then bang it on the furrowed rim.

Isom drew the blade from his Adam's apple to his chin. He said, Who all was down to the ball field?

She'd known he would ask, decided to not risk a lie. She hesitated, watched a fault line form on his forehead, then found her words.

Vivian, the Hall boys, Peanut Maynard, some of the Akers kids and some kids from over on Tomblin Branch.

Isom dabbed the corner of the towel at a spot of blood on his chin. He turned to face her, said, Them half-breed kids of Sol's? That mean that Ellis boy, too?

Her sweat-damp shirt went cold against her body. Yes, sir, she'd said.

You know he was gonna be there?

Cold water swirled up inside her. No, sir, she lied.

Inside the house, a pot lid fell in the kitchen, vibrated like a cymbal against the cement below the yellow linoleum. The odor of boiling cabbage wafted through the screen door.

Isom eyed June. The V-neck of his T-shirt sagged, showed the sheen of pale skin stretched thin over his puffed-out rib cage. She pictured the lungs beneath it, full of coal dust and quartz crystals, pushing against his ribs, eating away at muscle. He looked so much older than he was.

He said, What did I tell you about that Akers boy? They's no way I'll ever allow that. Solomon can keep his half-breeds on their side of the mountain.

I didn't know he would be there, she said again.

She fought the impulse to run but kept her eyes on his. In her memory, he had never struck her—maybe he was too sick and worn-out by the time she came of age—but she had seen him throttle a silent, flinching Tom with the backs of his knuckles when the coal bucket got empty or there was melted plastic in the burn barrel. And not very long ago, when he learned of Rena's pregnancy, she had seen him force her sister into the corner of their bedroom, threatening her with a belt, Rena crying and screaming the whole time. Bethel had finally stepped between them, and June still wondered if he would have actually hit Rena. Not too long after that, Rena and Watt ran off to Pikeville to get married, six months before Charlie was born.

Isom hung his towel on a peg and picked up the wash pan, pitched the soapy water into the yard, said without looking at her, You're not to be around that boy or his people. Last time I'll tell you.

He opened the screen door, said, Next time they show up

at the ball field, you come home. They ain't got no business in this holler.

After he'd gone into the house, she'd stood rooted to the porch, thinking, *Again and as always, Isom, you're plumb too late.*

Tom

TOM CAME FOR HER IN A BORROWED CAPRICE WITH Michigan tags. His own car sat in the front yard back home where he parked it when he left for basic training. He'd given the keys to Beauty to hold and promised to teach June how to drive when next he came home.

He opened the door and grinned, his face leaner than in the photo he sent home at the start of training. In it, his subtle smile was only a faint echo of his tenth-grade school picture that hung in their front room. Now, there were harder lines to his jaw, and his face was tanned from days in the Kentucky sun.

Junebug? He hugged her, his arms strong cords around her. What are you doin here? Is somethin wrong?

No, I just wanted to see you is all, she said. I haven't seen you for weeks.

He studied her face, asked, Do Mama and Isom know where you are?

She nodded, so weary of pretending.

Tom's brows dipped toward the bridge of his nose. He knew she was lying but didn't pry. He said, It's nighttime, Junie. Where are you gonna sleep?

I have some money, she said, thinking of the folded bills she'd borrowed from Rena and Viv that were tucked in her pocketbook. I thought you'd help me find a little motel. Just for tonight.

There's one or two round here, he said. We'll find you one. You hungry?

Yes, she said, thinking back to the peanut butter sandwich she threw away in Bowling Green. She'd downed two Pepsis instead, and now they burned beneath her breastbone.

Tom followed 41-A, a shimmering chain of taillights leading north, toward Hopkinsville. June asked him whether he'd missed home and Lena Faye, and he told her that some of the other men made fun of the way he talked, called him Gomer. She studied the buildings along the highway—night clubs and gas stations, car lots and grocery stores—could feel him glancing at her as they talked, still studying on her lie.

Inside the Waffle House, lights glared on glossy countertops. Couples and small groups of soldiers sat at tables and booths, pouring syrup or salt over heaps of food. Men hunched over plates, eating with their heads down, eating like they'd been hungry for all of their lives. Others, plates empty or already picked up, laughed and talked into the smoke-thick air, the room alive in a way that June didn't recognize.

Tom lit a cigarette, said, Why don't you want to take off that sweater? It must be soppin wet.

She kept her seat, took off her sweater, and gave it to him to hang over the back of an empty chair. Even though he probably wouldn't notice the fullness of her belly beneath her shirt, she felt exposed. She shivered.

I guess I ain't used to this air-conditioning, she said.

I wish I had somethin else for you to put on. Maybe that sweater'll dry quick.

June shrugged, looked up, met the eyes of a soldier a few tables away who was staring at her. Her face went hot.

Tom said, How's Mama and Isom?

Good, she said. Isom's just working, like always. I think his cough is worse, and Mama's already fretting over Decoration Day—and worryin bout you.

The room grew too warm, the food smells too overwhelming. She pictured her mother standing in the kitchen the week before, gawking at her as she stood there naked and pregnant.

When their order arrived, June picked at her scrambled eggs, tried to not stare as Tom shoveled in his food with the same hunger she'd seen on the other men.

Are you missing a tooth? she asked.

He paused to touch the side of his face and said, It was bad. The army dentist pulled it. Said they don't want me getting overseas and have a tooth get to hurting me.

In her head, she heard the voice of Walter Cronkite saying *Vietnam*, but she couldn't say it herself. She pushed the eggs around the plate, asked, Are you sure you're going over?

I'll know for sure in a few weeks, he said. At the end of AIT. But I know I am. I can feel it.

She looked up then. The GI across the room was staring again. He grinned when he saw June looking at him. One of his front teeth sat at an angle, but the rest of them were perfect and brilliant. She felt a jolt of static on her skin, turned her eyes back to her brother. Before now, she'd told herself that the war would be over by the time Tom finished basic training or that he would be stationed someplace closer to home. But the forced casual look on his face told her that he truly believed he'd be going to war, and then she knew it, too. Something around his eyes gave it away. She would remember that look for the rest of her life.

Now, he said, bunching his eyebrows. You tell me what's really going on.

Greyhound

THE BUS RIDE HOME WAS HOT AND SMELLED OF SWEAT and stale cigarettes. June had been to the lavatory twice, each time navigating the aisle on the verge of vomiting, hoping that she actually would so she might feel better. She wanted to open a window, but the latch was in the row ahead of her, and the man who sat there was asleep, his blond hair mashed against the glass like a sunstruck crown. She leaned back against the seat, watched the hills and road cuts of Kentucky flash by.

The first time it had occurred to June that she might be in trouble was a few weeks before, on another bus ride—a school field trip to Charleston—her friend Vivian Taylor in the seat beside her. June's lunch bag had lain between them, its brown paper smudged with grease from the fried bologna sandwich she had made that morning. June had picked up the bag to roll it tighter, and it released a salty, meaty smell, one that she usually savored, but just then, the memory of its taste caught in her throat, tremored to her belly and back again. Chips shattered inside the bag as she wadded it into a loose ball. Vivian watched, eyebrows raised. Even the sound of the breaking chips made June retch. She shoved the lunch under the bus seat and lay her head in Vivian's lap, tried to shut out the odors and noises of the bus—tried to shut out the idea that had begun to rise up in her mind, a mist that settled into the dark hollows of her brain where she didn't want to tarry. She felt Viv's hand raking through her hair.

The night before, in the parking lot of the Waffle House, she'd finally told Tom about the baby. After a few beats of silence, he'd asked, Are you sure?

I'm sure. I've read up on it, she'd said, watching his face.

She hadn't told him details: the sickness, the missed period—was it one or two?—the aching fullness in her breasts—how, lately, she couldn't stand the smell of onions or boiling chicken. The visit to Grannie Carrie's for confirmation.

His shoulders fell. Seeing the air go out of him like that had cut her to the quick. He asked, Does Mama and Isom know?

Her voice quivered. Mama does, and I'd expect Isom does by now, too. She tells him ever thing, don't she?

He put an arm around her, said, Oh, Junebug.

She waited for him to ask about the baby's father but knew he'd already assumed it was Ellis. She wondered how to tell him the truth—that she wasn't even sure.

Oh, God, he said. And for the first time since she'd been sick on the school bus ride—since she'd *known*—she let herself cry to someone other than Carrie. Tom held her tight, let her sob. It wasn't until after he'd settled her into a motel room in Oak Grove that he asked what she was going to do.

I don't know, she said.

He picked at the chenille bedspread, then asked after Ellis. He said, Isom will kill him, no joke. And I'm afraid he won't let you keep an Akers baby in his house.

June weighed what to say, but Tom spoke again.

He, for sure, ain't gonna allow you to marry one, he'd said.

Just then, her mind split in two directions. She thought of Ellis, who she hadn't seen often since he quit school and went into the mine to work the dead shift and sleep away most of the daylight. She only saw him when he had showed up at the ball field on Saturdays or when he called while she was at Aunt Beauty's—or when they'd slipped off somewhere. Then, she recalled the flash of another man's white shirtsleeve as he drove past the house last Friday, on his way home to Columbus. Through his open car window, a wisp of a Johnny Rivers song, then brake lights as he drifted around the curve. At that moment, she'd known it was the last she'd see of JT, who never showed up for work on Monday. Someone must've told him that she was pregnant. Word moves fast in a holler.

Tom said, Don't let Isom get mean. You need me, you know you can call. Or go to Beauty's.

She knew he was thinking of Rena and the belt.

I will, she'd said.

He'd touched her arm then, said, And you finish school, you hear me? Only a couple of months left to go. Don't do what I did and quit.

Later, she wished she'd told him what the English teacher had said about the essays she had written, but just then, she was thinking of Granny Carrie's predicted due date: October or November. *No telling where Tom'll be by then*, she thought.

Forty-seven miles outside of Myrtle Gap, June pictured Isom waiting for her on the porch, furious that she'd been gone overnight. She stood, teetered down the bus aisle, made it to the lavatory just in time to vomit into the shiny, metal commode.

Carrie

ON THE AFTERNOON JUNE PASSED THROUGH CARRIE Vance's front gate and stood in the yard staring at the door, she, just on the other side of the screen, must've known why June was there. She could've told by the look in her eyes because she had seen that look on many of the girls who had stood in that same place.

Well, come on in, Carrie told her after she finally knocked. Hit's too windy out there!

Granny Carrie was sixty-eight but could recall the story of every baby she'd delivered. Even though the exact dates and times had gone off into a hollow of her mind, she could conjure the correct season of the year and whether it was daylight or dark when the babies were pushed or tugged into the world, most of them swollen-eyed and wailing. And, too, she could tell the names of the mothers that delivered pale, silent babies, still warm from the womb but never to draw a breath.

Inside the house, Carrie's low-ceilinged rooms were tidy, her kitchen full of shiny objects that caught the light and held it: hanging strings of broken glass, canning jars of amber tinctures where leaves and flowers floated, on the windowsill three drying morels and a jelly glass with a sprig of pussy willow in it. The kitchen smelled of bacon, like June's own, and, beneath that, something earthy and ancient that brought her a curious comfort.

June sat down at the small wooden table and accepted the glass of iced tea that Carrie offered with her twisted fingers. Carrie's hands resembled the roots she gathered in the woods and kept to remedy the illnesses of those who still believed in their power. June studied the chamomile flowers that floated in her drink, tried to think of how to say what she'd come to say.

Carrie folded her thin body into a chair on the other side of the table. Her cotton blouse, missing a button, gapped in the middle of her chest. She wore no bra, and June could see Carrie's caved-in breastbone, its shape the opposite of Isom's rounded chest, made that way by his constant reach for air.

Carrie talked to fill the silence, said, You was born of a morning—a day in early summer. Shag come around to the house to get me on that old black horse he rode back then. Said the truck was out of gas.

June had never heard this story. Bethel and the other women hadn't talked much of their personal business when kids were around, or if they did, they spoke in quiet code that June had tried to figure out. What June did know about childbirth she'd learned from the traveling health nurse and Rena's baby books.

Carrie reached for the tea pitcher and said, Since you was Bethel's fourth—and I'm acountin the one she lost right after Correna—you come fairly quick and with no trouble. You was a tiny one, about two weeks early by my count, and Bethel wasn't yet ready.

Just then, the old woman leaned forward, stabbed a knotty finger toward June, said in a measured voice, And you was born with a caul.

June had heard that part of the story but never thought much of it. It was supposed to mean that she was special, born with second sight, but, as far as she knew, that was only partly true. For instance, she hadn't known she was pregnant until she got morning sickness. She didn't know who the father of her baby was.

Carrie said, You was so peaceful beneath that veil. Never made a peep until I snatched it off your face. After I did, you locked eyes onto mine for the littlest while. It was like you was already remembering something from another time. Then you scrunched up and went to squallin when the air hit your face.

Once, June had heard her mother tell about how her real daddy and the other men had waited out Tom's birth under a tree in the yard, passing around a bottle of homemade wine. When Shag finally heard the baby bawl, he ran inside and looked between the baby's legs and found it to be a boy. He got so excited that, as soon as Granny Carrie had wrapped Tom in a cloth, he snatched the baby from her and stumbled back down the porch steps. He held Tom in the air above his head and declared, Look around, Thomas Paul Branham, this here is your home!

Bethel said, All that time, Tom caterwaulin and me cryin, Shag! from the bedroom and Granny Justice yelling at him from the porch, Shag Branham, bring that baby back here afore you drop him! Finally, Daddy carried him back in to me, but not before he'd set Tom's feet into the dirt of the daylily bed, said, West Virginia soil, boy.

Carrie ran a kinked finger halfway down the side of her tea glass. Drops of water skittered ahead of it, then pooled on the oilcloth.

She said, With you, Bethel was awarshin' windows when her bag a waters broke. And your mama kept saying she wisht she could finish cleaning afore climbing in the bed to birth ye. Tom was still yet a little thing then, running around in droopy diapers. When I laid you on Bethel's breast, he crawled right up there and patted your wet head. All that black hair—course it changed to auburn later. And Lord, those blue eyes. Branham eyes.

June's body felt heavy, as if she were trying to breathe underwater. She closed her eyes, wished she could go into Carrie's front room and lie down on the couch. When she opened them again, Carrie, leaned forward, said, Is there something I can do for you, honey?

June searched the room for something else to think about, settled on the jars on the windowsill.

Honey, are you in trouble? Carrie asked.

The words June had planned to use left her. She nodded. Tears trailed down her burning cheeks.

Carrie's fingers darted in and out of the crown of braids on her head. She said, Well, then, does your mama and Isom know?

June shook her head, looked down at her lap.

Carrie said, I don't spect Isom will take it well. Does the baby's daddy know?

The air rushed out of June's lungs, then from the emptiness it left came a sob. She put her arms and head down on the table and let herself cry, replaying in her mind the night she tried to tell Ellis.

She featured him in his truck with his elbow against the driver's window, swiping his coal-dusted forehead with the sleeve of his other arm. His hair, the same color as the dust on his face, and longer than usual, curved over his coat collar, lay matted against his head where the helmet had crushed it during the shift. When he turned toward June, she startled at his brilliant hazel eyes fixed in his coal-smeared face.

What were you doing out here at this time of night? In this cold? he had asked.

I needed to talk to you.

Isom will kill the both of us, he said, looking at her again.

He don't know I'm gone. He's sick with a fever.

Your mama?

Too worried about him.

He stopped on the bridge over Dry Fork, said, I'm takin you home with me. We can talk up there.

You're plumb crazy, she said.

He said, Nobody home. Mama and Daddy have gone off to Huntington for Daddy's doctor's appointment tomorrow. They got a motel.

Are you sure? she asked.

He reached across the seat for her hand and said, Positive. They packed up and left out this morning.

Going to Solomon Akers's house had been the furthest thing from her mind when she sneaked out to wait for Ellis at the underpass. She had decided to tell him everything, especially what JT had done, but she knew that Isom would be furious if he knew where she was. Besides, she wasn't sure how to describe agreeing to go for a ride with JT in the first place—how something that she hadn't expected had overtaken her when he'd asked.

June watched the houses of the lower right fork go by as

Ellis navigated potholes and frozen puddles. She squeezed his hand and felt a warmth rise up inside her. Until Ellis had stopped the truck after she stepped from behind the trestle and told her to get in, until she breathed in the warmth of the cab and the smell of his skin beneath all the sweat and dust of the mine, until she saw the shape of his hands on the wheel, she had planned to tell him about the baby, but now she was losing her nerve.

Ellis's headlights cut a swath across the frozen yard, washed out the single yellow bulb burning on the porch ceiling, lit up the front of the shingle-covered house sitting high on its cinderblock foundation among the bare, towering trees. June had only seen the house during daytime, and only in summer when she ventured up the right fork with Tom or one of their visiting cousins, and until then, she had only seen it from the road.

The truck engine knocked and sputtered after Ellis shut off the key.

Damn if it ain't cold, he said, then, I want to show you something.

As June climbed the stairs to the porch, Solomon's coonhounds started up baying somewhere at the back of the house. She froze, looked toward the road for headlights.

It's OK, Ellis said. Daddy usually has fed them by this time. I'll be right back.

He went around the house, calling the dogs by name. June sat down on the cold floorboards, pulled her coat up around her face, studied a raft of lighter-colored, shinier boards near the porch's lip. She ran her gloved hand over it.

Ellis came back into the pool of light, pointed at the spot, said, That's what I wanted to show you. That right there is where your stepdaddy nailed Garvin's huntin boots about a week after Garvin got killed. Three years ago, now. Right here where Daddy would have to walk by them when he got home from the mine.

The thought of Garvin sent a slice of pain through her. She didn't know what to say.

Ellis said, Pointed them right at the front door, like Garvin's ghost was comin in or somethin. Made Daddy so mad, he pried em up with a crowbar, boards and all. Threw them over the creek bank. I went and got em, though. In my closet. Saved em for you.

Ellis opened the unlocked door, said, I cain't remember too many times I've come home and had this house be empty.

He switched on a pole lamp by the door. The front room was small, low-ceilinged like most of the other houses in the holler. Heavy drapes covered single-paned windows. Rocking chair, upright piano, a green low-backed vinyl couch. A haphazard grid of black-and-white and color photos hung above the piano, some of them faded and others showing baby faces with pink painted-in cheeks. Ellis's eighth-grade picture, a mirror of the one she kept in her wallet, tilted toward a black-and-white photo of Solomon in his army uniform. Some of the pictured people had lighter skin—Ellis's mother's family—and others were dark, Solomon's people.

Ellis kissed June's hair, said, It's cold in here. Come in the kitchen and set by the range while I get the coal stove going.

In the kitchen, familiar smells of coffee and bacon. Ellis flipped on the overhead light, then led June to a chair by the cookstove. She pictured Merkey, Ellis's mother—or

Solomon—sitting there on an early morning, waiting for the house to heat up.

Ellis turned the oven knob, opened its door. He said, Set right there. I'll be back in a minute.

The kitchen windows began to let in the hint of light that was rising from the east. She'd have to get home soon.

June scratched a fingernail at a clump of dried egg yolk on the stovetop while Ellis fumbled with newspaper and kindling in the front room. She heard him cuss under his breath, pause, then the *whomp* of fresh flame. He slammed the iron door, then he was back and filling the teakettle with water from the tap, putting it on the stove burner to heat.

On school days, she said, Granny used to warm my clothes on a chair by the oven door, feed me overcooked oats.

Ellis smiled, pulled a chair near June, sat down, took her hands in his. I want to kiss you, he said, but don't want to get you dirty.

He pulled her hands to his mouth, breathed on them. Thrill and dread collided in her rib cage.

Now what did you want to talk about? he asked.

She'd tried to conjure up her nerve, said, Let's wait until you're cleaned up.

He winked, said, Oh, I get it. You really did just wanna see me.

She rolled her eyes, pulled a weak smile, then up came the images of her and JT parked under the leaning trees at Mud Branch and shame swirled through her.

A wool army-green blanket hung over the only window in Ellis's room. Dim overhead light, shirts and jackets hanging from rods in the corner, a pile of work clothes in front of it making the space seem smaller than it probably was. She pulled back the blanket, and what was left of the night seeped into the room. She'd taken advantage of Isom's sickness and sneaked out, left a note for Bethel that she couldn't sleep for his strangled coughing and had gone to Beauty's, who never locked her doors at night. June knew it wasn't plausible, that she'd likely be found out, but last night, she truly hadn't been able to sleep for thinking of telling Ellis that she was pregnant. She had to do it then.

She sat on the edge of Ellis's twin bed, waited for him. She scanned the room, recognizing some of the shirtsleeves dangling from the clothes rod like useless arms and, on a metal shelf, the Reds ball cap he wore in summer. She resisted the urge to poke and pry, searched with only her eyes for something of herself, found the chain of gum wrappers she'd made for him hanging over a corner of the mirror. Stuck under a bracket in the opposite corner was her eighth-grade picture, taken a few years ago. She could find nothing in the face in the photo that looked like it might recognize this later version of herself.

She thought of the years before, when Tom was still in school and Garvin still aboveground, alive and cracking jokes with Isom. No boarders yet, come to build the four-lane, no JT among them. No day, last fall, when she'd walked past the makeshift sleeping quarters tacked to the side of Jewell Estep's house and seen JT standing shirtless at the horseshoe pit, a cigarette hanging from his lips. She didn't know his age but knew he was a grown man, felt him watching her. It had stirred in her something that she didn't completely recognize, something she'd only felt the edges of when she sat close to

Ellis. JT said something that made the other boarders laugh, and the next evening, when she passed by again, he asked her to go for a ride. And she did.

He picked her up past the house, past the drainpipe, and drove them to Mud Branch, parked behind a screen of blackberry bushes. A Gerry and the Pacemakers' song on the radio crackled with nighttime and distance—the singer's voice telegraphed from somewhere far away, WLS in Chicago—sending static toward them, toward other cars occupied by only two, parked in the shadows of mountains, the air inside them charged and brittle with longing.

He pointed toward the radio and said, The Mersey is a river in England.

Even in the dark, June could see JT squint his right eye, collapse his cheeks around the cigarette filter. He smelled of Dial soap and some brand of aftershave she didn't recognize.

Oh, she'd said.

JT hung his cigarette out the window, flicked the butt with his thumb. It's a good song, he said. Then he asked, You want me to roll up this window?

I'm OK, she said. Somehow, letting him roll up the window would seal them completely off from the rest of the world, make them more alone, which is what she'd thought she wanted since the first time she saw him in Jewell's orchard. A man, looking at her.

He cranked up the window, turned to her, cupped her right shoulder with his hand.

Why don't you come over here? he said.

She scooted across the seat toward him, drawn by something she didn't understand. Up close, she could smell the cigarettes on his breath, the scent of washing powders in the fabric of his shirt. She closed her eyes, felt the world spin like a record on the faraway turntable. He moved his face closer then kissed her. She shivered, didn't know what to do with her hands. She put her arm around him. Muscle tensed under her fingers, frightened her. She thought of Ellis, pulled away.

JT turned off the radio and they sat in the ringing silence until she asked him to take her home.

In a minute, he'd said, brought the glowing coils of the car's cigarette lighter to another Kool dangling from his mouth then began humming the Mersey song. She thought of getting out of the car, walking home, knew she could find her way in the dark, but it would take more time than she had to get back to Beauty's on foot. Her thoughts returned to Ellis, how he'd always felt safe to her. June realized that she didn't feel safe alone with JT, shouldn't have gone.

When JT stubbed out the cigarette in the car's ashtray, she waited for him to start the engine. Instead, he kissed her again.

Open your mouth, he whispered before he pushed his tongue into her. She struggled against him until a nerve at her very center gave way—a tight thread that finally snapped, told her that she couldn't, shouldn't, fight him.

Afterward, he drove her as far as Jewell's and let her out to walk the rest of the way up the holler alone. She could smell the aftershave on her hands, still taste his cigarettes. Shame and anger roiled up inside her—she wished she could take a bath. She imagined the scene if Isom knew what she'd done, pictured herself screaming back at him, It should be OK with you. He's a white man!

Beauty had already gone to bed. June tiptoed through the

front room to the spare bedroom, undressed and climbed beneath the satin bedspread, then let the last hour play in her mind. She remembered JT's weight on her—the fossil imprint she'd carry on her body forever. Ellis would never want her if he knew. She let herself cry.

•

Ellis was in the doorway, shoeless, wearing a clean white undershirt and jeans. She could smell his aftershave from where she sat.

He whispered her name, then kissed the top of her head. She resisted when he tried to nudge her back onto the bed, so he sat down on the floor at her feet, laid his head on her lap.

She pulled her fingers through his damp black hair, let it curl around her them. Tears singed her eyelids.

Your hair feels like corn silk, she said.

He was quiet for a while, then said, We're all alone, June. Nobody comin home just now.

She leaned over and kissed his forehead, said, I know. I'm just scared.

He opened his eyes and stood up. He reached for her top coat button. It's alright, he whispered. She shut down her mind, let him find her again.

After, they lay close together on Ellis's bed, her ear to the spot where his heart galloped beneath his skin. She felt safe—wanted to fall asleep to that sound, to follow those wild hoofbeats as they rushed toward something familiar she hadn't known she could miss.

She felt the catch in Ellis's breath. She cried, too, let the sadness overtake the wonderment of his tastes and smells, the weight of his hand on her hip, the fact of his breath in her hair. She wanted to stay in that room a while, let the truth live somewhere else.

He drove her home, dropped her, as she asked, just shy of the house. He cut the engine, watched her walk away. Just then she'd felt her mother watching her from behind the kitchen window as she came up the road, head down, carrying a pair of old work boots. All that now seemed like a lifetime ago.

•

She felt Carrie's warm hands on her shoulders, heard her ask, Hon, you going to keep it?

It took June a while to comprehend that Carrie was talking about the baby. She'd heard it told in whispers that Carrie had teas that women who'd been worn-out by birthing and raising baby after baby—or who'd had men force themselves upon them—could take to end their troubles, but she'd never heard it said aloud, for grown women held their secrets close. Even though, a few times in the last weeks, she'd let herself think about asking for the medicine, she'd weighed the fact that JT had forced her—had he?—against the fact that Ellis hadn't and would probably hate her if she took the tea, but she hadn't let herself dwell too much on it this day. It was too late. She could not bring herself to do it past the quickening that was coming any day. She could not bring herself to do it for the chance that the baby belonged to Ellis.

Carrie's voice again, Come on, honey. Lie down a while.

June swiped her arm across the damp spots she'd made on the tablecloth, then across her mouth and nose. She let Carrie lead her, still sobbing, to a tiny bedroom. Carrie pulled back the quilts and told her to get in, then she pulled off June's tennis shoes. Before she left the room, she said, Rest awhile now.

A few minutes later, Carrie was back to lay a cool washrag on June's head, then she said, I ain't going to ask who the daddy is. Hit's none of my business. But just know this, you ain't the only one's ever had secrets.

Too tired to talk or cry anymore, June waited for the spasms below her ribs to stop. She pushed thoughts of Ellis and Isom, JT out of her head, let herself slip into the sound of the creek running past Granny Carrie's window.

Deputy

AFTER RIDING THE BUS FROM FORT CAMPBELL, JUNE was bone tired, but she walked all the way from the bus stop to the mouth of the holler. Too tired to answer to Isom for a night away from home and wholly unwilling to involve Tom.

Near home, she rounded the curve at the drainpipe, saw Isom standing near the rose of Sharon gesturing at a Mingo County sheriff's deputy. As she got closer, June recognized the set of his feet, the lie of his gaze—the pitch of his voice. It was Bud Canterbury.

Isom carried a layer of yellow clay over the coal dust he usually wore home, except for his face, which shone like the moon. Most of the grime was gone, maybe sweated off, except where it darkened the crevices around his eyes and the deep ravines alongside his nose.

Her mind ran in two directions at once. The garden soil smelled of something alive and comforting. She wanted to lie down among her mother's Good Friday potato hills and sleep. At the same time, she wanted to walk right past them into the house and lie in the patch of sunlight that washed across her bed of an evening. She didn't care if the deputy was there—there, surely, because Isom thought she had run away.

She skirted the garden, away from the men and toward

the backyard. Between the rows of Isom's work shirts and a load of gray-tinged undershirts and socks hanging on the line, Bethel's bushel basket on the new grass. And Bethel, herself, stood by the well, watching the men, her face washed out, hollow.

June felt the shame rise up, squeeze her heart until the blood strained against her eardrums. Lightheadedness weakened her legs. She leaned back into the warmth of the horse chestnut.

Isom's voice rose again.

Damned if I know, he said. Lock me up, I reckon! Everybody knows you all are tight with Sol and all them other darkies over there.

Lock up Isom? June's mind churned. *Canterbury's not here for me?*

The deputy shook his head, walked to the edge of the yard, dropped his cigarette onto the road. Sunlight exploded from the polished toe of his shoe as he ground the butt into the sand. He walked toward his car, exhaled a jet of smoke. When he had hauled himself inside the cruiser and slammed the door, he poked his balding head through the window, said, Brother, don't let me have to come back up here again. Stay away from Solomon Akers, or next time, I'll have to carry you back over to Myrtle Gap with me.

Isom nodded once in the deputy's direction then stood rooted to the yard, feet apart, hands tucked into his armpits. He kept his eyes on the black cruiser until it made the curve at the edge of the garden, left a fin of dust behind it. June was too tired to think, wanted, needed to escape into sleep. She slipped into the house through the front door.

From her bedroom window, June watched Bethel meet Isom on the back porch.

What in this world? Bethel asked as she reached to swipe at a fleck of blood on his swollen lower lip. He winced, turned away, sat down on the porch swing and grabbed at a bootlace to untie it.

Isom? Bethel asked.

He worked the leather laces like reins, crossing them then pulling them free of their hooks. He lifted his head, said, Get me a drink of water, and tell June to come on out here.

Something in Isom's voice brought all of June's nerves awake again, caused her heart to pound, the nape of her neck to go damp. She sat up on the bed and waited for her mother to call her, listened to the water dipper scrape and thud against the bottom of the bucket in the kitchen, heard the first boot thump on the porch floor.

On the porch, June leaned against the rough-shingled wall, crossed her arms. Bethel sat on the glider, hands folded in her lap.

Isom looked directly at June for the first time in days. His eyes burned out of the moon of his face.

How come that Akers boy didn't know you're havin a baby?

June couldn't think. She could smell the stale dampness coming off his sock, and it made her sick.

How come he had to hear it from me?

Her mind grew thin, strained to keep up. A rivulet of sweat slipped down her backbone. She tried to speak.

I don't . . . You told me . . .

Her mouth went dry. She couldn't shape the ends of the sentences.

Isom aimed his voice in Bethel's direction. I know I swore to you after the last time that I'd not go around to Sol's again, but that boy has to do right.

Bethel threw an arm across her belly, rubbed the side of her face with her free hand. She spoke.

Isom, what did you do?

Sweat slid down the backs of June's knees. Isom had gone back to fussing with the bootlaces. Gnats swarmed around his sweat-matted hair. He said, I ought to send her around there to live. Let them people take care of her!

Tears stung June's eyes. She thought of Ellis's room, the blanket-covered window.

Bethel's eyes brimmed. She whispered, What did you do?

Isom wouldn't look at her. His voice lurched as he worked the bootlaces.

That ole boy and me just about had an understanding until Sol came home drunk, like usual, and come at me with a tire iron.

June glanced down the road, willed the deputy to come back.

Bethel uncovered her mouth, said, Did you hurt somebody?

Isom kicked off the boot, pulled off the dingy sock and swiped at the gnats with it.

Not hardly, he said. I had it out with the boy, then when Sol come home, I threw that iron across the yard then knocked him on his ass.

Daddy, June began. She pictured the pistol he kept under the truck seat, fought for breath enough to say, Did you hurt him?

I like to have. Still yet might if he don't do the right thing.

What do you mean? Bethel asked.

Well, I sure as hell am not going to marry my daughter into that bunch of half-breeds, but at least that boy can pay doctor bills and support.

Bethel wiped at her eyes with the backs of her hands. Well, then, she said.

Isom stood, spit into the yard. He pointed a dirty finger at June, said in a voice that had gone hoarse, Sis, you done done it now.

A chill rose over her, raised goosebumps on her bare arms. Up on the mountain, a thin hem of remaining light backlit the trees.

Isom opened the screen door, said, Goin to get my bath.

Bethel stood to follow him, then turned and went to June, put her arms around her. Her shirt was damp against June's face. She said, You have to finish school, June. No matter what.

I will, I promise, Mama, June said into her mother's hollow breastbone.

When Bethel had gone into the house, June sat down on the swing, her mind racing in every direction, water with no place to go.

Bethel

SOLOMON COME A AGE BETWEEN WORLD WAR II AND the Korean War and found hisself one of the few survivors of his infantry unit after the Battle of Taejon. It's no wonder that he drunk so much after he come home all broodin and gaunt. Some nights, he'd raise Cain until sunup then go to work in the mine. Come most evenings, he'd start all over again.

I've known Sol since we was in school, just kids, him a few grades ahead of me until he quit his tenth-grade year and, like most every other man round here, went into the mines.

Sol was really dark-skinned, and for that reason alone, Daddy wouldn't have let me go with him. Lord, he were the prettiest man I ever seen. Had them eyes and dark skin and coal-black hair. When Elvis Presley came along, he reminded me of Sol. I think Daddy was afraid because he couldn't tell whether Sol was mixed colored and white or Indian and white or all three together. Daddy was awful afraid of what he didn't know or understand, and for that reason, we had to hide from him and just about everybody else.

We never really got together until I slipped off from the house and went to a basketball game over at Redwine with the Dempseys. Brookie Dempsey was my school friend, and just after the game started, she pulled at my coat sleeve, said, That man on the far bleachers over there keeps starin at you.

Just then I looked up and met those black eyes that was already on me. They burned into me like hot coals. By God, they lit a fire in my chest. Then I realized it was Sol Akers, and I turned away. My daddy woulda killed me for just lookin back at Sol, acknowledgin him. All through the game, I felt his eyes and that burn spread out over me like warm molasses. A grown man had never paid me any mind before.

After the game—I couldn't tell you who won it—my legs could hardly carry me down the bleachers. I didn't let on to Brookie at all, had told her I didn't know him. We rode home in the back seat of Mr. Dempsey's Buick with her talkin a streak because we won the game and me feeling relief and longing churnin my insides, my outer edges chilled and the fire inside cooling. I hardly understood it. Closer to home, I begin to git scared. Honey, I tell you, I was a-stewin on how to slip back into the house, but Lordy, I made it. Mommy never knowed.

The next Monday, he waited for me in the parking lot after school. I knew I shouldn't get into that car, that I would surely get whooped for running off like that, but I done it anyway. We dated in secret all that year, or so I thought, and until around Thanksgiving time the next one. Daddy wouldn't even let him in the house, and Mama didn't never too much like him. She said he was fast. After Daddy was gone, Mama let him come to the house but warned me, Girl, if you burn a blister, you've got to wear it.

Sure enough, by November of my junior year, I had missed my monthlies and knew I was in trouble. Then here come Shag. Lord, but he was a caution. Could make me laugh like no other. I was moonin over Sol but had done give up on him marrying me. I thought I was doomed to bein alone till I run into Shag at a dance over at Delbarton. I wasn't showin much then, and Mommy had let me go with my cousins. It all started when he asked me to dance.

The first song we danced to was "Sioux City Sue." Honey, he took me all over that floor, light as a feather on his feet. A course I could dance, for I had big brothers who taught me, me standin on their shoes as they waltzed. I kept up with Shag just fine, and when some people was a-lookin on, disapprovin, I just let em gawk. I didn't care.

He hung around where I was a-settin, offered me some whiskey from his flask, but I said no thank you. It was near the end of the night when the band played "Ole Buttermilk Sky" and he took me by the hand and led me to the floor. That become our song. When we was married, he bought a record player, and we about wore that record out, dancin on the porch or in the kitchen and Rena in my belly right there between us. Sometimes I'd stand on his shoes to make him laugh.

Of course I told Shag from the git that I was pregnant. He said that didn't matter, that as soon as he seen me, he knew we was gonna marry. When he asked me, I had to decide whether to wait on Sol or go for the sure thing. We was married in Mommy's livin' room during the milk moon. Mommy made me a dress, and I carried a bouquet of snowdrops. Rena was borned bout five months after that.

He was so handsome and a real good daddy to our three kids. Rena never woulda knowed the difference if she wasn't so dark complected. Shag, he had blond hair and periwinkle eyes. Tom and June got his eyes, but they got my strawberry hair.

A Secret

JUNE COULDN'T SLEEP. UP THE CREEK, JIMMY BAISDEN'S coonhounds made a racket, likely pining to get out of their boxes and into the moon-washed woods. Besides the train whistle down at the coal tipple, it was the loneliest sound she knew. She missed the comfort of Tom's clock radio at the other end of the attic, playing music into the early-morning hours. She thought of getting up and turning it on but didn't. Nights in her room were usually quiet—a sanctuary from Isom's and Bethel's disapproving eyes, a place where she could breathe—if not for the droning undercurrent of Isom's television.

Sometimes a slideshow of memories played in her head. Rena running after Tom with a lit sparkler one Fourth of July, Isom opening bottles of grape pop at Maynard's and handing them to her and Tom. How icy the Nehi had been, how she could barely hold it in her small hands. A picture of Ellis carving their initials into the tree, his tongue between his lips as always when he concentrated.

Often, she let herself think about marrying Ellis and living in one of the old coal-camp houses, abandoned years ago, that still stood in the rough brush over on Dove Creek. The world was changing, and mixed marriages were becoming more common. Folks would leave them alone. They'd put in new windows, sweep it free of dirt and litter, bring it back to life. She'd get Beauty to help her scrub it down and make curtains. Rena, who would be their neighbor, would lend them bedding and towels. She pictured a garden, a flower bed full of zinnias and marigolds. She'd wait on the porch of an evening for Ellis to come home, him smiling through the dirt on his face, her holding their child. The primitive hatred between Isom and Sol would die when she and Ellis married.

June kept the images moving, tried to not let any one of them linger enough to affect her, but she couldn't help herself. Ellis stayed in her mind. She pictured him standing in the doorway of his room then walking to her on the bed. Thinking back on that and what had come after woke an ache she had to push deep inside herself.

•

The air in the room was warm and still, and her nightgown stuck to her skin. She tried to imagine the baby moving inside her, making itself real, claiming space. Rena said that at first, Charlie had felt like a butterfly swooping through her lower belly, then, quickly enough, he became a bowling ball jarring her ribs. Just then, June couldn't feature any of that, even though she knew the time was coming.

Two days ago, when she'd finally told Rena that she was pregnant, because she knew Bethel or someone else would soon tell it themselves, Rena had cried a little then asked, How do you know for sure?

I been sick of a mornin. No monthlies. Besides, Granny Carrie did a exam on me, June said, recalled the peculiar, uncomfortable feeling of Carrie's hand inside her.

She said, Due in the fall, October or November.

Rena said, Why didn't you tell me?

What could you do?

She could see that Rena was stung. Rena said, Are you going to keep it?

June said, It's probably too late, but I want it, anyways.

Rena picked at a pool of chipped coral polish on her thumb. Before Charlie, she'd kept her nails painted all the time. She said, I could've talked to Isom for you. Could've told him not to be so hard on you as he was me. I'm not scared of him now.

Well, he hates Ellis, so it don't matter, anyway.

He always has, Rena said. She added, Has hated Sol even before Uncle Garvin died, and I know why.

What are you talkin about? June asked.

The air in the room thickened. Rena gnawed at her nail polish.

He's jealous. Something about Sol and Mom—before Isom or Daddy, Rena said. I overheard Beauty and her talking about it one time.

Mama and Solomon? June tried to picture them both younger—together—but couldn't. There were hardly any pictures of Bethel before she was married to June's father.

I'm not sure what all. I wouldn't dare ask Mom, Rena said, then, Does Ellis know yet?

June was lost in thinking of her mother as a young girl.

June, Rena said. Does Ellis know?

June nodded.

What does he say?

I don't know. Isom caught him at the house, told him yesterday. Might've beat the lights out of him had Sol not just then come home.

Rena's face went white. She said, Isom went over there again?

June nodded, heard herself say, But he might not be the daddy. I just don't know.

What do you mean? Rena whispered.

June felt the floor drop from beneath her, felt herself tumbling, told Rena most everything, just as she'd told Vivian at school the day before.

•

Baisden's dogs had stopped howling. Downstairs, Isom cried out in his sleep. The bedsprings creaked as he groaned and coughed, then came the sound of him hacking black, gobby phlegm into the coffee can he kept by the bed. She heard her mother murmur, then the house went quiet again. She let herself fall into a half dream of Bethel as a young woman, before Isom, before them all, and before Sol went off to war in Korea. Before Garvin's dying in the mine. She dreamed of her mother as a beautiful girl, as she had surely been, with dark, intelligent eyes and a head of wavy auburn hair. Through a window in time, June watched her mother, at sixteen, step into a car and drive away with Solomon Akers, her laugh and bronze ribbons of hair floating out the open window.

Last Days of School

THE CREEK BEHIND THE SCHOOL GAVE OFF THE SMELLS of early summer, the essences of living things coming awake after a deep winter sleep. June stretched her legs down the steps, leaned back on her elbows, offered her face to the mid-May sun. For a moment, she didn't care that she had exposed her body to the other kids, for word of her pregnancy had gone around a while before.

Because of the nearness of graduation day, she was allowed to come back to school for the last three weeks, even though she was unmistakably pregnant by then. Some students gawked at her, stopped speaking to her altogether except to taunt her, one boy calling out to her in the crowded hallway, Heard that baby is a Akers. How's it feel to be incubatin a darkie's child?

She let the racket of school bus engines and slamming doors float past her as she waited for Viv and replayed her earlier talk with Miss Cline, the English teacher. Miss Cline had pulled her aside after class to tell her that she was as good an artist as she was a writer. She said, June, the drawings in your commonplace book are just wonderful. You could make a writer and an artist.

And, once again, she encouraged June to enroll in college. June knew that she'd have to have a scholarship to attend, for

Isom said he was not about to pay for her to go off "with all that free love going on." He'd said, Besides, nobody in this family has ever gone to school afore, McCoys or Fields.

June had wanted so badly to remind him that she was not a Fields and that Shag's mother had trained to be a teacher.

Before June was allowed to return to school, Miss Cline had been her homebound teacher, had parked her red Ford Falcon a few feet from the porch on Thursday afternoons. If it was raining or muddy, she walked to the door on the toes of her high-heeled shoes. She wore a pink car coat over the outfit she'd worn to school that day. She kept her blond hair high in the back, teased like Rena did. Each time June opened the door to let her in, a whisper of White Shoulders and cigarette smoke came in with her.

Hello, June, she'd said each time.

On Miss Cline's first home visit, June looked down at her high heels and shiny stockings then folded her arms over the flannel shirt she wore.

She'd lead Miss Cline through the front room to the kitchen where Bethel was cooking or peeling some of the fall apples she kept in a cardboard box.

Bethel always commented on the weather with a question such as, Chilly out, ain't it? and Miss Cline would affirm.

Miss Cline would set her orange vinyl tote on the supper table, and June would take her car coat from her. She'd seen one like it in the Sears catalog, envied it. Every time she laid it on her faded chenille bedspread, it looked like a party favor.

That particular day, Bethel had draped a dish towel over the bowl of apples and went outside to work. At the Formica table, Miss Cline pulled papers from her bag. She pointed at the top of one, where a B+ had been jotted in red ink—June's report on activist Helen Matthews Lewis.

This is really good, June, she said.

June flushed at the attention, said, Thank you.

Miss Cline nodded toward the papers, said, It just needs some better transitions.

She touched June's hand then with her elegant fingers. Her engagement ring gleamed. She went on, I think you could be a writer.

June picked up the paper she had written in longhand cursive and read the comments in the margin: *"Appalachia" is capitalized!*

June worried the edge of the first page, said, I'm afraid I won't be any good.

You know better than that. I wouldn't tell you if I didn't truly believe it, myself.

I cain't go to college, June said.

Miss Cline nodded, said, I know, but you don't have to. You can gain more writing skills by reading good books. Then, maybe you can go to school when you get situated.

She glanced at her watch, said, Plenty of writers never went to college. I can help you, though, if you want to apply.

Just then, the baby had flickered inside June's belly, but she didn't mention this. Miss Cline had rarely asked her about the baby, even though it was right there between them when she made her weekly calls. Hardly anyone talked about the baby, save Beauty or Rena. She felt as if she had a disease, as if she were going to die and disappear in the fall. June wished that Miss Cline would ask how she felt or whether she had any names picked out.

Miss Cline pulled a brown clothbound book from the tote, *Intermediate Algebra* in gold lettering on its spine. June liked solving equations, the messiness of it, the erasing and backtracking to find the missing idea that would mend the arrangement of numbers and letters and restore order. There was only one correct answer.

Will you please excuse me? June asked.

Of course, hon, Miss Cline said as she opened the brown textbook to a page marked by a slip of paper with June's name neatly written on it.

In the drafty outhouse, goose bumps had risen all over June's body. She tugged at the elastic waistband of the hand-me-down pants that Rena gave her then stood there, cradling the squirming baby inside her with icy hands, watching a spider crawl along the edge of the wooden door.

The words *I think you could be a writer* replayed in her head.

Without disturbing the spider, she opened the door and stepped out, watched Bethel chop at a cornstalk with an axe. June thought about telling her about the B+ on her paper, but didn't. She walked back to the house with Miss Cline's words haloing her head, as they would until the baby was born.

•

Viv plopped down on the school steps, brushed away the fallen maple seeds they called *helicopters*, and said, Law, it's hot. I need a smoke.

The armpits of her pink blouse were saturated with sweat, and June could smell the scent of Ban Roll-On coming off her. She picked at a scab on her shin.

June said, Miss Cline is after me about enrolling in school again.

Viv flicked the scab off her leg, licked her index finger, dabbed at the fresh blood. She said, What'd you say?

Told her the same thing as last time. I cain't go to college with a baby at home.

As she said it, she wondered where home would be. She hoped it would be with Ellis.

Don't give up on yourself so easy, June. You might yet go. Or, we can go somewhere else. Cain't we still go to New York?

Viv opened her purse, began ransacking it. She said, I almost forgot. Got you something. It come in the mail on Saturday.

She brought out a wad of green Kleenex, opened it. Inside was a polished metal bracelet that matched the one she wore.

Here, she said. It's your own POW bracelet. It's in better shape than mine.

June had admired Viv's own POW bracelet, which she never took off. She accepted the gift and ran her fingers over the engraved name. The date below it was written in the way Tom dated his letters home after he went into the army: 17 June 66. She put it on, whispered the name that was written on it, held it up to glint in the sun.

Thank you so much, she said. She turned to hug Viv then, hoped she'd never see her brother's name on a bracelet. When Viv pulled away and stood, she said, I'm out of cigs. Let's go to the store before we go home.

I need you to help me up, June said.

At that moment, she felt happier than she had in a long while. She was over her morning sickness, graduation was coming, and the sun felt like a balm to her. She kissed the bracelet that warmed her arm and made a vow to wear it always. Years from that day, when Viv would be dead of ovarian cancer for some time, June would come across her senior picture. In it, Viv smiled at something off camera, backlighted, ethereal, a faint shadow of nicotine on her front teeth, her long diaphanous blond hair framing a strong jawline. She would have lived in Mingo County the whole of her life.

Bethel

ALL I EVER WANTED WAS FOR MY CHILDREN TO GET A education. I was so proud of Tom for goin into the service. I have hopes he'll come out, catch up on his schoolin, and use his GI Bill to go to a trade school. But it's God's will. And, honey, sometimes I let myself get mad at God.

Law, but he takes after Shag. I don't think of Shag much now that Tom's not here to remind me. That boy is him made over, and sometimes it'd catch me out and I'd have to go off by myself for a while. It was something. When he got to be a man and I'd hear him call out, I'd think it were Shag. He was a ghost of his daddy, down to the way he walked and supped his coffee. I figure he'll marry Lena Faye Hall when he comes home and they'll raise some babies. Lord, but that girl was pitiful at the bus station when he left.

Rena's a good mother. I just wished she'd graduated high school and not dropped out. It woulda made her feel good about herself. She seems content, though, is doing a good job raising Charlie. Better than I did until Isom come along and saved us.

June is my brightest one, takes that after Shag's people, always readin books and askin questions, talkin over stuff. Law, she about wore my ears out when she was little. She learned to read before she even went to school. Wasn't no kindergartens then. Now we have the Head Start, and the bus runs all the way up this road. I spect Charlie will go if the bus runs up their holler over on Dove Creek.

Of all my kids, I mostly thought June woulda gone to school, maybe even over to Marshall, but that idee's gone now that she'll have a youngun to take care of. She is verily talented at writing and drawing. I got some o' her pictures in the scrapbook I keep.

We had Shag's Social Security all through the years, but Isom was a good provider, too. My kids never went without shoes nor writin paper and pencils like I had to, but I don't fault Daddy and Mommy fer that, for they done all they could. The times we was in back then was rough.

On the day I married Isom at the courthouse in Logan, I come home and overheard Rena, June, and Tom out in the yard a-talkin. They was discussin what to call him, Daddy or his given name. At the time, they weren't old enough to know much. June suggested they call him Daddy, but Rena wouldn't have nothin of it. They couldn't agree, so they decided each would call him what they wanted. At first, June and Tom called him Daddy, but eventually they called him Isom, just like their sister did. I cain't feature what changed their minds.

I'll allow that Isom's been rough on my kids. He don't believe in mollycoddlin, but I think they've had it a lot easier than him and me did a-comin up. Why, I was afraid of his daddy. Like my daddy—like most of the old people around here—he was prejudiced. And he was mean as a snake. Beat on them kids all the time. I was glad when he died 'cause I was afraid he'd beat on mine, too. I couldn't have stood it.

June Meeting

THE CEMETERY WAS CLEAN, ITS BINDWEED AND CRAB-grass gnawed at by a dull mower blade at least once since the winter thaw. On Decoration Day, the week before, the grounds had been scoured by families who came to clear away last year's bled-out ribbons and bleached plastic flowers that were wind-flung against the fence. They were replaced with vivid artificial tulips and roses, their wire stems jabbed into the gravelly clay graves, or honeysuckle vines and pink and white peonies that had been stuffed into tinfoil-covered coffee cans and leaned against the stones.

June fussed around the warped plank tables that sat under the tulip poplars and basswood trees. As people arrived in church clothes, she accepted their baskets and covered dishes, arranged jars of iced tea and jugs of sweet-smelling Kool-Aid, the powder on their lids staining her fingers red and orange.

She had been there since early morning, dressed in the same yellow cotton shift she'd worn under her graduation gown last week, now a sure tightness at her waistline, summer sandals on her feet—had been there since the breeze, cool on her bare legs and arms, moved off the creek and through the gravestones like the last sighing breath of the dead.

While she waited for the preaching to start, she went

among the newly decorated graves, reading the stones that were legible, the familiar names of those who had perished aboveground in fires, or by gunshot, or from the Spanish flu, and those who died belowground in cave-ins and explosions. She recalled stories of floods that scoured whole towns, tucking the dead away in trees and drainpipes before a proper burial.

Everyone from Twenty-Seven had someone buried there. Mounts, Deskins, her own people: Sturgills, Branhams, Justices, McCoys. And there were Akers stones, as well, even though many didn't think they should be there. Someday, she and Ellis would be buried there, too.

She could not allow herself to dwell on Ellis for long. He had changed shifts at the mine, and she had not seen him since that night in his room but wasn't ready to face him because she couldn't possibly know if the baby was his.

Two graves were new that year, their gravel-strewn mounds marked by temporary funeral-home plates, the typed names and dates blurry beneath frost-shattered plastic. Old man Adkins from the head of the holler, passed away in early January, and Odell Mahon, the thirteen-year-old grandson of Cap and Dreema from the right fork, killed in a car wreck over at Matewan just after last year's June Meeting. Like the other kids, June had called him Red, and he hadn't seemed to mind. He'd had a face full of freckles, the greenest eyes she'd ever seen. He had sometimes teased her on the school bus about her big feet.

There were older graves, their now-illegible names long ago scratched onto shards of sandstone and time-shrouded by lichen, that might have been mistaken for mere rocks had they not been in a graveyard. Upright hickory and oak markers with names and dates carved into them. The small stones of children, some containing arrowheads or marbles pressed into concrete, the toys of the dead. Uphill, in the shaded corner, June's nearest kin. Shag Branham, her own daddy, Great-Granny and Grandpa Branham, Grandpa Justice, dead awhile before June was born, and now Granny, almost two years gone. There were aunts and uncles she barely remembered, the small stones of their babies scattered among them. Aunt Lorena, Uncle Dick's first wife. Uncle Garvin's memorial.

June smiled to think of Garvin, wearing black tennis shoes when he wasn't wearing work boots or his church wingtips. She pictured the Fourth of July he shinnied up the big maple in Granny Justice's yard. All they could see were his legs, those high-tops dangling among the leaves. Beauty stood on the porch, seesawing a Virginia Slim between her fingers, yelling at him to come down. Two years later, he would be trapped down in the mine with Solomon Akers and his men.

June knew it would've been just like Garvin, when they smelled the methane gas in the mine that day, to tell those that could walk or run to go on ahead. He would have told them to get out right then, to stop trying to lift the hunk of slate off his leg because it was no use. But everyone knew he hadn't really been doomed just then, because after an able-bodied Sol and some of the others had gone off and left him, after the second blast sealed off Garvin and his injured men from any hope of daylight or fresh air, Garvin had somehow gotten free and crawled to the phone box, had talked to the mine boss and emergency crew outside—had spoken for the others who were drifting into bottomless sleep, clutching just-scratched-out notes to wives and mothers who'd never read them. He talked until the phone lines burned up—had calmly whispered *Mommy*, then *Beauty* as gas filled the tunnel—and when the last explosion came, there was nothing more, just static and Uncle Garvin's rusted-out Plymouth sitting among the other empty cars in the smoke-shrouded lot, its green fins gathering ashes as they fell.

•

Uncle Dick was tuning his guitar. Ronny-John, his son, played "Farewell to Trion" on the banjo, and Curtis Salisbury played along on the fiddle. People shifted toward the folding chairs set out on the level section of the cemetery. They stopped to hug or shake hands before sitting down for the preaching. Bethel, holding Charlie's hand and carrying a folded blanket to sit on, started up the path. Isom remained with three other men under a stand of trees beyond the fence where he'd likely stay to roll cigarettes, one after another, and visit, never come up for the sermon at all.

June took a chair between Rena and Beauty, who smelled of the Brocade cream that she'd bought from the Avon lady and that the humid air lifted off her tanned skin. June's chair was warm from the sun and it made her sleepy. She rested her head on Rena's shoulder, listened as the women talked about how hot it was for June, how there seemed to be more people than last year.

Their voices carried June in and out of her dozing until she felt Rena draw a sharp breath. She opened her eyes, lifted her head, looked around. Ellis stood at the outer edge of the row, staring at them—at her. His face was a canvas of worry, his high cheekbones flushed beneath the creamed-coffee skin, his left eye bruised and bloodshot. June glanced toward Isom and the men down the hill. She stood, smoothed her dress, and walked toward Ellis. She didn't care that Isom might see her following him into the woods.

She waited to feel the force of everyone's eyes boring into her back, especially Isom's, then tried to shut down her mind as they climbed the slope into deeper woods. She watched the shoulder and arm muscles move beneath Ellis's shirtsleeve, remembered his room and her head against his chest, the smell of his clean T-shirt.

She had followed him into the trees like this once before, on a warm autumn afternoon when she was thirteen. He took her into the woods beyond the drainpipe, first leading her beyond the rust-colored ditch into weedy undergrowth and then up into the timber. They had moved through the drapes of light that fell between the frost-stripped branches and climbed until they stood in front of a high beech. There, Ellis had pointed to fresh wounds in the bark. He took her hand and traced the weeping shapes he had carved the day before: *EA + JB*.

I love it, she said.

He squeezed her hand, said, It's us. Long as this tree yet stands, we'll be right here.

They stood there, feet crumpling the paper-dry leaves, looking at each other, then away by turns. June thought he would kiss her then, but he wouldn't for another year, when he'd walked her most of the way home after a softball game. They'd stood out of reach of the yard light when he bent to brush his lips against hers. For the next few days, each time June thought of Ellis's mouth on hers, she felt that what she'd known of herself—her own bone and muscle—had shifted into something new. A strange landscape with newly discovered spaces where Ellis's breath and touch had settled.

Now they stood beneath an early summer canopy as she wiped her damp hands against her hipbones beneath her dress, swallowed to wet her lips and tongue.

He spoke first. Why didn't you tell me?

She told him she wasn't sure why, then she added, I couldn't.

You couldn't?

June, unable to hold his stare, looked down and noticed her filthy feet inside the new sandals, the twig trapped beneath her toes.

He touched her arm, said, Is that what you think of me? That I would run off?

She looked at him, at the still-pink scar below his eye—Isom's work. She reached out, let the tips of her fingers brush it. She said, I'm sorry Isom done that.

Ellis pulled her to him, rubbed her back. Forget about Isom, he said. I'm scared, too, but we can do the right thing.

June backed away from him, said, I'm so sorry.

He frowned. No, it's both of us, he said. We both did this.

No, she said.

The word spewed out of her, tainted the air between them. He drew into himself like he'd just been rib punched. She had to look away.

Sometimes, in the dark of night, June had let herself imagine something with Ellis that she couldn't with JT—the two of them married and living in Granny's old house or maybe in downtown Myrtle Gap, an old coal-camp house or an apartment over Main Street. No one would ever have to know the baby might not belong to Ellis. Then, if she let herself think too long on it, a deep loneliness would set in and then the recognition that she, herself, would know or might always wonder, and all of it would be too heavy for her to carry.

He put out his hand to touch her belly but didn't. When's it due? he asked.

October, she whispered.

The world spun. Then she said, It's not yours.

Uncle Dick's guitar droned from the cemetery and a cloud passed across the face of the sun. She shivered.

What do you mean? Ellis said.

She said, I mean I don't know.

His chest rose and fell in quick, shallow fits, then he asked, What do mean you don't know, June?

The first strains of "I'll Fly Away" rose up from below. June wanted to run home and lie down. She couldn't stand the thought of Ellis thinking she'd done him wrong, but she couldn't make herself tell him the truth. She was ashamed. It was her fault she'd gotten into JT's car that night. She deserved what had happened.

Never mind, she said. I'm just too tired and mixed-up to think.

His face went deep red, his eyes darkened. He said, You're being crazy, and he turned from her, started down the mountain. She waited until he disappeared into the trees before she sat down and began to cry.

Bethel

I WATCHED THEM KIDS GO, WATCHED ELLIS LEAD JUNE into the skirt of trees at the bottom of the mountain, prayed that Isom wouldn't take notice. I couldn't help it. As they disappeared, first him and then her, I got a last glance and saw how Ellis favored his daddy in the way he was built. For the shortest while, I couldn't blame June for loving him. Might've knowed how she felt.

Soon as I told Sol I was with child—his child—he run off to work in the Goodyear plant in Akron. I had to walk around for nearly a month, pretend I weren't sick or tired, clutchin my secret with all my might. I was right mad when I heard he was sending money home to his mama and daddy. After that, I had to tell.

My own mama, for Daddy had died by then, took my news pretty good, said she knew it was bound to happen and that it took two. Lord, she cussed Solomon Akers up one side and down the other when he come back from Akron. I about keeled over to hear her talk like that. Of course Sol couldn't stay away long from the mine or his people. He come back home when Rena was about six weeks old and never even come around to see her one time. Then he married that girl America Hatfield. I knew her as Merkey in school, though. She was nice.

I have no earthly idea when it was that Sol first laid eyes on Rena—I always imagined it to be when I had her with me somewhere in town—but he woulda knowed she was his from the start. She had that dark Akers complexion. If everybody hadn't already known, they would've fairly easily guessed she didn't belong to Shag, what with her unusual eyes and that curly black hair. I was relieved to know that she had not got his bad temperament. Those Akers people are known for their easygoing ways until you cross one of em. I cain't say I blame them. Folks was often mean to them, called them ugly names. Sol could be real tender toward me, though. Most don't know that.

Sometimes I ask myself if I ever truly loved Isom like I loved Sol and Shag. I tried to imagine how I would feel if he were to die, and I cain't. All I know is I've growed used to him, and he has kept us in shoes and clothes and there's food on the table. It puts me in mind of those arranged marriages that people have over in India. Eventually, people get accustomed to one another and settle down to just plain live. That was me and Isom.

Isom, he's never once laid a hand on me, except in the tenderest way. But I sometimes, when I'm a-walkin in the woods, allow myself to imagine being married to Sol Akers.

Flying

JUNE STEPPED BEYOND THE SWATH OF BEAUTY'S PORCH light into the shadows of the yard, leaving Beauty inside in the front room, smoking and reading the *Grit* magazine one of the Hall boys came selling that afternoon. June had waited all evening for Ellis to call before he went to work, but he hadn't.

Why don't you just call him? Beauty had asked.

I couldn't stand it if he hung up on me, June said.

She swept her flashlight beam back and forth across the road, watched for copperheads that might have crawled out from the underbrush to collect the warmth of its sandy surface. Up on the strip, bright lights washed out the stars, burned through mineral-clouded air like the eyes of night creatures. Diesel engines growled as machines gnawed at the flesh of the mountain, brought up coal from its dynamited wounds.

Evenings at Beauty's were quiet now without Garvin. No longer was he here to tell what he called the critter tales that used to frighten June or sing off-key to the Andy Williams record on the hi-fi: *moon riverrrr.*

Beauty and Garvin were never able to have any children of their own, but they hadn't seemed to mind the noise and mess of nieces and nephews who passed through the small, orderly cabin they'd bought from Granny Justice.

Now, June often visited Beauty to keep her company and to get away from Bethel and her Bible-reading silence, the sound of Isom's gurgling cough. Tonight, she and Beauty had made cheese pizza from a boxed kit they'd bought at Maynard's store, then they'd played rummy, but June could hardly concentrate.

The night air calmed her. She followed the sandy road whose curves she knew by heart, knew where she was in the dark by the sounds the creek made in certain places. If she hadn't known, she could've told the time of year by the smells rising off it. There had been a rain shower that afternoon, and the water smelled of mud and leaf, the scale and shell of creatures that lived around it.

When they were kids, she and Tom would race all the way home in the dark after evenings at Garvin and Beauty's, cutting through gnat swarms and ghosts of warm air coming off the creek. Sometimes, before the mine explosion, they imagined themselves dancers—Lords a-leaping, Tom said. They caught air in stretching bounds, conjured images of snakes, tried to keep their feet off the ground as long as possible. For a few breathless seconds, they flew. And now she carried a child, no longer free to run and leap, and Tom had disappeared into a jungle where there surely were plenty of snakes to jump over.

From the edge of her yard, she heard the kitchen radio and briefly mistook it for Tom's. It played the Grand Ole Opry at a volume that told her someone was listening from another room.

The smoke of Isom's rolled cigarettes wafted through the screen door. Moths that had clung to the mesh just before scattered like torn paper when she opened it.

He was lying on the couch, his socked feet propped up on

the arm, an orange beanbag ashtray on his chest that rode the waves of his breathing. He sat up, hung his head over his knees, and coughed. The ashtray tumbled onto his lap, then to the floor.

Goddamn, he wheezed. He brushed ashes and cigarette butts off his lap into an open hand.

June bent to pick up the ashtray, said, Isom?

She knew he'd seen her talking to Ellis at June Meeting, but he seemed too weak for fury.

He stared at the trash in his palm. Go on to bed, he said.

I had to talk to him, Isom, she said.

It's too late for that, he said. Now get on to bed.

June waited until she was in her room to cry. She had wanted to tell him about JT but was relieved she hadn't. It wouldn't matter to Isom, anyway. She had lain with Ellis Akers, and there was no forgiving that.

She heard Isom open the screen door, then the whisper of him brushing ashes off his pants. Then the door again and the sound of him pulling the string to turn off the overhead light.

Hours later, just as the sun came over the mountain, June rolled onto her back. She listened again to wisps of music coming from the kitchen radio, straining to hear where Bethel was in the house. It was in that time of morning quiet that she most noticed the brushes of movement in her belly. She placed a hand below her navel and waited. A few heartbeats later, she felt it again, the baby's awakening. Each time, a thrill surged through her. She closed her eyes, pictured a honey-skinned girl coming into form.

Snapping Beans

JUNE FLICKED THE END OF A STRING BEAN OFF HER lap, over the porch rail and into the yard, picked another bean from the dishpan and snapped it. An explosion up on the mountain nearly jarred her glass of tea off the rail. An echo shivered through the holler, caused the baby to turn in her belly, a kicking tumble so much stronger than those first movements like moth wings brushing a lampshade.

The birds went quiet. Bethel had been on her knees in the garden patch across the road, pulling summer squash from a tangle of vines. She struggled to her feet and wiped her hands down the seams of her dress.

I wisht they'd quit that, she said. She turned, gazed up toward the head of the holler where a swarm of dust settled over the trees. In that moment, a shaft of sunlight struck her brown hair, glinted off the strands of white running through it, made her the peasant in *The Song of the Lark*, an oil painting that hung on the wall of the school library, her body a cage of bone, save the soft rise of belly beneath her shirtwaist.

June recalled a mine strike the winter she was twelve. Isom refused to cross the picket line at Twenty-Seven, said he'd damned sure not buy any coal from the company. All that winter, Bethel walked her kids along the railroad tracks in early mornings, carrying a bushel basket, stopping to pick up chunks of coal that had fallen off the railcars as they headed out of the mountains. Isom fussed, said he didn't want his wife having to pick up coal, especially coal that still belonged to the company. He didn't want the foreman or the men who walked the picket to see his kids scrounging, his wife all stooped over.

One evening during the strike, Solomon Akers stopped by on his way home from work to offer coal from the bed of his truck. He had expected Garvin and Isom to be gone, on the picket line, and he told Bethel he'd brought it for her, but Isom had been home. He cursed Sol and told him to get off his property or he'd get his gun. Goddamned scab, he'd yelled.

By the end of the following summer, the bowels of the mine would shatter, splintering rock and timber, and Isom would blame Sol for leaving Garvin to die in the dust-thick darkness.

The strike lasted into the still-cold mornings of early spring, and when all but the fist-sized or smaller coal ran out, Isom went to hacking up the old corn crib behind Granny Justice's barn. He took an axe to it, gashing up its sides then smashing and grunting at the old boards, pulling them apart with a claw hammer. Tom, ordered to be out there with him, sawed splintered boards into stove lengths and stacked them into the wheelbarrow with frozen, bloodied fingers.

•

Up on the mountain, another explosion. June pictured tree roots wrenched from the earth, dirt and rock bursting up from the ridge, peppering back to ground the same way the muted explosions of Vietnam came across Rena's TV.

Bethel cupped her chin, rubbed her cheek with dirty fingers. June imagined her to be thinking of Millard Deskins, killed in the war—how his mother Ruby claimed she saw the mortar blast on the TV news and right then knew it was her boy they were carrying on the litter. She said she'd recognized his double crown cowlick showing from under the end of the muddy blanket they'd covered him with. Then came the gossip that there wasn't much left of him below the chest to send home. A closed casket.

June was certain that, at the moment, Bethel was thinking mostly of Tom, who had joked in a letter home, *They call us being here being "in country." I was already IN THE COUNTRY at home. Ha!* he'd written.

June, too, was thinking of Tom. Last night she heard him call her name. She'd sat up, expected to hear his radio playing on the other end of the attic or to see him standing in her doorway, telling her where he'd been and all he'd seen. She hadn't slept the rest of the night, watched the curtains shiver in a draft from the window.

She recalled learning in physics class that matter is neither created nor destroyed, that it only changes forms. *Well then,* she wondered, *where did the heat go after Isom threw wood into the stove that spring? How far away do particles from the top of the mountain travel after a blast? Where do people go when they've been blown up and there isn't much left of them?*

June called across the road to her mother, who was back on her knees in the dirt. Mama, I've about got these beans done.

Bethel didn't move. June realized she was praying, and just then, the question came. When the baby comes, what part of her—what matter—would have changed forms to make it? Ellis or JT's? Would nothing of her own self be lost? She closed her eyes and listened for the birds to start up again.

Maynard's

ELLIS'S PICKUP WAS PARKED IN FRONT OF MAYNARD'S store. Scattered in its bed were fishing tackle, a canvas tent, and an ice chest. Empty Vienna sausage and pork 'n' beans cans spilled from an overturned cardboard box.

That's Ellis's truck, she whispered to Rena. She wondered if he'd run off to the woods for a while and had just come back, was relieved to think that might be the reason he hadn't called. She longed to see him, talk to him, touch him again, but she was also afraid.

As they walked past the truck, she heard the engine tick, wanted to open its door, climb inside, and wait for Ellis to come out of the store. She'd make him listen to her. Even though she had written a letter telling him how sorry she was, she still hadn't told him about JT and the night on Mud Branch. She longed for another chance to see him, in case Sol or Merkey had intercepted her letter. Maybe she could tell him everything now.

She followed Rena through the door, her legs hollow, electric charges coming alive just under her skin. Inside, the familiar mingled smells of fresh light bread and the sweetness of peanut butter cups, tobacco, and wood smoke underneath.

She scanned the room for Ellis but found no one else in the

store. Rena said, I cain't remember a time when Mikey or Hazel wasn't in here. Must be around here someplace.

June's mind rummaged for an answer, some kind of a sign that would help her make sense of the empty room and the green pickup parked outside. Dread rose up from some knowing place inside her.

Rena shrugged and walked toward the shelf where Mikey kept the washing powders. Then, muffled laughter from behind the store.

Rena pulled a box of Rinso off the shelf, said, They're probably out there telling tales and lying. You want a Nehi?

No, thanks, June said. I done had one today.

Well, at least get you something you want. We've got to hurry and get back home.

June was reaching into the candy-bar rack when the back door opened. Mikey stuck in his freckled, bald head and said over his shoulder, I told you there was somebody in here.

He stepped into the room, trailing smoke from his cigar. Hey, pretty ones, he said, the words coming out too loud because he'd been drinking.

Rena giggled, said, You better not let Watt hear you talk that away. He'll have your hide.

Wisps of smoke drifted through the door's opening, trailed gray tendrils that reached around the doorframe. June stood fastened to the floor, dread and yearning boiling up inside her.

She heard him before she saw him, knew enough of his voice to recognize it. Solomon Akers hunched his frame through the door, looked around at the three of them then closed it behind him. He nodded at Rena, said her name, then set his eyes on June.

Well, there she is, he chirped. I heard a rumor you was in the family way and now I see it's true.

June glanced at Rena, then Mikey. She edged closer to the counter, then Rena was beside her, dropping soup cans and the box of Rinso onto the scarred wood surface. June could feel Sol's eyes scouring her. She pulled her overshirt tighter around her.

Hey, he said in a low voice.

She turned to see him mimicking holding a basketball or watermelon in front of his belly, before he pointed at her. The gesture made her ill.

Honey, it's way too late to hide that, he said. And you sure wasn't going to hang it on my boy after layin up with one of them boys from the road crew.

How does he know that? Tears seared the rims of her eyes. She gritted her teeth, willed herself to not cry from the shame she felt. She looked at Rena, who shrugged as if to say she didn't know how he knew about JT. She would later offer that maybe Sol had a lucky guess or that one of the boarders had told it.

Mikey hunched over the steno pad where he did his figuring. He was working out Rena's bill with a pencil stub but looked up long enough to say, Sol, that's enough now.

Solomon moved closer then, said, I'll tell you what's enough. My boy was so tore up about this mess that he enlisted.

The words poured over June, froze into a shell around her. Sol nodded at her, pointed, said, He gets killed, it's your fault.

As June and Rena left the store, Solomon called, The Lord sayeth, Let justice roll down like waters, and righteousness like a ever-flowin stream!

Come a Storm

JUNE WALKED TOWARD THE MOUTH OF THE HOLLER under a gunmetal sky, the air as heavy as she felt. The leaves on the trees, already beginning to change colors, had turned their silver bellies to the sky.

Granny Carrie had said that June was in the last trimester of her pregnancy. She hadn't given up on trying to hide her body, had put on one of Tom's old long-sleeved flannel shirts that she often wore when she went out, though everyone knew of her condition by then. That day, the shirt had gone sodden in the humidity. She imagined a rubber diving suit against her skin. At the same time, the shirt was a comfort, so she kept it on. She smiled to think what Tom would say about her wearing it without his permission.

She and Tom had not often quarreled, but they had fought like most brothers and sisters. Before he left for the army, they'd mostly argued when June borrowed his clothes and didn't hang them back up after she wore them. They had never once struck one another, although Tom accidentally hit her with a corncob once when he'd aimed to huck it nearby to scare her. She never told on him, could never bring herself to strike Tom at all. She'd seen Isom do enough of that.

She had just turned around at the underpass and started for

home when the late-summer sky broke open, releasing fists of warm rain that pounded the hard-packed road. She walked faster, passed the simmering slate dump and its burnt-rubber smell, passed the water impoundment toward a four-room house that squatted by the road. She hurdled onto Nettie Hatfield's porch, the soaked clothes sticking to her thick body.

Lord God, you're about drownded, Nettie said. She shut the screen door behind her, gestured at June's belly pushing against the wet shirt, then the porch steps, said, You got no business hoppin up on porches now!

She handed June a dry towel from the clothesline strung across the front porch, said, You cain't afford to get sick.

The rain came in waves, letting up for a few seconds then returning to pummel the porch roof, requiring them to pause their sparse conversation. Nettie seemed to understand that June didn't feel much like talking and so didn't ask questions. In one of the lulls, a roar rose up out of the impoundment dam down the road, the roiling water behind it angry, thundering like a drunken uncle.

Honey, mark my word, Nettie said as she nodded toward the dam. One of these days that thing's a-gonna bust. I only hope I ain't still around fer it. Hit'll kill us all and the government will call it a act of God.

Surely not, June said.

Lord God, I hope you're right, Nettie said.

When the rain finally stopped, sudden sunlight bathed the holler. Tree leaves, roadside weeds, and Nettie's grass had been washed clean of coal dust and now threw off sharp light that made June's eyes ache. She thanked Nettie and started home, carrying a bag of fresh kale for Bethel.

Just past the Estep place, the last house for the next half mile, tires splashed through the potholes behind her. She moved over into the tall, wet joe-pye weeds at the road's edge and turned to watch a shiny green-black car crawl past her. Rivulets of rain beaded its hood. Inside it, two uniformed men stared at her as they passed. The white-lettered words on the door registered with her then: *United States Army.*

Oh, God. She stood rooted among the dripping weeds, the hard sunlight pounding down on her head. *Oh, God.*

Her mind traveled the road ahead of them. Her thoughts stopped at each house that had sent a boy to war. First would be the Mounts's place, Dewey gone off a month ago. Navy, she remembered. Not out of boot camp. Past her own house would be the Gillman's. Lark Gillman was in the army infantry, same as Tom. It would be one of the two of them.

She yearned to run but was afraid for the baby. She wished another car would come along, maybe Beauty herself, back from Charleston, to carry her the rest of the way home.

She rounded the last curve before her house, breathless, took a shortcut through the muddy garden, stepped high over shriveled potato leaves and glistening pumpkin vines. She made it to the yard, could see the driveway and the green car in it, shiny as coal in the raw light beside Isom's truck.

She dropped the bag of kale. Oh, God, she whispered. Oh, God.

Bethel

THE MORNING BEFORE WE GOT THE WORD ABOUT TOM, it was a blue jay flung itself against the kitchen window, left a indigo tuft stuck to the muddy smear on the glass. All day, I felt uneasy and watched for other signs. A day later, it come a rain shower and washed all that off the window.

It was late summer, and that day, I had all that gardening to do, mostly by myself. June was too big to bend over, so she sulked and spent most of her days alone, walking the hills and holler like she'd done that day, September 18—a Wednesday. It was she that come breathless into the house after I'd let them men in, before they told me about Tom. I recollect I was somehow worried about the baby and made her set down.

I don't recollect much of what the soldier said, him looking no older than Tom when he ducked his head under the lintel. I just remember the floor coming up, hittin me on my knees like I was making a beseeching prayer, but it was all backward. It seems to me that beseeching is all I ever done after that.

They didn't know what to do with me, and June just set there on the davenport like a statue, all the color gone from her face.

Ma'am, is there someone we can call?

Just then, somebody was passing by, maybe Press Newsome,

I don't know, lookin to see what was going on, I reckon, and they sent him to the mine to get Isom. All I remember of what came after that was taking to my bed—had I stopped the clocks?—and waking up in the dark with Isom huddled up agin me, trembling. I put my hand to his face and felt the tears. Every night after that, I was afraid to go to sleep, for I'd not wanted to wake up of a morning and start that grief all over again.

I wanted my son back so bad. The man who come to the house said we'd git a thousand dollars because Tom had been killed in action. I didn't even care about that. I'd lost a child before, but it was a stillbirth and happened before I had a chance to get to know him, had nursed him, or could've still found him in the dark by his smell. That was nothing compared to this, and no amount of money would make it right.

It was nigh to ten days before we got Tom home for a funeral. We got a telegram from the army telling us when to expect the *remains*. Remains *is a odd word*, I thought. Then when we got him, they wouldn't let me see him—had his casket bolted shut, tight. I found myself wondering if he was really in there. They wouldn't let us bring him to the house, either. I guess it was Isom and Beauty planned it all with the army. I just couldn't do it.

Granny Justice

HIT WERE JOHN HENRY WHO COME TO GET ME WHEN my own time come. I had just closed my eyes and here he appeared in my room, back from the dead and holdin two babies—our twin girls that was born in 1919—all of them grinnin. I could feel Little John and Jarvis, Mommy and Poppy with them, too, but couldn't make them out. Hit's all still a mystery.

John been dead thirty-odd year when he come to get me, but he looked just the same as when we was young. I wonder how I looked to him. He said nary a word, but that smile made me feel so warm all over, like the first time I laid eyes on him in grade school, but it were such a pure, holy love he gave off just then that I somehow knowed come from the Lord. They lingered only awhile then left me standin where I was and walked back into the beauteous light. I somehow knowed I couldn't go with them, that I had unfinished business to tend to. At the time, I didn't know what that was.

I give John Henry Justice seven babies in all. I think if he had lived, he woulda ventually wanted more, but I had already had the change o' life when he passed away. Honey, I didn't want no more kids. I was plumb wore-out with carryin seven to term, cept the twins, which was two months early.

John Junior, or Little John, were my first. He lived to twenty-three, was killed when a log rolled on him and drownded him in a splash dam over on Yellowjacket. I didn't think John Henry would get over that, but he did, with the Lord's help. He was saved and baptized a couple of year after that, over at the church on Cyphers' Creek where his people come from. I never expected that but was grateful when it occurred. I guess his oats was sowed, although he was faithful, far as I know—and a woman knows what kind of man she's picked. He was unusual for his time. Mostly, women in these mountains do all the churchin for their men, hopin their own dutiful service will save them at the Rapture, which I know now is nonsense. Ain't no rapture. I have no idee if that works—women attendin church in the stead of their men. It ain't for me to know.

My next baby were Custer. He went into the service then settled up in Cincinnati with his Italian wife. He had been loggin when Junior was killed, but he went into the service right after that. I allus suspected he was deathly afeared of water, but don't you know they stuck him on a island first thing. When he come home, he moved over to Lincoln County and tried to grow tobacco for a while. He was awful loyal and visited me oncet or twicet a year, usually in the summer. His wife Eloisa was allus good to write. They never had no kids. I don't know why.

Then along come Jarvis and Jupiter after Custer. A set a twins. Jarvis was sickly and died when he was but two days old. Somethin was wrong with his intestines, the doctor over in Williamson said. He couldn't nurse. Ever thing I fed him came right back up. I felt so helpless.

Jupe made a career out of the army, just like Custer, for he allus thought Custer were a shinin star. And he was. Jupe was wounded in Italy. He come home and married a Deskins girl from over on Huckleberry, but she died givin birth to their first child while he was in the woods, cuttin logs for T Bone Lively. He never remarried, but he still yet lives over there on Huckleberry. He didn't come home much, and when he did, I could tell he was most of the time in his cups. I don't think he could forgive hisself for not bein there when Doskie and the baby died. Maybe he thought he could've done somethin, but they wasn't a thing that could've been done, and I told him as much.

Next come my girl twins, my first girls. They was borned too early, right after the peak of the Spanish flu, on July 12, 1919. I had the Spanish flu at the end of 1918 and like to have died. Never had a fever like that one before or since. I didn't know it at the time, but it affected the babies I was carryin.

John Henry thought I would surely die and made arrangements for my mommy to raise the least uns, Jupe and Custer, if I did. But I didn't. My daddy had already milled some pine boards for my coffin, but he wound up makin a little casket for the twins instead. I can still recollect how them nails sung as they went into the boards. We nested them angel girls together in that box and buried them up on the family cemetery at the mouth of the holler. I named them Mary Magdalene and Salome, after the scriptures.

Bethel were my last borned, delivered by Carrie Vance's mother, Oma Jean. The rest I done mostly on my own with Mommy helpin me, but she was gone by the time Bethel come along.

She was a beautiful baby. Bald as a cue ball at first till her hair come in red, and she had them blue eyes like I seen on the twins when they come to fetch me out of my deathbed. I reckon it were the Scotch comin out in her, from my McCoy side. All of my boys had red beards like my brothers and my daddy and granddaddy.

Bethel were a easy baby. I lay that off to her brothers watchin after her all the time. She were a tomboy from the start, but when she turned twelve and thirteen, she were a wild one. And that was just the beginnin. Her daddy and me was terrified that she would turn up pregnet like many of the other girls her age then, and she did, sure enough. She ran the roads with Sol Akers ever when she could slip out of the house. John whupped her for it oncet, before he passed over about six months later, but it never did no good. She still turned up expectin Corrina.

I guess I was plumb wore-out by then and had give up and was kindly relieved that John wasn't there for that because he never did like Melungeons or any people who was differnt, and Sol's people was Melungeons for shore, somehow kin to the Goins bunch outta Tennessee. You could tell by the dark skin and thick, wild hair. Them strange eyes. They're a fine-boned and pretty people.

The joke was kindly on John, though, for I never told that my Grandmommy Clay's mother was a Indian from Kentucky. I'm right proud of that. It was her taught my mommy the roots, among other things. Yes, I hear tell Granny Jince was dark, but the rest of us that come after was mostly light-skinned and you couldn't hardly tell the Indian in us less you was a-lookin for it. I had a picture of her somewhere but cain't recall where just now. Long black hair made up into a bun at the back a her head, wearin a regular dress, but you could tell she's a Indian if you know what you're lookin for.

Aunt Esther allus said Grandmommy was ashamed of her mother bein Indian or Portygee or whatever they call it. That made me sad. I remember goin' to visit Granny Jince once when she was still yet alive. I was little then, and she had a rooster I was fraid of. I'm named after her. I got her close-set eyes.

They was one more pregnecy after Bethel, but no one ever knowed about it, save me and Mommy. Not even John ever knowed. It was three months after Bethel was borned, and I knowed I was in the family way again. I was wore-out with a new baby and them boys runnin around like banshees. Mommy had told me that, if a body fed her babies at the breast, she wouldn't get pregnet until she weaned. I guess that don't always work.

I was over at Mommy's and she was a-puttin up corn. Hit was a hot summer mornin—we allus done our cannin in the cool of the day if we could—and I was lookin the beans for her, pickin out the sticks and rocks, for they was to be supper that night. Bethel were a sleepin in the little dresser drawer I'd fixed up for her, lined it with a quilt. Law, she barely fit she was so big by that time! I guess it were the heat and the smell of that raw corn. When I stood up to dip water for the beans, I fell out on the floor and took the water bucket with me.

Mommy stuck me up in a chair again and said, Look at me, Jincy.

I was still addled, but I looked her in the eye. Right then, I come to, and then I knowed what she was a-thinkin. I said, It cain't be true, but I knowed it was. I realized my monthlies hadn't started up again. I was so used to it by now, with all my pregnecies, and I was so occupied by lookin after my kids, I didn't notice it. I went to squallin then. I cried, Mommy, I'm plumb wore-out. I cain't do this agin!

Mommy went quiet. I thought she were mad at me, so I run my fingers through them beans to soothe myself and tried not to be sick because the smell of that corn was all a sudden too sweet. After a while, Mommy said, I don't think you can, either, Jincy. Carryin seven babies and lookin after four little uns is enough.

What am I a-gonna do? I asked her.

Mommy was at the stove, a-puttin jars into the cannin pot. She turned around and said, I'll tell you a secret I never told nary a one, and as long as you live, don't you dare tell it, either.

She dried her hands on her half apron and said, I made plumb sure five children was all I ever had.

Funerals

JUNE PUT ON HER DARKEST-COLOR DRESS, A NAVY A-line, for Tom's funeral and found it scarcely fit. It strained over her swollen breasts and stretched around her torso, and the tension in the fabric made her feel angry and anxious. She couldn't breathe.

For the past ten days, she'd slept only in Tom's room, where her private grief came in surges. She ate her meals there or lay on the bed staring at nothing, unable to concentrate on reading or listening to the radio. She'd think she was too wrung out to cry anymore, and then some small trinket or memory would set her to bawling again.

That morning when she woke, she'd felt Tom in the room with her and was reminded of waking on another overcast autumn day a few years before, a November afternoon when she and Tom had been home from school with the flu. She had awakened from a restless nap to the gravity of a body sitting on the edge of her bed. When June opened her mattery eyes, it was Tom, who brought the smell of coffee and boiled chicken in his clothes, his own eyes red, his face just beginning to hint at the acne that would bother him, follow him into the army.

She noticed the distended skin around Tom's eyes, realized he'd been crying. He said, They done shot the president.

June, disoriented and fever-addled, said, What?

Tom took her hand, blurted, JFK is dead . . . shot in Dallas!

For the first time since waking, she registered the silence of the house. No coffee spoons clinking in cups, no scratch of Bethel's house shoes on the linoleum, no gospel music on the radio. The world had shifted while she slept. The president was dead.

June and Tom had followed the election and Kennedy's presidency, and the past April, Rena had gone on a school trip to see him when he had flown into the Kanawha Airport. It had been raining that day, and Rena's teacher held up an umbrella so JFK could stand under it as he shook hands with people across the chain-link fence. Rena had been close enough to touch his blue suit coat. She said it felt like a bolt of electricity went through her. When she'd come home that evening thrilled and dreamy, Isom bragged at the supper table that he'd voted for Nixon and added, I hate that Catholic mobster. Number one, he's a communist nigger-lover, and two, he just shows up here so he can say how sorry he feels for us poor folks, but he won't do a damned thing about it. Mark my words, he'll get us tangled up in that mess in Vietnam, and Tom, you better be ready to go.

Hearing Isom say those things had made Rena cry and June so sick to her stomach that she couldn't eat. She couldn't help thinking that her own father would never have used those words.

Tom squeezed June's hand, said, I wanted to tell you myself.

For a time, they sat there on the bed, tears raveling down their cheeks.

Too weak to put together questions from the thought

fragments that darted through her fevered mind, she would ask them later, get details from the news that she, Bethel, and Tom watched at Beauty's in the coming days. Bethel had even let them stay home from school the following Monday so they could see the funeral.

•

June tugged at the bodice of her funeral dress, tied back her hair with a fat white strand of yarn, studied her red eyes and suntanned face in the mirror. She heard Bethel in the kitchen, crying. Then her own hot tears returned. The world was all wrong. There was no hope, no place for all of her love to go.

Granny Justice

HIT'S A DIFFICULT POSITION BEIN IN LIMBO, ON THIS side of things and not bein able to communicate like I'm of a mind to. I'm not complainin. I think I will miss bein on this creek, but I cain't comfort the livin like I could when I was still yet alive. My heart hurts for Bethel and June and Rena. I feel helpless.

I wish I coulda been the one to get Tom when he crossed over, but I guess that ain't why I'm still here. I learned about him gettin killed the same way as ever one else. Asides, I think John Henry musta come from Heaven itself when he come to me that day. I don't believe he left any unfinished business. He surely must've growed outta his prejudice and has gone to his reward.

Law, but I loved that Tom dearly, called him my Tom-boy, for he were the tenderest—hardly put up a fuss about nothin. He put me in mind of John Junior. He helped me out, mowed my yard with that old push mower, collected eggs when I had them chickens. Anythin I asked him to.

Course I love all them kids like my own. Turned out they was the only grandbabies I'd get. I loved it when they was little and would come over to spend the night. I fairly spoiled them. We'd eat popcorn I cooked on the stove and drink pop that

I got for em when I done my tradin over at Maynard's. Then we'd all get up in the bed like a pile of puppies, and I'd read to them from the Holy Bible or some poetry. They specially loved Robert Service poems. Made em giggle. I helped them memorize Psalm 23 and the Yeats poem that my mommy loved so. Rena even said both of em for me at my funeral. It moved me. I was so proud.

I'm kindly glad I'm still yet here to stick close to June and Rena and Bethel in this time. I know what it's like to lose a grown son. It ain't for the weak. Maybe they can feel me and my love around them, for that's all what I got to give.

Going to Ground

ISOM, WATT, AND THE OTHER MEN FROM THE CREEK had dug Tom's grave next to Garvin's, and the preacher from Parsley Bottom came around to do the service and would take no pay for it. The army sent soldiers, too, and at one thirty on a Thursday afternoon, after Bethel had been handed a crisp, folded American flag, the men laid PFC Branham into a nest of clay and fragrant sassafras roots. Then came three sets of gunshots that volleyed off the ridges.

In the weeks after that, after supper and the last dish was scrubbed and scalded and the well bucket refilled for the night, Bethel disappeared, leaving June to sweep the floor. Isom, shut up in his own thoughts, sat in the chair by the front window holding a cigarette between yellowed fingertips. Many times, he'd leave it to burn in the ashtray on his lap as the dark came down the mountain and he wiled the time before his shift. Sometimes he sipped a glass of Cutty Sark from the bottle that Uncle Dick had brought him just before the funeral.

When the last light had gone from the day, Bethel would come in, her face still bruised with grief. After some weeks, she stopped going wherever it was she had gone every night, but she still sometimes disappeared during daylight. Her sorrowing seemed to come in swells, and for the rest of her days, it would never really leave her.

June had often heard Bethel say, When a body gets troubled, it's time to go to water, and this is what she had done when she worried about money or when death had taken Grandpa Justice. June had not been alive when Bethel miscarried, but she imagined her mother going to the creek then, too. This time, though, June was sure that when Bethel disappeared, she went to ground, where her son lay among the many others she'd loved.

Palimpsest

JUNE WENT TO THE CREEK WITH A WISHING JAR SHE'D started after she and Viv made plans to go away, with a pen and steno pad still embossed with shadows of the letters Bethel had written to Tom. She sat awkwardly on the bank and wrote her own letter to him, layered her words over her mother's, and then wept as she tucked the folded paper into a knothole in a tree. When she was all cried out, she curled up on the ground, knees to the expanse of her belly, and dozed. Later, she made a list of girls' names, as Carrie had predicted the sex of her baby, and she knew, could feel it to be true. She wrote the names of family women and characters from books, tried combinations of given and middle names, realized she never knew any part of JT's real name. Her mind burned through that thought. She willed the baby to be Ellis's.

She dumped out the contents of the wishing jar—among them a piece of rock quartz, a folded dollar bill, the hollow wing bones of a bird—and used her fingers to scoop dirt into its opening. When it was half full, she screwed on the cap and ring and set it aside to take home with her to hide beneath her bed. Soil for her baby to stand on. She studied her streaked fingers and recalled the colored layers of dirt in the walls of Tom's grave—the dank, sweet smell that rose up from the ground.

Thinking of Tom unseated a pebble in her throat, sent it sinking into her chest. She thought she might be sick. More tears welled and slid down her face. Above her, dry, dying leaves floated on a pond of sky. The world was upside down and would never be right again.

When they were kids, June and Tom would go to the woods to explore or dam up the creek with chunks of glinting sandstone until it formed a knee-deep pool. If it was too cold to swim, they floated leaf boats and stick rafts then threw rocks at them while Tom yelled, Strafe em! They played Indians, pretended to stalk game, cooked their imaginary kills over flameless fires made of piled-up twigs. Or they hunted for arrowheads. The best time for finding them, Tom told her, was after a storm, when they had tumbled down the holler in the churning water and caught on a sandbar. Tom had been better at finding them than June, and most of those still in the lard can under her bed had belonged to him. He spotted them by crawling along the creek bank while June wandered upright, distracted by animate things—wildflowers and bugs. Tom had studied the scrapers and points, cataloged them, knew each by its heft and edge. He was so adept that he was able to identify them as soon as he picked them from the dirt or water. Before he pocketed an arrowhead, he'd hold it up and describe its features, imitating the announcer on Mutual of Omaha's Wild Kingdom:

This here's a Hardaway side notch. This southern Appalachian artifact is composed of jasper. It's from the Middle Archaic Era.

June brought her fingers to her face, sniffed the dirt that was a time capsule filled with things so much older than her and Tom or Isom and Bethel. Older still than Great-Granny McCoy and all the old ones before her.

When she was a girl, she would sometimes lie on her stomach in the yard and pull clumps of grass to expose a few inches of ground. She watched ants carry their loads—food crumbs, grains of sand—in and out of the frame of that tiny world into which she peered. She wondered at the scale of it all, how tall the surrounding forest of grass must've seemed to the ants, wondered whether they even knew or cared that she was there or whether they were aware of the hovering sky so high above them. Thinking of all this, the sudden pulling back of the lens to the trees and mountains around her had made June, herself, feel small, that only she possessed knowledge of this secret world.

The first time she had eaten dirt was a few days before. She'd been puzzled to find herself digging a tiny hole in the yard with a spoon, bringing the soil to her lips. She let her tongue taste last summer's rain, from the time before there was a baby, before Tom and Ellis were gone. Then the dirt became something else. It sated her hunger, her desire—and so she had pushed the whole of the clump into her mouth. It sat on her tongue for a bit, then she worked it to her back teeth. In the chewing of it, she learned it, recognized the stones that had made it, the wind and water that had worn it down into the thing it now was. Then she swallowed it, took all of it into her, took in the crumbled twig and bone of everything that had ever lived on the creek. She tasted the bones of her ancestors. After that, she craved it, welcomed it into her blood, imagined the dirt settling into it to form the bones of her own child.

Myrtle Gap

BEAUTY'S FAIRLANE FLOATED OVER THE NEW ASPHALT of the four-lane, headed toward Watson's Department Store in Myrtle Gap. In the passenger seat, Bethel giggled, said, Law, Beauty. I've never in my life gone this fast!

Early fall had settled over the mountains, the highway corridor from Williamson to Charleston finished for three weeks. All of Jewell's boarders were gone, her orchard quiet again.

It was June's first time on the new four-lane, too, with all lanes wide open. She glanced at the speedometer. Beauty was driving sixty miles an hour, a speed faster than any of them had ever experienced. She handled the steering wheel with hands whose nails were filed to points and painted a bright pink, blew cigarette smoke out her window, which she'd rolled down just enough.

Earlier, at the mouth of the holler, they'd passed a stray dog, pitiful and gaunt, in the weeds by the railroad tracks. June wasn't sure anyone else had seen it sitting there on its haunches until Beauty remarked, Looks like somebody's huntin dog's got into the neighbor's yard one too many times.

She's right, June thought. If the dog had been standing, its bloated belly would've dragged in the dirt. Its legs were too short for hunting racoons, but it had the unmistakable nose of a hound.

On a summer day when he was twelve and June ten, Tom came up the road and into the yard cradling a small, brindled mutt against his sweated-through shirt, the dog too weak to walk. He handed it to June, who was sitting on the front porch waiting for the mail car.

Where'd you find him? she asked. She picked a sticktight out of a buff-colored patch of hair on the dog's neck.

Down by the tracks. Guarantee you, somebody left him up on the strip, Tom said.

June pictured the wild dogs and feral cats that lived in the woods bordering the steep, rocky grade to the strip mine—where they were left to fend for themselves when no longer wanted. She had only gone up there once, had walked up with Tom the summer before, looking for pop bottles that hadn't been shattered by gunshots. When they'd gotten to the first dozer cut, they were turned back by the stench. Someone had been up there for target practice, and June and Tom didn't have to go farther to know that there was at least one dead cat or dog up ahead, rotting in the humid July air.

I'm going to get something for him to eat out of, Tom said. He went into the house and came back with a tin pie pan. In it was a biscuit and milk gravy from the stove warmer. The dog writhed in June's arms, kept his eyes on the food as Tom set it on the porch. When she put him down, he limped over to sniff the biscuit, whined once, then began to nibble.

He's mangy, June said. Isom ain't gonna let you keep him.

Tom squatted by the dog, clasped his hands behind him, said, I'm naming him Barney and Isom don't have to know.

Barney, June said, remembering what Papaw McCoy had said about names: Once you give it a name, it's your responsibility to keep care of it.

They never knew how Isom found out about the dog. He never said. But one afternoon, as he left for work, he said to Tom, Get that damned dog out of the barn before I knock it in the head.

Tom was stunned. He had made a pen for Barney in the corner of Granny's falling-down barn across the creek, where Isom seldom went, and over a week he had kept him watered and tried to sneak him table scraps, had doctored his pitiful skin. He and June had hoped that if Isom heard him barking, he would think it was another dog from somewhere up the holler. But he had not barked.

Isom slammed the truck door, said, If that thing has give my coonhounds the mange, then I'll whip you. He'll not make it, anyways. He's too wormy.

Tom swallowed hard.

Isom started the truck, said, Be a man, Tom. Take my .22 and put it down.

Tom blanched, blinked several times.

Isom lit a cigarette with the truck lighter, said, He ain't eating. He's gonna die anyways.

Tom jammed a thumb into a belt loop of his jeans, twisted it until it went white. When Isom was gone, tears traced his cheeks.

Tom? June said.

He shook his head, motioned down the road and said, Sometimes, I'd like to kill him.

He started for the barn. She waited until he was across the

road to follow. When she, too, had crossed, she stopped to slap the spot on her calf where a sweat bee had stung her then followed the path Tom had worn through the tall weeds on the hill, unmindful of snakes. Ahead of her, he took long strides, stopped twice to swipe a shirtsleeve across his forehead.

In the barnyard, she paused, watched him slide through a space between the barn's rough timbers. Inside, the dog whined.

Barney? She heard Tom whisper it like a question.

She stepped in, let her eyes adjust. Weak light fell through holes in the roof onto the dirt floor, drifted in from cracks in the walls. Tom was on his knees in the far corner, leaning over the pen he'd made with cast-off chicken wire and the old, splintered tomato stakes that their mother wouldn't miss. Inside it, Barney lay on his side, panting.

She stood beside the pen, watched Tom dip his fingers into a coffee can filled with old motor oil, watched him bathe Barney's wounds with it. He said, Uncle Garvin told me used oil is the best thing for the mange.

He stopped to swat away the flies that bothered the air around them, drawn by the pools of watery shit in the pen.

Tom, she said, he's sufferin.

He wiped his fingers on the straw bed of the pen, then sat back, stared at the toes of June's tennis shoes, said, I know.

Is he going to die?

Tom looked up at June, shrugged. He started to cry. Tears coursed down his reddened, dirty face.

Go get the gun, he said.

When she returned with the .22 and an old pillow case, he had taken down a section of the wire. He lay on his side in the straw, his hand closed around one of the dog's front paws.

Is he dead? she asked.

Tom shook his head. He sat up, took the gun from her, checked the safety. Then he rested the rifle across his knees. A current of silence moved through the barn. June had cried then, too. There was only the sound of Barney's ragged breath that June could still sometimes hear when she thought about it.

June watched the dog's ribs, counted his breaths, let herself hope they would stop on their own. Fly buzz brought her awake and she heard herself say, Maybe he'll die anyway, before Isom gets home.

Tom shook his head again, swiped oily fingers through his hair, said, We don't know that for sure.

Somewhere down the hill, a bucket rang hollow against a stone well wall. After a time, he whispered, I cain't do it, June.

She took the rifle, counted to one thousand to give Tom enough time to get off the hill. She tucked Barney up to his neck in the pillow case, cradled him for a bit, then lay him on the straw bed. He tried to lift his head but couldn't.

By the time she racked a shell into the chamber, she knew Tom would be crouched inside the drain pipe down the road, where the sound of water would muffle the shot. Her hands shook, eyes stung. In her mind, she heard the sound of Isom's belt slithering out of its loops. She drew a jagged breath and sighted in on Barney's head.

I'm so sorry, she whispered. I'm so, so sorry. She drew one more breath and held it, then squeezed the trigger.

•

In the front seat, the women talked about Jackie Kennedy's hair and clothes. June stopped listening. She watched the fresh road cuts and the weeping trails of water on their faces sweeping past them. The floating sensation of the car made her drowsy. She thought they might've gone airborne. She tried to not think of the dog they'd passed at the mouth of the holler.

There was, on that day in Beauty's car, still so much for June to be sorry for. She thought of Tom—wondered if he'd been scared that day on the Mekong Delta or if he even knew he'd been hit. *Small arms fire*, his records said. She was sorry about Ellis, who was slow to answer her letters. She was sorry for herself and for the starving dog. Then she thought of the baby, who had been lulled quiet inside her during the car ride, and a wisp of happiness rose inside her, something that felt close to what might be the grace she'd heard about in church. She listened to the road singing beneath the car and the rush of air past Beauty's open window like a river of time.

Bethel

YESTERDAY, WITH ISOM GONE TO SLEEP AFTER HIS shift, I put on my boots, walked up the holler, and climbed the hill past the Indian rock shelter. Some of the trees I've knowed since I was little had fell over or sat real awkward on their rotting stumps. Tender little saplings grew all around them. By the time I got to the fire tower that looks out over Suttle's Gap, I was sweatin under my jacket and had to pull it off. I stood there at the bottom step in the harsh sunlight and wondered how it could possibly be fall without Tom. It was his favorite time of year.

Oncet, my brothers and I climbed that same tower. We'd played all day, had ranged farther and farther, and it was gettin too late to make it out of the woods by dark. Hit was dog days, then, and we were surely to get whupped when we got home for being out when it was so bad for our health, or so Mama said.

The tower very nearly took my breath, first from the climb, then at the top with the suddenness of so much sky. It were the first time, outside of picture books, I'd seen so many ridges at oncet. Honey, under the trees that grew on them hills, it were a jumble of worn-down pyramids like in Egypt, stretched to the end of the world. And it were the first time I ever seed the actual end of a day. Not the kind I knowed, where mountain shadows begin to fall down over the holler in the middle of the afternoon. I had thought the whole world was like that. Just then, it were the whole of the pink sky changing from day to night. Dusk laid there in all that peachy rawness. I felt like I was a part of it.

That long-ago day, my brothers lost interest and started back down the wood ladder, threatenin to leave me. I ignored them and watched the blanket of light pull back and slip over the ridges.

We was all filthy and hungry and sure to be in Dutch with Daddy and Mommy, but that marvel made it all worth it to me. Many's a day after, I slipped up the ridge, climbed the tower just so I could stand in the sky. Ever good thing seemed possible then.

Yesterday, the tower steps was too slick with moss and near too rotten to climb. Some of the boards was gone off the tower itself, and it looked like a piano missin some of its keys. I still longed to climb it, though.

I turned and looked out over the mountaintops and saw some had been carved clean until the layers of rock showed, like slices of a big ole stack cake. I had seed some of them from the road, but looking at them from on high like that was a shocker. They was valleys had been filled up with the pushed-over exploded rocks and dirt from the tops. It's what they call the valley fill, and the tops was unnaturally flat, covered in some sorry vegetation that don't even grow here natural. I put my coat back on and started back to the house. I wisht I never woulda went up there.

October 24, 1968

IT STARTED AS A GUST OF PAIN LOW IN HER BELLY, LIKE an early morning wind come to shake the remaining leaves off the trees in the yard. Before the day was over, June would feel as if she, herself, had been uprooted, blown inside out, her bloodied roots exposed to the sky.

A few days before, Carrie told June the baby had dropped into place for the birth, and that it would come early, probably due to the strain the family had endured. June had been anxious, wanting—not wanting—the day to come. She was ready for it to be over, to hold her child, and at the same time, she was terrified. Carrie had prepared her on what to expect would happen and had promised to put an axe under the bed when the time came to cut the pain.

Those last few days, she slept and read the shiny-paged magazines that Rena brought her, *Ladies' Home Journal* and *Redbook*, and helped Bethel put up a fruitcake for Christmas. Then she cleaned the kitchen and front room, heavy-bodied and driven. She arranged the layette that Viv bought her at Watson's and the diapers Rena had gotten with Green Stamps. There had been no baby shower, but a few weeks before, Rena had made an Italian cream cake for her, Viv, Beauty, and Bethel. They'd even had a punch that Beauty made. Miss Cline had been invited to come, too, but she was on her honeymoon. That day, Beauty gifted June a beautiful nine-patch baby quilt made from green and yellow calico. She had hand-quilted it in secret and had even cut up one of Garvin's shirts to use for one of the blocks. Being told that had moved June so much that she cried a little. She cried easily then.

When the pains came, she avoided Isom, who had hardly spoken to her in weeks. She waited for him to leave for the mine, then made several trips to the outhouse, her feet bare inside Bethel's galoshes, her shame nearly as strong as her fear. Each time she went outside, she wanted to keep walking away from the question that hung over her, to go into the quiet woods, to hide from what she knew was coming. Instead, she returned to the warm house, pacing the finite spaces of the kitchen and living room. After she went upstairs to try to sleep, Bethel appeared at her bedroom door, and the question June had been avoiding showed on her mother's face.

Are you feeling puny? Bethel asked.

I don't know. Maybe something I ate didn't set right on my stomach.

Two hours later, when it had started to snow, June had to stop pacing and fold herself into the pain. Bethel put on her coat, snapped the elastic bands around her boot buttons, and tied a scarf on her head. Before she left to use Beauty's phone, she said, Go lay down. I'll be back directly.

The house went quiet, save the sound of coal sputtering inside the stove and June's panicked, uneven breathing. She lay on the couch, her eyes closed against the pain and the cold gray light coming through the window. Between spasms, she sank into the cushions until she had to sit up and cry out. After a time, she found herself on the floor on hands and knees. She rocked herself back and forth until the pain passed.

Mama, oh, Mama, she repeated as she crawled to the window. Bethel and Beauty were coming down the road, and when Bethel saw June's face behind the glass—its lack of color, her tortured mouth—she sprinted toward the yard, startling a redbird out of the holly bush. It skimmed her hair as it lifted into the sky. Bethel stumbled, landed on her knees at the edge of the coal pile. When Beauty pulled her up, her hands were blackened, a tiny bit of coal wedged into the flesh at the base of her thumb, where it would remain until her death.

June didn't remember Bethel and Beauty coming into the house or how she, herself, got up to her room and into bed. She didn't remember Carrie and Rena's arrival. What she would remember was Carrie's face looming over hers, a watery curtain of space between them. She would recall Beauty's smooth hands swiping the hair from her burning face, pulling it to one side. Her mother's voice, from far away, saying her name, and the stutter of Isom's boots on the porch.

She would remember the animal sounds she heard herself make, then the room suddenly spinning into silence as she splintered wide open. The sultry, wailing girl laid against her chest, her arms forming a cradle around her, the impossible heft of the baby's head in her palm. The sound of her own voice saying, Aubrey Grace, then the room gone quiet enough again to hear Bethel's crying. The sleeping girl's skin and hair were dark against June's own. Her tiny eyelids translucent as a bird's. Ellis's child.

Lying In

JUNE OPENED HER EYES TO THE WEAK LIGHT OF AUtumn dusk and plumes of frost on the window glass. She shifted beneath the quilts, flinched at the soreness of her body, registered the rough strip of terrycloth between her legs. Her hands went to her belly, found the raw-dough mound of it. She took in the silence of the house, thought Bethel must have taken Grace into the front room.

She got out of bed and opened her bedroom door, wondered if she had dreamed of taking Grace out to put her feet in the dirt or if it had actually happened. She couldn't remember.

The coal stove crackled in the front room. Carrie would've gone home to rest and Isom would soon be getting up for work. She checked the front room, then padded into the kitchen. Bethel and Beauty sat at the table. She looked around for Grace.

Bethel hadn't yet pinned her hair back up, and it drifted around her drawn face. Beauty hunched over the table, her head propped by a hand, her free hand scissoring a cigarette over the ashtray. She stared at the Formica tabletop.

Mama? June whispered. Why did you not wake me to feed Grace?

Both women looked up at her. Tears slipped down Bethel's face.

Mama? June repeated. Icy wind swirled through her rib cage.

Beauty covered her mouth with the tips of her fingers, red fingernails in contrast to the color of her winter-paled skin, turned her face to the frozen window.

Where's the baby? June asked.

Beauty stood up and walked toward her. She reached for June's hand, said, Come set down.

June stiffened, a pillar of ice. She could not breathe for the sheer need that overtook her then—something entirely new that turned her inside out. The sore places in her body throbbed. She looked into Beauty's eyes, forced out the only words she could think.

Where is she? Where is my baby?

Beauty turned to look at Bethel, then back to June. She said, Gone, honey. She's gone, and she began to cry softly.

What? June whispered. Yesterday flooded back over her—the breathing, crying baby against her body, its tiny mouth at her breast before she, herself, fell asleep. She looked at her mother and asked, She's dead?

Bethel shook her head, said, No.

Beauty finished the sentence for her. Isom took her, she said.

What did he do? June yelled. She felt a gush of fluid between her legs.

Beauty touched her arm and said, Your daddy took her away last night and he won't tell where. Come and set down.

June, Bethel said, he said he give her away.

To who? she screamed, unconcerned with waking Isom.

She folded into herself then, lay down, put her cheek against the cold linoleum. She felt the warm blood trickling down her thigh, realized the towel that had been there to catch it was gone.

Grace. Oh, Grace, she sobbed.

Searching

JUNE WOKE FROM A BRITTLE SLEEP AND SOMETHING that sent her running out into the near dusk. The early snow clotted the hemline of her nightgown and filled the spaces between her bare ankles and the undone boots she had jammed her feet into.

In the backyard, she followed faint footprints to where Granny Carrie had thrown the bloody wash pan of water from the birthing cloths. It lay there, a pale pink shadow against a drift. She stopped to stare at it, remembered the warmth of the washrags Carrie had applied to her aching body yesterday. She pushed her hand into the stain, then darted to the frozen rose of Sharon bush, then the horse chestnut. Crows cried out in the woods. She didn't know where she was going. She had heard what Beauty said earlier and scarcely had processed it before they gave her a glassful of Isom's whiskey and put her to bed: Her baby was gone.

Yesterday, when she'd seen the baby's dark skin, she knew that Isom wouldn't let them stay, but she never dreamed he'd do what he'd done. Tears seared June's cracked bottom lip just as the whiskey had. Disoriented by the snow, she had to swivel her head until she found the garden. She went to it, began clawing away its layers of ice and leaves. Again, she wondered whether she had put Grace's feet in the dirt, remembered the jar under her bed.

The back door opened and Bethel's snow-muffled voice came across the yard.

June? June!

Where did she put it, Mama?

June dug with snow-scalded fingers until Bethel, still wearing her house shoes, stood behind her. She touched June's shoulder, said, Hit's not here, honey. I told you what Isom did.

June had not heard the door open, but she heard Beauty's voice, just beyond Bethel's, say, She's looking for the afterbirth.

Oh, honey, her mother said.

He should've let us take her to the hospital, Beauty said.

Bethel ignored her. She took June's hand, said, Come on in the house, Junie, before you catch fever.

June broke her mother's grip and lay her body down on the frozen ground. She let the snow soak the front of her thin nightgown, let the fire of it burn into her skin. She clawed through the snow to the dirt, tried to loosen it, craved to eat it.

As Bethel and Beauty tried to pull her to her feet, a picture flashed into her mind—a painting she once saw on a book cover over at Watson's. *Flaming June*, it was called, and it depicted a woman, dressed in a gown the color of wild persimmons, resting on a bench. She could just as well have been in the school bus seat, with her head in Vivian's lap. *That's me*, she thought, as her mother called her name. *My baby is gone and every part of me is afire. I am burning.*

That night, Rena opened the door to June's room, said, Junebug, let's get you a bath. She came farther into the room, said, Oh, honey, you stink.

June stood, let Rena pull the still-damp gown off her body, which seemed to belong to someone else—the soft belly and, every other place, skin straining over her bones. In her mind, she heard one of Granny Justice's favorite Bible verses: *Your body is a temple of the Holy Ghost, which is in you.* Had Granny been in the room yesterday, witnessed Grace's birth?

In the kitchen, where Bethel had pinned the curtains shut, Rena poured warm water over June's back. June didn't even care that she was naked in front of them. The water brought her awake enough the register the smell of warm biscuits in the oven and the ring of a car's tire chains out on the road. June washed herself then dried with a stiff towel that must have been folded on the shelf for a while, for in it lingered the faint warm light of a summer day on the line.

Bethel wound a strip of muslin around June's chest and pinned it tight with one of Charlie's diaper pins to keep her milk from soaking through. We'll need to change this directly, she said.

My body is a temple, June said.

She dressed herself, then gave in, bent over the sink and let Rena pour warm water over her head. Rena's nails felt good on her scalp as she worked in the shampoo. As she stood there, squeezed shut her eyes, let herself fall into the darkness, a long-ago memory came back to her. Isom, still young, standing beside Bethel at the sink, lifting an aluminum water pitcher to pour ribbons of water over her long, cinnamon-colored hair. Steam had risen off her head, and she sighed an animal, otherworldly sigh. Afterward, Bethel sat in front of the stove while Isom combed her hair that dripped onto the hearthstones.

Upstairs, June's bedroom window was halfway open, the

dirty linens in a pile at the foot of her bed. From the doorway, she watched her mother pull a clean sheet over the mattress, startled by the tears slipping down Bethel's face. Bethel bent, picked up the corner of a dirty sheet and wiped her eyes, then said, Hit's done. Nothing we can do.

Rena came to tuck her in, but June refused the warm biscuit and apple butter, gulped the glass of bitter whiskey she brought. It burned all the way down. Rena pulled the fresh sheet and then the quilt over June, said, He had no right, June. No matter who the father was, and the God's honest truth is, that baby is Ellis's. I can see that.

June wanted to shut her eyes and drift away, but she lay there recalling the sounds and smells of the night before, disjointed images that came and went from her mind. She featured that Granny had, after all, been in the room last night, standing at the foot of the bed, her face full of love, and then she landed on the memory she was searching for—the baby's dark complexion, so much like Ellis's. She had planned to let Ellis know when the baby came, but she knew she'd now have to tell him everything. She'd write him, even if he didn't write her back. Maybe he could help.

She lay there burning with whiskey and burning with want, trying to think of a way to get her baby back. She called Rena back to the room.

Did anyone take pictures? she asked.

Rena shook her head, said, Go to sleep.

Granny Justice

HIT'S A MYSTERY AND A THOUSAND WONDERS WHY I'M still here, up in this holler, plunderin around this empty house and stretch o' the creek. I ain't been able to help Bethel through her grievin. June neither, and I shore ain't yet been able to help her through all the trouble she's endured.

My mommy knew the roots—she could cure the thrush just by blowin smoke three times into a baby's mouth—and if I was still yet alive, I would have boiled up some tea with pennyrile and the other secret ingredients they's not many knows anymore. We woulda got June's monthlies started agin and she could've got on with it. My mommy did that for me oncet, and I expect that were why I lived to such a old age. I was so wore-out back then I might woulda keeled over dead if I had any more young uns. I sometimes think it would've been better for June, too.

Most of em cain't see me now, nor hear me, but I'm still here. June registers me at times—I was there for the birthin, feelin useless, hoped she could recognize the touch of my hand, but she didn't let on to no one. I cain't touch the others, not even that baby, though I tried. I cain't stop the rain or heal those that's sick or hurt no more, so I don't know how

I'm sposed to help anybody. So I wait and watch them machines gobble up the mountain, rock by rock, helpless. In the meanwhile, I trust that the Lord will appoint me my purpose in his time.

A Christmas Card from Vietnam

Dear June,

I can't tell you how awful I feel about what your daddy done. We will find Aubrey Grace and get her back, I promise! I don't know for sure when I will next get home. Likely as not until the end of my tour. But will you see what you can find out? But I know you. You've already started looking.

I think Aubrey Grace is a really pretty name. I'm glad you named her after your great-granddaddy. Mama said he was a good man and she always admired him. No matter where she is and what somebody else might name her, that will be her name, for I know she is still alive. Isom is mean as a snake, but I don't think he's killing mean. And I want to give you and her my name. She will be Aubrey Grace Akers. We'll be a family.

How did you know where to write me? You're smart, so it probably wasn't hard for you to figure out how to get the address. Anyway, thank you for writing to tell me. I wish you only had to tell me that she was born and that you're sure she's mine. But, even if she wasn't, I'd marry you anyway.

It seems strange to write this, with everything that has happened, but I want to wish you a Merry Christmas and tell you

I'm sorry for how I acted at the June Meeting. I was out of my head and didn't know what to do.

I drew the redbird and the trees with mistletoe on the front of this paper, but I guess you've already figured that out. It's not as good as what you could draw.

It don't really seem like Christmas here. It's too hot and muggy, worse than high summer at home. But one of my buddies got a package with a little Christmas tree in it and we used the lids off of our C rations to make ornaments to hang on it. Christmas day, we all eat our rations while setting around it. These boys make fun of the way I talk, but I'm used to it by now. Plus, they're all good fellers.

I don't expect that it seems like Christmas to you, either. We'll get her back, June. We will. Please take care of yourself and see what you can find out. I am sorry for not writing you before. I am thinking of you all the time.

Love and merry Christmas, Ellis

Time to Go

BETHEL STOOD BY THE COAL STOVE, PULLING A TORtoiseshell comb through her hair. From across the room, June could smell the Tame cream rinse she had used, and she wanted to scream at the ordinariness of her mother's movements. She was worn-out from searching through her mind for all the places Isom might have taken her baby, and she had stopped talking to any of them. She felt so helpless and exhausted from hating him that she could hardly feel her own skin or taste the food Bethel begged her to eat. She no longer felt or heard much of anything but the roar of hot anger in her head and the icy branch water threading through her veins. Yesterday, she had watched Isom eat his Sunday dinner and let herself wish for him to die in the mine or for the black lung to take him earlier than the doctor predicted, and then she wondered if she was capable of actually killing him herself.

Bethel said, Remember that time I put glitter in your hair before the New Year's Eve party at church? It was so sparkly and pretty, but it itched you until the next morning when you could warsh it out.

June watched her mother pull a snarl of hair from the comb, open the stove door, and throw it in.

She sighed, said, June, I'm ashamed what Isom did. But you cain't put it on me.

How long was he gone that night? June asked. The sound of her own voice seemed to come from the other side of the room.

Bethel's eyebrows went up. She backed up to a kitchen chair and sat down, said, Listen to me, June. Sometimes things works out for the best.

Mama, he took my baby, she whispered.

Bethel raked her thumb over the teeth of the comb. Her own words came quietly. I've lost a baby before, she said.

A rumble started in June's ears, like a storm churning up the holler. She said, I know! It's not the same. You never even nursed it or much held it!

Then she thought of Tom—of Bethel's losing Tom, whom she had nurtured for eighteen years.

Bethel shrank into herself, closed her eyes, sat so still that she might have been asleep. Then she said, No, a stillbirth ain't the same. Even still, I know.

I'm sorry, Mama, June whispered.

When I was pregnant with Rena, Bethel began, they told me I couldn't keep her.

They?

Bethel went on. I weren't married because the daddy wouldn't marry me. After I found out I was expecting and told him, he run off. Said he didn't want to come home to a ready-made family. A man who's lived through a war bein afeared of a family! My mama said it would be awful hard to support a baby on my own. She encouraged me to give it up after it was born.

June's mind whirled. She recalled the dream of her mother driving off with Sol Akers.

Bethel said, But your daddy marrying me is the only reason I got to keep Rena.

June tried to imagine life without Rena. She said, Does Isom know that Rena don't belong to Daddy?

Yes, Bethel said. I haven't ever kept a thing from him.

Does Rena know?

Oh, Lord, yes, Bethel said. She's the only one among us has dark skin.

June didn't have time to think. She blurted, Rena is a Akers?

Rena is a Branham, her mother said. She ran the comb back through her hair.

The truth sat like a wall between them.

Please help me, Mama, June said.

Bethel sighed, said, Isom was gone about three hours that morning, June. I begged him not to do it.

June ached to believe her.

Bethel

JUNE MOVES THROUGH THE HOUSE LIKE A APPARITION, her only sound the scritch of bare feet on the cold linoleum. She trails vapors of unwashed bedsheets, writes grief wherever she walks. She is rail-thin under the dirty nightgown, and this is way worse than the baby blues I had after Rena. She rarely talks or eats, and I can feel her hunger ever where. It chills the corners of the kitchen and front room, follows me to the bed of a night, fills my sleep with her pining. I wisht I could help her but I cain't. I'm too stewed in my own hurt. Rena remarked the other day that June resembles the ghost apples she seen in McClung's orchard up Yellowjacket Creek when she was a girl. She said all of June's essence has rotted, leaving only a icy shell of its old self.

I know Isom feels June's hunger, too, for, most times, he is sullen, even with the baby gone and his problem solved. He eats his dinners without talking, rarely says much before he heads out to work, never asks about June, for I don't think he can face her. Hard as he is, he knows what he done.

Isom weren't always this way, though he was always quick to anger. He's hardened over the years—same as his lungs. Each blow the Lord put on him slowed him a little more—first he lost his daddy, then Garvin, and, soon after, Tom. If he grieved over the baby we lost when we was first married—nobody else knows about that—he never let on. All the same, time has took more and more from him, and June getting pregnant by the Akers boy just about done him in. A person can only stand so much. Eventually, all that hurt turns to anger because that's the easiest road.

I live tween the two of them, daughter and husband, one drawed back into herself and one coiled like a snake that cain't help but strike. I go through this hard winter, warshing, cooking, breaking the skin of ice on the rain barrel. I hang basil over the door, but the haints are already inside the house. I gather charms but cain't mend up what's broke.

Balsam

RENA DUG THROUGH BOXES IN THE HALL CLOSET, THEN she and June carried the Christmas decorations to the front room where Watt had stood the Canaan fir he brought home from the woods. The tree rose a foot above the frame of the trailer window. Bits of ice and snow still hung in its lower branches. When June had arrived, the scent of it gave her a bittersweet feeling.

June had been relieved when Watt showed up to get her that morning. He'd even waited for her to eat and bathe. Although she spent as much time as she could at Beauty's, she needed to be out of the holler for a while. She could no longer think at home, had to go through most of her days avoiding Isom or not speaking much to Bethel, and she knew it was breaking her mother's heart.

Rena handed June a nest of tree lights and said, I don't know why he got such a big tree this year.

June worked at unsnarling the lights, willed herself to be cheered by putting up Christmas decorations. She said, Mama told me some things.

Rena stopped pulling decorations from their tissue wrappers.

June took a risk, asked, Has she told you who your daddy is?

Rena pulled up the sleeve of her sweater and gestured to the olive skin of her arm. She said, Look at me, June. It's fairly easy to tell I'm not a Branham.

I might have an idea who, June said.

Rena pulled down her sweater sleeve, said, It's a wonder Isom let me live in his house.

Town

A MAN SWIVELED HIS STOOL AWAY FROM THE COUNTER and coughed into a white hanky. From where she sat, June could see the hanky's crisply ironed creases, the coal tattoo on his forearm. The muffled, phlegmy sounds he made put her in mind of nighttimes at home with Isom. She turned away from the red-faced man toward the diner window.

Afternoon light skimmed the tops of the trees and the glass skins of second-story windows across the street, a sign that dusk—lately the hardest time of June's days—was coming. A feeling of loneliness stretched itself inside her chest, like fog settling into a ridge. It was the time of day that she longed for Grace the most. And Ellis and Tom.

June took a sip of Coke, ran her palm over the salt-gritted tabletop. She glanced at the wall clock. Rena would be there to pick her up anytime. At home, Bethel would have started cooking supper for Isom and given Charlie a bath.

That morning, when Rena picked her up, they hadn't driven more than half a mile from the house before Rena had said, I've got something to tell. Please don't be mad.

She tapped her pink fingernails against the steering wheel, said, I ran into Sol at the service station over in Holden.

What did he say? June asked.

He said that, that night, Daddy had brought Grace over there to leave her and, even though Merkey wanted to keep her, Sol wouldn't allow it. Said the baby wasn't Ellis's and to get her away from there.

June caught her breath, said, Did he say where Daddy took her?

Rena just shook her head.

I don't know how to feel, June said. If Solomon was lying and really did have her, he'd never give her back to me. But now, even though I think Isom took her to Myrtle Gap, I don't have any idea how I will find her.

She began to cry.

We'll find her, Rena said.

When they reached Myrtle Gap, June said, I keep thinking she has to be here.

What makes you think that? Rena asked.

I don't think Isom would've given her to anyone we know. It would be too easy for me to find out. I think he would've left her in a place with a lot of people.

What about Williamson or Pikeville?

I don't think so. Not if he was only gone about three hours like Mama said. After he tried to leave her at Sol's, this would be the only place he had time to go to and get back in three hours.

God, Rena said.

Will you leave me off at Watson's? June asked. I need to get some Kotex. I hate buying them from Mike.

Rena dropped June on Main Street and drove off to her appointment. June was sure that Rena was pregnant again but didn't want to tell June because it would make her feel worse than she already did. And it would. That morning, June woke with the thought, *And here I thought that Tom's dying was the only bad thing that ever could happen to me. I was too young when my daddy died to remember him very clearly. It's all too much.*

At the *Myrtle Banner* office, a boisterous woman from the front desk helped her search through stacks of newspapers until they found the edition for the week after Grace's birth.

What exactly are you looking for, hon? the lady asked.

Oh, just an obituary my mama wanted, she lied. She thanked the woman and sat down to scan the paper, relieved that the secretary had gone back to her desk.

June found the two-paragraph article on page two: *Local Police Take Custody of Abandoned Infant.* Words swam past her eyes: *newborn girl, cardboard box, Esso service station. Will be put up for adoption.* Afterward, she'd been too stunned to concentrate enough to remember what she needed from Watson's.

Rena pulled up to the curb across the street from the diner and honked the Impala's horn. June went to Rena's side of the car, said, I found her!

She fanned herself, said, I feel like I cain't breathe. I'd know more, but they ran me off from the newspaper office. Said they had to close early.

Rena said, Get in here and tell me then!

When Rena dropped June off at the house, its kitchen windows steamy from Bethel's boiling chicken or cabbage or pinto beans, June leaned back into the car and said, My mind is going a thousand miles an hour. Grace is safe!

She kissed Rena's cheek. Before she made it to the house, she turned and walked back to her sister's car. She said, If you're pregnant, you can tell me, OK?

Rena's eyebrows went up. She said, I was afraid you'd be mad. How'd you know when nobody else knows yet?

Not mad, June said. I'll be happy for you. When are you due?

July, she said, and her face relaxed. She smiled.

June said, Did you tell Sol you know he's your daddy? What did he say?

Rena shrugged, said, Not much. I told him, I know who you are, and all he said was, You do, do you? And then he kind of snorted and said, That was a long time ago. No use looking back.

I'm sorry, June said.

Rena shrugged again. It's OK, she said. Watt had already said that, knowing Sol, he probably wouldn't want anything to do with me. Anyway, Daddy was the one who raised me.

Daddy, June thought as she walked toward the shining porchlight.

That night, she lay in the darkness listening to the house that was once, at this hour, alive with the sure, steady breath of their sleeping—Bethel and Isom's, Rena's, Tom's. And for the briefest while, there had been the tiny sighs, the delicate quick breaths Grace took as she drank from June's breast. And while she had hoped that Isom hadn't done anything terrible to her baby, she was relieved to know that Grace was probably safe and sleeping in a house in Myrtle Gap.

In the tangle of her mind, she recalled a conversation between her mother and Isom about the four-lane road. Isom had said, It ain't nothing but a easier road out of here for folks who cain't be happy with what they've got. Especially the young uns.

He's right, she thought. Before the war, several of the boys from the holler had gone off to Richmond or Cleveland, looking for work. Some even as far away as South Carolina and north to Detroit. There in the dark, the words came to her: *You've got to go,* as sure as if someone had been there to whisper them in her ear. *It's time for you to go.*

Third Floor

JUNE STEPPED INTO THE DAYLIT LOBBY OF THE MERcury Theater. The scent of buttered popcorn reminded her of going there with Tom to see *The Sons of Katie Elder.* She introduced herself to Mrs. Mounts, the manager, then followed her up the carpeted stairs, over the worn-out places where years' worth of other feet had passed. She marveled at the thinness of the housedress stretched over Mrs. Mounts' ample body, the thick, veiny ankles always a few steps ahead of her, and marveled at how the laceless, run-over Keds stayed on the woman's swollen feet.

On the second-floor landing, Mrs. Mounts pointed to a door. The underarms of her housedress had gone transparent, and her hair gave off an ammonia smell from a recent perm. She wheezed, Projection room's in there.

Between the second and third floor, the carpet bloomed back to life. At the top of the stairs, Mrs. Mounts tried one key and then a second in the lock of a heavy gray door. Through a dirty hall window that overlooked the alley, June traced the path back down Grafton Street to the doctor's office, where Rena had gone for a prenatal appointment.

Mrs. Mounts twisted the doorknob, reached into the apartment, and snapped on a light switch. Sound echoed through the windowless, newly paneled room. Against the far wall, a mattress roosted on a wooden bedframe. On the opposite wall stood a green Formica table and one scarred ladder-back chair, a stove, and a new golden-yellow refrigerator, strangely out of place among the other worn furnishings. On the far end of the room was another door, and beyond it, a metal shower stall and low-hung sink tipped forward a bit beneath a small window.

June slipped her hand into her jacket pocket, feeling for the money that she'd brought—twenty dollars that Rena paid her for watching Charlie a few afternoons while she napped, along with the rest from the money she'd saved and kept hidden in her bookshelf between the pages of *Wuthering Heights.*

Mrs. Mounts said, This's only been a apartment for a few years. Used to be storage. She nodded toward the fridge, saying, Just about brand-new.

June took it all in: the dimness of the room, the used mattress, the smell of fresh paint, of rusted pipes and dust—the smell of endless, quiet days. A faint shiver ran through her as she featured lonely Sunday afternoons.

Does it get hot in summer? she asked.

Lord God, yes! I've got a box fan downstairs you can use when it gets too hot. Kinda hard to fathom right now, though, ain't it?

June traced a line through a coat of gray dust on the kitchen counter with her finger, revealed a trail of gold flecks that caught the overhead light. She flicked a dried-up fly into the sink.

How long has it been since someone lived here? she asked.

About six months, the landlady said. Kid who lived here got drafted.

June started to ask after him but asked, Will I be able to hear the movies playing from up here?

Depends on whether it's a wild one or not. Some of them movies can get pretty loud. Car chases and shoot-outs, you know. Steve McQueen. Clint Eastwood. You'll be downstairs working most of the time, anyways.

Mrs. Mounts scratched at a piece of tape stuck to the freezer door with a red fingernail, said, Course, it would just be you living here, wouldn't it?

June's face burned. Yes, ma'am, she said. She opened a cabinet door between them, peeked in to try to cover her shame. Shards of newsprint, brittle as the fly, drifted onto the stovetop.

How old are you?

Almost eighteen, June said.

Where are your people?

Over in Mingo. At Twenty-Seven.

Mrs. Mounts worked her mouth like she might say something else, but she didn't. June opened a drawer. In it, half a walnut shell, a thin red baloney casing twisted into an infinity sign, a green plastic clip from a bag of white bread. She picked up the clip, rubbed it between her finger and thumb, remembered that Tom sometimes used those for guitar picks.

June's next words come out in a rush: My brother was killed in Vietnam.

It was the first time she had said it to a stranger.

I'm sure sorry about that, Mrs. Mounts said. They's lots of boys getting killed. I still don't know what become of the boy lived here, though I heard he was killed, too.

The sky beyond the bathroom window had darkened, the air gone still, like the hills were holding their breath.

It's going to rain, June said. I'd better go.

You have a car? Mrs. Mounts asked.

No, ma'am. My sister brought me today.

Mrs. Mounts studied her. She said, It's a IGA store over on Dingess Street. You can walk down there for groceries. And they's a washer and dryer in the basement. You can use them.

June tried to imagine herself living in the apartment and working in the theater, tried to picture Grace living there, too. She looked around the room for a place to set up a crib that she had no idea how she'd get. Rena needed Charlie's for the new baby.

Mrs. Mounts leaned on the doorjamb, flopped her thick wrist back and forth. The keys on the ring chinked against one another like dull bells. She shifted her weight, asked, Are you interested in the job?

Yes, ma'am, I believe I am, June said. It might be a few days before I can get a ride back over here with my things.

How about you start work a week from today? Course, you can move in anytime you want between now and then. We won't been needin to use it.

Downstairs, June stepped out into an early dusk brought on by the coming storm. Wind raised the hem of her jacket. It moved through the trees above Grafton Street, startled their last brittle leaves. They lifted and fell, bronze tongues whispering something June couldn't quite understand. *Maybe it's the dead boy from the apartment*, she thought. *I cain't quite get shed of ghosts.* She walked toward the doctor's office to find Rena.

Bethel

THE POCKET OF MY GOOD DRESS STILL YET HOLDS A fistful of dirt I took from Tom's grave. Most folks keeps theirs in jars or boxes, but oncet I dropped that clay in my pocket, I couldn't take it back out, was afraid I wouldn't git none of it all in one place again, so there it sets.

When the army eventually sent home his footlocker, it come to Logan by bus and Isom had to go fetch it. I set and stared at it a full hour afore I opened it.

Inside was his wallet and the clothes he wore on the bus ride over to the induction center, his Zippo lighter, a deck of playing cards, the edges of the cards worn and filthy, the buckeye Lena Faye give him to carry in his pants pocket. There was also a small New Testament with a red leather cover, a paperback of *The Carpetbaggers*, which I hid away where June couldn't find it.

Scattered among the papers was a few photographs, mostly from home, one of Lena Faye in a white mini skirt and boots. Its edges was curled from him carrying it, but there was another one I never saw afore. In it, Tom, rail-thin and shirtless, stands among a group of other boys in front of a helicopter. Some of them are all smeared with grease, and all of them are smiling big, Tom's smile the biggest of them all. I wonder how many of them boys is dead now.

I never told no one this, and after all this time, I just remembered it the other day. The memory must've got lost in all the other things I had to fret over. On the night before the day the army papers listed as Tom's death date, I had woke up all alone in the dark bedroom. For some reason, I set up in the bed and a roarin started up in my ears. Like a freight train was comin. Then, something crashed plumb through me, front to back. Whatever that was hit me and kept on goin into the pitch-black night. When I recollected about that, I had June look it up in Beauty's encyclopedia, and sure enough, Vietnam is eleven hours ahead of us. I knowed then that sound was Tom, leavin this world.

Sometimes I think about Beauty, who has no handful of dirt to keep, for Garvin has no real grave she can visit, save the black belly of the mine. She's never took off her wedding ring. I suppose that's her own way of holding on to him. She is a true beauty for shore, and fun loving, and they's plenty of men who'd like to have her, but she never takes no notice. She keeps plenty busy and can do most anything a man can. I know she won't marry again, for Garvin was her one and only. It puts me in mind of my great-granny's sister, who was betrothed to a Union soldier who died in the War Between the States. She was sixteen at the time, and she never married, and don't you know that when she died at age seventy-four, they buried her in the wedding dress she never got to wear. It was still as white as when she sewed it all those years before.

I can remember when Garvin brought Beauty around here the first time. Her people are from over around Pikeville, most of them gone now. It was a Saturday afternoon. Beauty come into our house with her hair set and wearing a full skirt, plaid, as I picture it now, and a starched white blouse. By the end of the day, that blouse was wrinkled, but she never spilled a speck of food or tea on it.

Everyone loved her right off, even Mama, who dearly loved Garvin and called him her son, the same as she called Shag. It was real plain to all of them that Garvin worshiped Beauty. What impressed me most was how she got right down on the floor and played with Tom and June, as if they was still yet babies. She slid out of her patent leather shoes and played pretend with them and Junie's doll babies until it was time for her to go home. I knowed right then that she'd be a good mother, but that was not to be.

Half a year later, they was married in the Baptist church over at Marrowbone. They moved into the old log house up the holler here, and right away, Beauty set to making it nice, and it was. Still is.

She painted and papered the walls, had new kitchen linoleum put down, even had Garvin wall in the back porch so he could take his mine clothes off in there before going into the house. I might have envied her a little over the years. Even so, I count her as my best friend. I sure wish she coulda met Shag. Oh, we've had some fun times and we've sure had to lean on each other so much, specially these past years.

I must've been down on the floor with that trunk for a while that day Isom brought it home. When June come home from Beauty's, I showed her all them things except the book, which I had hid under the davenport. It's still yet there, come to think of it. She went to rifling through the pictures and papers lookin for somethin. Finally she found it and held it up by the chain. It were the Saint Christopher medal she given Tom the day he left. She inspected it close, said she wanted to believe he had wore it all the time. I knew what she was hintin at and told her I expect that whoever does the job of returning things would likely clean them up first. In fact, nothin in that trunk, save that one helicopter picture, couldn't have been things I'd found while cleaning under Tom's bed up there in his room. Nary an object would give someone who didn't know any idee it had been halfway around the world and in a war.

I carry that one picture taped inside the cover of my King James Bible now, goes to church with me ever Sunday. Most of the rest of it has stayed in the trunk under some of Tom's good clothes I finally took down from his closet. I took the small items—except the Saint Christopher—and stashed them in a little wood box I've had for a long time and tucked that back in with the clothes in the trunk. They's a flower carved in that box lid, inlaid with silver, and, just like my ivory comb Shag give me, nobody but me knows where that box come from. If Isom knew, he'd make me throw it away for sure.

This house holds Tom in more than just them few things. He's all around us, quiet as usual, but sometimes I can feel him. I even smell his smell. I know he sends me signs, and I keep the touchable ones on the kitchen windowsill. A owl feather, a rock shaped like a heart, a blue butterfly wing.

I've left his room mostly the way it was, and I still sweep and dust in there. There's no sense in heatin it right now, so I keep the door shut. Someday, when Charlie is big enough, he can sleep up there when he comes up to stay the night.

Part II

Water

Flying Again

THE PLYMOUTH SHOT THROUGH THE ROAD CUT, tripped the wire of a full moon. Its headlights fanned into the edges of the woods, igniting islands of dirty snow that remained in the undergrowth. June held tight to the steering wheel for fear she'd float away from the dream of freedom.

In the back seat was a box of food from home: ham, yeast rolls, and a thawing piece of Christmas fruitcake that Bethel took from the deep freeze to send with her. Also in the box, a small brown poke with four peanut butter cookies inside. Folded up and lying beneath was the wax paper with a crisp ten-dollar bill Bethel had hidden there. When June got home and found it, she cried.

That afternoon, June had stashed some of Tom's things into a clothes basket she'd take with her, and she waited until Bethel was in the garden to go beyond the attic walls and into the dark rafters to search among the cardboard boxes for her father's things. She found the Montgomery Ward box labeled *Shag* jammed under the eaves. *Nobody else cares about this now*, she thought. *They never even mention him*. She carried it to the Plymouth and put it in the trunk.

Once, Bethel had come into Tom's room and found them going through the box of their father's things. Funeral ribbons, cards of condolence, and Shag's personal effects littered the floor. Each of them picked up items and examined them, smelled them, held them close.

What are you doing with that? Bethel asked.

We're just looking, Mama, Tom said.

Put all that mess away right now. And quit making such a racket. Isom's asleep.

She called it a mess, June thought. *It's Daddy's things.*

After Bethel had gone downstairs, June took her father's Boy Scout pin from the scattered items and hid it in her sock drawer before stowing the box back in the attic. Later, when she and Tom looked for it, the box had been moved deeper into the rafters. They blamed Isom.

Shag and Isom had been friends—running buddies, Bethel had said. June had an early memory of Isom coming to the house a few times to visit her daddy. He'd been nice to her then. After her father died, it seemed that Isom came around more often to check on them. A year and a half after Shag's death, Isom and Bethel were married in Beauty's front room on a Friday afternoon.

June switched on the radio, stirred up a fizz of static. She glanced at its face and recognized the position of the dial—1190, WOWO out of Fort Wayne. Tom's favorite station. The red line on the tuner still held its place after all that time.

All reminders of Garvin, who bought the car brand-new nine years ago over at Pikeville, were long gone, save a bullet hole in the passenger door, put there during a mine strike. Garvin had refused to fix it, carried the scar like a war medal.

A year on, Tom's presence remained in the car, as fresh as the last time he drove it to Maynard's to get snacks for the bus ride to basic training. Shriveled tobacco lingered on the steering column, fishhooks clung to the sun visor, a whisper of English Leather on the steering wheel. Earlier, when June got in to drive to Myrtle Gap, she nudged the seat forward so she could reach the pedals. A root beer bottle rolled from under the seat and the sight of it pulled the breath right out of her. She had been with him on the trip to Maynard's when he bought it.

Tom was seventeen when Beauty gave him the Plymouth. Garvin had been dead for a while then, and the car sat next to their coal shed, accumulating dust since Isom had driven it home for Beauty when they all realized Garvin wouldn't be coming up out of that mine. Later, when he got the car, he had pulled it up under Granny's maple and spent a day cleaning it with buckets of water he carried from the creek, then brushed clear nail polish around the bullet hole so it wouldn't rust out. He changed the oil, then afterward took Bethel and June for a ride over to Lenore to get ice cream. And before he left for the service, he taught June to drive the car. After he died, Isom said he intended to keep it. And now, June was driving it away from home with the remnant of something freshly detached trailing behind her. Something else opened ahead of her, just out of reach of the headlights.

When she asked Isom and Bethel for Tom's car the first night of her visit home, Isom had said no and warned her to not ask again. The next morning, June overheard Bethel tell Beauty about it. That evening, Beauty came down the road and stood on the porch with her hands on her hips as she spoke to Isom. June and Bethel had been washing dishes in the kitchen and heard them out there, heard Beauty say, Garvin would want her to have that car. I held the title for Tom, so I have the say. I'm giving it to June.

June could hear the anger rising in Isom's voice. He said, She don't need to be runnin the roads. She's already been in trouble once.

Beauty lowered her voice, said, Isom, that's done and over. You saw to that. When are you going to let her alone?

Bethel froze, the dish towel suspended from her hand, her mouth shut tight. She closed her eyes, slowly shook her head.

June couldn't hear what Isom said next.

Beauty spoke again. You've pushed her away. That's the last I'll say on that, but you need to think about this: That car was Tom's. It's not yours to keep or give away.

She'd fallen silent for a beat, then said, Garvin would've wanted this.

Goddamn it, Beauty, Isom said.

After Beauty was gone, he had simply and wordlessly handed June the keys Beauty left, but he gave her a look that would have withered her had she been able to feel anything at all.

Watt had taken the Plymouth to the filling station in Holden, had the oil changed and the tank filled and wouldn't accept any money when June offered. He'd said, You'll need that money, Junebug.

Lights from the car behind her lit up a smudge of thumbprint on the rearview mirror, revealed a skin of cigarette smoke on the inside of the windshield. June reached up to touch it—Tom's breath still visible. She scratched at the film with her fingernail and shivered, turned up the heater.

"House of the Rising Sun" came over the radio, clear as

glass for almost a verse, then faded as she drove between the cuts. Bethel hated the song, said it was about a whorehouse, turned off the kitchen radio when it came on. Now June concentrated, strained to fill the gaps in the lyrics as the song wavered in and out.

The rain started up near Holden, at first a thin veil then thick enough to blur the porch lights of the houses sitting so close to the road that June could usually make out the programs on the TVs inside them. She was grateful for the new windshield wipers Watt had put on. The sudden dampness of the night sharpened the scent of coal smoke rising from the chimneys. When she passed beyond them, the smell faded, like the music on the radio.

As she drove up the ridge, she tuned to the movement of pavement beneath the car, thought of the places she might go to find Grace if she couldn't find her in Myrtle Gap. She had never gone further than Charleston in one direction and Pikeville in the other. Now, she could go anywhere she wanted. Someday, she wanted to go west to Oregon, had been thinking about it since Uncle Lovell had written a letter home about riding stretches of fence lines, and how, on the train out, the wide emptiness grew in proportion to the distance he'd traveled from the mountains at home. He said he had welcomed it, and she wanted to see it.

By the time she parked on a side street near the theater, wet, quarter-sized flakes were falling—another late-spring snow shower. She knocked on the glass door of the lighted lobby.

Mrs. Mounts shambled across the room wearing a man's flannel bathrobe.

Lord God, June, she said. What are you doing here?

I figured I'd come back a little early, get myself settled. Sorry. I haven't yet put my theater key on the chain with the car key. It's in my suitcase.

Car key? You got a car?

June nodded, said, My brother's.

Mrs. Mounts tilted her head then and smiled. Aw. That's nice, she said. You have a license?

Not yet, June said. I can drive, though.

Light flickered through the crack in the green velvet theater curtains. Mrs. Mounts said, Oh, that's Shep. He had to do a splice and he's running it to make sure it's fixed good by Thursday. Running it without the sound up.

June picked up her suitcase and started for the stairs. Thank you for letting me in, she said. I'll see you tomorrow.

As she passed the theater curtain, she glanced at the screen. Doris Day was kissing Brian Keith in the rain without the usual music.

Mrs. Mounts called her back, said, I almost forgot. You got a letter in the mail yesterday. Since you wasn't here, I slid it up under your door.

Go Down, Miss Moses

ALTHOUGH THERE WERE FEW CARS ON THE ROAD, JUNE walked against oncoming traffic, like Tom taught her. The soles of the water buffalo sandals that Viv's sister had given her skimmed the gravel. She tried to stay off the hot asphalt, only stepped onto it to avoid weedy patches or the dead blacksnake turning to jelly in the first heat of summer, except for its head, which was smashed as thin and perfectly as if it were on a page in a picture book.

She retraced the route she'd driven last Sunday. That day, though, she walked because the Plymouth had stalled out and was parked under a towering basswood in a turn-out. The road paralleled the creek, dipped into the curves of the mountain. As she passed the places where water willows trailed branch tips in the water, strands of cool air brushed her skin. Although she hadn't walked far, she was grateful for the relief. Just a little farther up the road, where the white clapboard church sat at the head of Blackburn Holler, the asphalt would turn to red dog and the creek would curve south.

Her sweaty palm gave off the metallic tang of the car key, and the POW bracelet chaffed her wrist. She watched for poison ivy and hummed the melody of a song she'd heard in *Easy*

Rider for the past few nights as it played in the theater. *I pulled into Nazareth, feelin about half past dead.*

She didn't worry about the car or how she would get back to Myrtle Gap. She thought only of where she was going that day and how she had gotten to the unfamiliar place because of an envelope Granny Carrie had mailed to the movie house with a folded newspaper article tucked inside—a recent story about a preacher and his wife filing papers to adopt the newborn baby girl found at the Esso station. It said they lived just outside of Myrtle Gap, near Blackburn Fork. Across the top, Carrie had written in wobbly cursive, *I thought you deserved to know this.*

June had been elated, but knew she couldn't be certain that the baby was Grace, would have to lay eyes on her to know for sure. And soon—before the adoption went through.

It was nearly time for the service to start when she reached the red-dog road. The people outside the church hadn't noticed her. She stopped at the edge of the creek to unbuckle her dusty sandals, waded in to her ankles, bent to swipe the dirt from the tops of her feet. The cool water sent a shiver through her. *Take a load off, Fanny*, she hummed, hoping to slow her wild pulse.

When she looked up again, the church steps were empty. From the road, June heard the piano start up, then voices singing. She recalled the stiff back of the piano player from last Sunday, the blond curl that swayed from her updo when she reached for the high keys. When the preaching started, the woman had left the bench to sit in the front pew. Her face was thin, faint acne scars showing on its cheeks, no makeup. It held a quiet kindness.

The preacher, Brother Brewer, was stout, wide-hipped like a woman, his voice an octave higher than Isom's. June could see why some might think him handsome, except for the thin, oil-black hair combed across a bald patch on the top of his head. He, too, had kind eyes, except during the more dramatic portions of the sermon when he closed them and yelled at the ceiling or turned them on the small congregation.

That day, she hadn't gone through the double front doors but turned left and walked past a bed of yellow buttercups to a side entrance. The handrail to the basement was warm and slick under her palm. At the bottom of the stairs, she stepped into a cool, dim hallway that smelled of old book pages and mildew, listened to the muffled rise of the singers' voices in the church above her. Her feet, still cold from the creek, carried her hesitantly along a wall that led down the hall.

The first door was locked, and the second opened to a closet full of old hymnals and Christmas decorations. Further down the hall, on the opposite side, was a door with a glass window. Light shone around a small, white piece of poster board taped to it. When she was close enough, she could make out the words *Quiet, Please. Nursery* printed in square capital letters. In its upper right corner, a pasted-on picture of a bluebird carrying a yellow ribbon in its beak.

June had waited all week for this. She pushed the door. Green, leaf-patterned linoleum, crib, rag rug, a woman, older than Bethel, in a rocking chair, smiling at her. She froze.

Hi, honey, the woman said. She shifted a sleeping infant—*Too small to be Grace*, June noted—to her other shoulder then resumed rocking and patting its back with thick, callused fingers.

Sorry, June whispered.

She tried to take in as much of the room as she could before excusing herself: the woman's yellow double-knit dress, a basket of picture books on the rug by the rocker, a toddler on the floor, chewing on a green plastic stacking ring. *Short pants*, she thought. *A boy.*

Honey, what can I help you with? the woman asked.

The baby on her shoulder grunted, arched its back, nuzzled its face into the woman's neck. June's stomach pitched.

I needed air. Decided to look around.

Her eyes tracked to the crib. Inside, a nest of dark hair at the end of a quilt tucked around a small, sleeping child. June made herself look back at the woman then say, I love babies.

Heat swirled across her cheeks.

Oh, they ain't nothing better. That's why I'm down here. Been in this nursery for close to twenty year, since mine all growed up and moved away.

June squeezed the key chain in the hand behind her back, leaned into the door. Her mind sprinted to keep up with the images. The child in the crib. The small fist at the cheek. The crown of dark hair. The tiny hiccup in the rhythm of its breathing.

The woman said, I'm Granny Letha.

My name's June.

She hadn't meant to use her given name. The rise and fall of the blanket had addled her. She pointed to the crib. How old is that one? she asked.

About seven months. Preacher's baby. Nobody knows her exact birth date, so they made up one—October 25.

October 24, June thought. Her mind slipped into slow motion.

She watched the little boy on the floor toss the plastic ring. It bounced off the wall and wobbled to rest under the crib.

I've not seen you here before. Where you from, June?

Over on Scarlett, she hears herself say. Twenty-Seven. My people are Justices and Branhams.

Letha nodded. The boy on the floor reached in the direction of the green ring, opened and closed his hand as if it would come back to him.

Oh, now, Granny Letha said to him. I cain't get up.

I'll get it, June said.

She knew that Letha had been about to ask why she was there at Blackburn Fork. She dropped to her knees, crawled across the cool linoleum toward the crib, tried to keep her dress down over her hips. She reached under the crib and grabbed the spit-covered ring. A whiff of baby powder and lotion, and, when she looked inside the crib, hazel eyes staring at her, the fist, opening into long, elegant fingers—Ellis's fingers and face.

She grabbed the bars of the crib, steadied herself, pulled herself to standing.

June probed for information, said, I'm sorry, I think I woke him up.

It's a girl, hon. She'll go back to sleep, Letha said. Plumb cried herself out.

June bent over the crib, held herself aright on the bar. Grace's eyes were closed again. Upstairs, the preacher's fevered voice.

I should go back now, she said as she picked up her car key.

Come back and see me anytime, Granny Letha said. I don't think I know your people. Only Justices I know are over on the Tug. Branhams, I don't know.

June smiled. Probably no kin, she said before she turned for the door. Behind her, the green-and-yellow quilt burned like a beacon. She couldn't allow herself to look back.

Outside, clouds gathered into bundles overhead. The preacher's voice faded as she walked down the road and tried to reconcile the need to get away from the church with her yearning to stay with Grace. *I'll get her back even if she's legally adopted*, she thought, but that didn't dampen her agitation.

She left the road to sit in the cool woods and wait for the people from church to pass on their way home. Three milk cows clustered under an oak in a corner of the next field. June watched them chew and lumber until she had calculated that all of the cars had left the church; then she walked back to the road.

On the blacktop again, she registered the sound of a car coming up behind her. It was Granny Letha, driving a black Ford truck with rusted livestock racks on the back. A tall girl sat in the passenger seat.

You're afoot today? Granny asked.

Yes, ma'am. My car quit on me before I got to the church.

You should've said something! Letha swatted a bee back through the truck window, said, Well, get in. Let's go find it and see.

The girl scooted to the middle of the seat, smiled at June, extended a hand, its nails short, unpolished. Several leather bracelets, some with knots and beads, orbited one tanned wrist. On the other was a POW bracelet.

I'm Mary Margaret, the girl said.

She's a VISTA, Granny said. From Massachusetts, but says she ain't a Kennedy. She winked at June, said, I let her into my house to talk after she promised to come to church with me.

Mary Margaret rolled her eyes then nodded, said, I'm going to cook her Sunday dinner. She leaned toward Letha, who said, Brown biscuits and brisket. I haven't had corned beef in a age!

June slammed the door, winced because she hadn't meant to be so forceful. Isom would have yelled at her for that.

She had heard talk of the VISTA workers and had met one just once before now—back home. He, not any older than Rena, had come walking up the road one day last spring wearing khaki pants and a plaid button-down shirt under his windbreaker. When he introduced himself at the door, Bethel had been polite and invited him in for a cold drink. She answered his questions about the coal stove and their drinking water, the outdoor toilet. They'd tried to make small talk, but after he'd told them he was from Chicago, Bethel's attention drifted, and she gave up on trying to find something they had in common. After he left, they never saw him again.

Mary Margaret's long, straight hair smelled of Breck shampoo, and June could tell she put something on it to get that shade of blond. She was wearing a white shift and black leather sandals with gold chains for straps.

Whereabouts is your car? Letha asked.

June pointed, said, Just around the curve.

Mattie

MRS. MOUNTS COUNTED THE NIGHT'S TICKET MONEY, stopped often to scribble figures on a scratch pad. She frowned, mumbled something June couldn't hear.

True Grit was playing in the theater, near the end of its run. June wiped down the counter with bleach, pictured Mr. Shep up in the booth, drinking a beer, blowing cigar smoke into the projector beam, waiting for the movie to unspool so he could shut off the bulb and go home to bed.

She was able to call up the exact scene in the movie by the swell of the soundtrack. On the first night, Mrs. Mounts let her sit in the back of the theater and watch it all the way through, and since then, when she got a chance, she slipped into the dark auditorium to watch parts of it again. Her favorite scene, when Rooster took the reins in his teeth and charged his horse across the meadow, shooting it out with Ned Pepper, gave her a wild thrill. And the Technicolor sky, the twisting gold leaves of the trees in that scene caused a longing in her that she couldn't name, like a long-ago memory she tried to call up but couldn't. It had some kind of hold on her. She was fascinated by the wide-open scenery that reminded her of Lovell's descriptions in his letters, the flint-knapped ridges of the mountains in the background. She loved the crisp lighting that caused her to feel the chill air, to smell the leather and wood smoke. The lather of horses.

Most of all, June admired Mattie, the main character, appreciated her sass and orneriness. No one pushed her around or told her what she could or couldn't do, and the scene in the livery stable where she bargained for Little Blackie made June's heart swell.

June often thought about Mary Margaret, the VISTA worker, since she'd met her in Letha's truck the Sunday before. She decided that she admired her, for at eighteen, she was on her own in a place about which she knew little. Even though she spoke differently, she didn't seem out of place like the VISTA boy in the windbreaker.

Mary Margaret went to Letha's often, to help in the garden, which she pronounced as *gah-den*. Letha was teaching her how to put up beans and corn, and in turn, Mary Margaret collected Letha's stories and recipes, even songs, wrote them down on a blue steno pad where she kept the others she gathered. June envied her freedom and intelligence, thought of talking to her about Grace, but in the end, she was afraid Mary Margaret would judge her, think what June planned to do was wrong, and tell Letha. And, surely, Letha, who adored the preacher and his wife, would warn them.

Before she rented the apartment, June had thought about asking Rena and Watt if she and Grace could live with them, for she was certain that Isom wouldn't let her come home again, especially with Ellis's child. But now there would be another baby in Rena's house, so she didn't ask. She also knew she couldn't stay in Myrtle Gap once she had taken Grace back. Even the law would be looking for her, so she thought about moving to Charleston, but the new fuel pump she had to put on the Plymouth had taken most of her savings. She felt the friction of time as it sprinted past her. Soon, Grace would be walking, and June would have missed so many parts of her growing up.

Laurel

ABOVE THEM, THE PIANO LAUNCHED INTO "IN THE Sweet By-and-By," and Letha hummed along as she changed Grace's diaper. She turned to smile at June as she came through the door, then said, Little Laurel, here, is up and at it today!

Hearing Letha use that name for Grace rattled June. She'd have to be careful not to say her baby's true name aloud.

Letha set Grace down on the floor and then herself into the rocking chair. She said, Honey, you staying down here with me today?

Grace crawled over to Granny, tried to pull herself up on the arm of the chair. June's arms ached from the want to hold her.

Yes, ma'am, she said, keeping her eyes on the baby. I like it better down here.

Don't tell nobody, Granny laughed, but me, too. She pointed at the ceiling. My daddy was a preacher, and I've about done heard enough preaching for two lifetimes. Besides, I can hear everything from right here, anyways.

She patted the hand that Grace gripped the rocker arm with and said to her, Don't you tell, neither, miss. She threw back her head and stifled her laugh with her hand.

Can I hold her? June asked. The words nearly clogged her throat.

Why, sure, Letha said. She's the onliest one in here today. We're going to spoil her.

June stooped to pick up her daughter. The baby squirmed and tried to twist away. She put her hand on Grace's back, said, Shh. It's OK. Grace stiffened, reared back to stare into June's face, those hazel eyes scorching into hers. It's OK, June said again. She wanted to say, *We know each other.*

June wished she had a place to sit but walked around the room while Letha, still rocking the chair, told about the New England supper Mary Margaret made last Sunday. Letha interrupted herself to ask, That car running alright?

Yes, ma'am. I really appreciate you taking me to town. It needed a fuel pump. I guess the car sat for too long after my brother left.

That can happen, Letha said.

Grace began to relax against June's body. June could feel her leaning into her shoulder, could feel her own heart beating against the front of the tiny pink dress. She wanted to believe it was the sound of her voice that soothed Grace.

Letha said, I've got to go outside for a minute. I drank too much coffee afore I left the house this morning. Will you be OK?

June nodded.

After Letha was gone, she sat down in the rocker, which was still warm from Letha's body. Grace had fallen asleep. June closed her own eyes and let the baby breathe on her neck. She calculated whether she would have time to take Grace and run before Letha got back, then remembered that Letha and Mary Margaret knew her name and could describe her car. She'd have to think of something else.

Why, look, Letha said when she came back in. How in the

world did you get her to sleep? she whispered. Earlier, she was carrying on so!

June said, I've got a nephew, Charlie, who's almost three. I've had practice.

Upstairs, the sound of conversations and shuffling feet.

Sounds like church has let out, June said. I should get going.

Honey, why don't you wait and meet Miss Regina, Laurel's foster mama? She always comes right down to get her.

Maybe next Sunday, she said, handing Grace to Letha, but when she turned, Regina Brewer was already in the doorway, smelling like Avon, smiling, holding out her arms for the baby.

This is Sister Regina Brewer, Letha says, and Regina, this here's June.

A shadow crossed the woman's face before she remembered herself and smiled. She held out her hand, and June took it, noted again the short fingernails, the simple gold wedding band. June became self-conscious of her own poorly painted nails.

We haven't seen you in church before, Regina said.

It was a question. June scrambled for an excuse, stood there wishing she was already back in Myrtle Gap.

I think she likes it down here with us, Letha said as she bent to pick up a pull toy full of colored plastic balls.

Well, it's nice to meet you, June, Regina said. I hope you'll come to services some Sunday.

Thank you, June said, watching Grace tug at a loose hairpin in Regina's hair.

Regina grabbed Grace's pink diaper bag from the counter, said, Now I've got to go. I know I'm not supposed to do this on Sunday, but if I don't do some packing, we won't ever get moved.

And they were gone.

Moved? June regretted not running away with Grace when she had the chance.

Letha rubbed her lower back, must've noticed June's panic. She said, Regina and Brother Brewer are moving into that little double-wide just down the road on the creek side. I was over there yesterday, helping Regina put newspaper in the cabinets and drawers. They've fixed it up real nice inside.

June scanned the nursery for her pocketbook, found it hanging on the crib. She rummaged for the key chain and Letha continued, Some of the men will be helping them move their things over from Naugatuck on Friday. It'll make them a nice home, praise the Lord. Looks like they figure on stayin here with us for a while.

Stay, June thought.

Wyla

JUNE STEPPED THROUGH THE HOSPITAL DOORS, WHERE she had left Rena drifting in a twilight sleep and Bethel and Isom holding Charlie up to the nursery window to see his newborn sister. The baby slept in a clear plastic bassinet, tiny fists pulled up to either side of her china-doll face. All morning, June had held Rena's dry, limp hand or smoothed her ratted hair as she murmured strings of words that June couldn't make out, or she stood at the nursery window, staring at the baby girl through Charlie's fingerprints on the glass. Finally, a nurse said, Honey, you've been here all night. Go get you something to eat.

She crossed Grafton Street toward the row of maples that threw their shadows across parking meters and the cars parked along the river's edge. Heat rose from the asphalt, burned the soles of her flip-flops, coiled up her pale bare legs.

A few yards ahead, at the place where the creek threaded into the river, a bridge and a stand of willows leaning over it as if listening for something to rise from the muddy creek bottom. In the slow yellow water, a half-submerged tire coated in rust-red mud and the end of a metal pipe that pointed toward the sky. On the rocky bank, a tangle of vines, silver leaves open to the sun like the pale mouths of snakes.

It was the Fourth of July. Later, people would line the riverbank all the way to Three Mile Curve to picnic and wait for the fireworks show. June had seen it once—she must've been five or six—when Garvin and Beauty brought her and Tom. They'd sat on a blanket, drinking pop and eating leftover potato salad and pie until the show started, then they lay back in the dark and stared into the erupting sky, the tips of Garvin's and Beauty's cigarettes echoing the bursts of light above them.

On a bench beneath one of the maples, June let down her guard, let the tears come. Happiness for Rena and Watt, a longing for Tom and Grace. She let herself miss Ellis and, finally, reckon with the look on Isom's face that morning when he first saw Rena's baby girl. It was a look of wonder and gladness that she'd only seen on him when he first saw Charlie—must've been the same look he wore when Tom was born, for he had been there in the yard, waiting with Shag. A smile nearly as big as Watt's. His expression had both angered and saddened her, but she couldn't let on to Rena. She felt herself drop into that bottomless well inside her that hated Isom, then heard Granny's voice in her head reciting a Bible verse about forgiveness, but June was lost and couldn't allow herself to forgive anyone. She ached to be on Blackburn Fork with Grace and Letha.

Last Sunday, Letha invited her home for dinner, and she had gone. Mary Margaret was there when they got to the house, tending to the chicken and dumplings Letha had put on before church, and she seemed truly pleased to see June. Letha explained why Mary Margaret had skipped church, had winked and said, Mary Margaret here is Catholic. Could only get her to our church one time, so she might as well cook!

They'd eaten a meal of dumplings, fresh kale, and homemade light bread. For dessert, Mary Margaret had made an apple crisp, and they took bowls of it and glasses of iced tea out onto the front porch.

June loved spending time with them, didn't want to leave when dark began to fall. She felt easy with them, as neither of them pried into her business.

Before she left for Myrtle Gap, she thanked Letha for introducing her to the preacher and Miss Regina.

Well, I figured it was about time, Letha said. They are very fine people to know. Miss Regina is so much happier now that they have Laurel.

When she had cried herself out, she ran her fingers through her unwashed hair and looked toward the theater down the street, her third-story hallway window lit up by the sun. She longed to lie down on her own bed and nap but wanted to be at the hospital when Rena woke. She stood and crossed the bridge again.

Only Watt and Charlie were in the maternity-ward waiting room. Watt looked dazed and Charlie happily ripped pages out of a hunting magazine. When he saw June, he held up his arms for her to pick him up. Watt looked up at her, his face a picture of worry, then stood. He'd been waiting for her to come back.

What's wrong? June asked.

He blanched.

Panic rose in her. Is Rena OK? she asked.

He nodded, said, It's Isom. They've taken him to the emergency.

June tried to feature what he was telling her. What happened? she asked.

Watt took Charlie from June, said, He passed out in the hall up here. They couldn't wake him up. He stopped breathing but they brought him back with that new CP or something or the other.

She found Bethel sitting in the hallway in the emergency room. A nurse sat beside her, rubbing her shoulders, trying to get her to drink from a paper cup. But Bethel shook her head. She was crying too hard to talk or even catch a breath. The nurse looked up at June, told her, They're working on him right now. You the daughter?

Stepdaughter, June said.

Bethel

I WAS DOZIN IN THE ROCKER THE MORNING ISOM TOOK that baby from my arms. It startled me, for I've not known him to care to hold newborns. He never hardly held Charlie until he could sit up by hisself.

I jolted full awake.

What? I said.

He held her in the crook of his arm. Don't say a word, he said.

The room was chilly, and he set her down on the davenport, began to wrap her up in a lap quilt. She never opened her eyes that whole time.

I stood up and moved to take her up again, but he shook his head, said, I made up my mind.

What are you about to do? I whispered, although June was plumb wore-out and still dead asleep and wouldn't hear a thing. He went into the kitchen, and awful thoughts began to run through my mind. I seen him trap kittens in gunnysacks and throw them in the creek to drown, do away with stray dogs when the kids wasn't looking. He'd walked them dogs into the woods carrying a shovel and a rifle on his shoulder. Most times, the dogs went willingly, their faces so full of trust it like to broke my heart.

I froze where I stood, wore my fear like a red-hot shawl. I eyed the gun rack, the rifle still hangin on it, untouched, like it had been for a while. I wanted to pick the baby up but knew that I might need to take up that rifle and it would take both hands.

He come back from the kitchen with a pasteboard apple box, lined with newspaper and a old bath towel. He slid the hot water bottle under that towel.

I'll buy you a new one, he said without looking at me. He was feeling guilt, for I knowed right then he'd planned this, had had everything ready.

You cain't do this, I grunted from somewhere in my belly, tryin to conjure up fear in him.

He picked the baby up from the davenport and laid her in that box.

I have to, he said, tucking the quilt in around her. We've had enough business with them Akers. No more.

Later, I would come back to that remark meant to hurt me, but right then, watching him take such care with the baby caused the thinnest veil of relief to settle on me. I realized he wasn't going to harm her. But still yet.

Isom picked up the box and moved toward the door.

I tried to stop him, realized for the first time in my marriage that I might be afraid of him. I sobbed, No! She'll get hungry . . . will need to eat soon.

When he gave in, I knowed then he'd seen me eying that gun.

That baby made nary a sound as she suckled her sleeping mama for what I feared was the last time, and turned out it were. All at the same time, I willed June awake and also wished her to sleep on and be spared this. Isom had made up his mind. If I stopped him then, he'd a just took her later while I was asleep.

She come away from June's breast making little smacking noises that made me ache. She unclinched her fists and fell into a deep, deep sleep. June, herself, never once stirred or opened a eye. Just then, she changed into a grown woman before my very eyes. She would have to learn to carry this grief, too.

I could hear Isom's truck idling out front. He came into the bedroom and took Grace from me, wiped the milk off her chin with his thumb. My body heaved. I could not take my eyes off them but soon could no longer see for my tears.

Stay here, he said. I'll not hurt her.

I sat there until I could no longer hear the truck, all the while wondering who he meant he wouldn't hurt. For he'd hurt all of us then.

He come home a few hours later, bypassed June's rage, and went right to bed. That evening when he got up, he didn't say nary a word to me. Or her.

A Picture of Grace

JUNE OPENED THE HALL WINDOW, LEFT HER APARTMENT door ajar to air out the mustiness that had gathered in the week she was away helping get Isom set up at home. She tried to push away the disappointment that there had been no letter from Ellis waiting for her when she got back to the apartment.

She had a little time before she had to go to work, so she put away the clothes from her suitcase then opened the box that Bethel sent with her. Inside it were three jars of raspberry jam, a slip of devil's ivy tucked into a damp paper towel inside a baggie, a crocheted rug Bethel made from plastic bread bags. There was also fifty dollars—half from Beauty—to help pay that month's rent. She hadn't wanted to take it, but she'd had no choice.

She thought about Bethel, now home alone to care for Isom, for he was too stubborn to accept help from anyone else. The thought of Bethel's asking her to move home permanently, to help with Isom, terrified her. Would she be able to say no? What would she do about getting Grace back?

It occurred to her then that, if the stroke had killed Isom, she could've probably brought Grace home. It sickened her to realize she wished him dead.

When everything was put away, she took out the box of stationery Beauty gave her for her birthday and began a letter. She tried to write her sentences straight on the lineless paper.

Dear Ellis,

Here is a picture I drew of Grace last I had her in the church nursery. Granny Letha thought it was a good likeness. Of course I didn't tell her who I was doing it for. I drew her how she is now, and I hope you'll see that she is just you made over. Sometimes I try to recall what she looked like the day she was born, but I've watched her growing like a weed for too long and can't remember. I'm going to get her back. I know I will.

I'm sure that by now, someone has written you that Isom had a stroke on the same day that Rena's baby girl, Wyla June, was born there in the same hospital. Mama is all tore up about it. She told me that when he does die, for he hasn't got long, she will tuck his carbide light into the casket so he can find his way home.

I took some time off working at the movie house to stay at home and help Mama with Isom. Mrs. Mounts was nice about it and said to take however much time I need, but I am back in Myrtle Gap and working now. Still trying to get Grace back.

Mama tried to do all the regular things she does in the house, but I know she is tired. She's aged years in the past month. She's lonely, too. Rena has the new baby and Charlie to take care of, but Mama can't be over there as much as she wants to. Law, how Mama and Isom sure do cheer up when Rena takes the kids to see them.

Beauty helps out a lot. She takes Mama to the store because you know Mama never did learn how to drive—maybe I'll have to teach her. And she's helping Mama fill out all the paperwork so they can draw Isom's disability and miner's pension. The doctor over at Huntington finally signed the black lung paperwork.

Beauty tried to get Mama to go to Myrtle Beach for a vacation, but she wouldn't. She said she might would go after the garden is put up and Isom is better. I want to believe she will go, tho I can't quite picture her on the beach in a bathing suit. In the meantime, Mama will work as hard as she always has. She seems to be going downhill a little since Isom got sick. She sleeps a lot more these days and doesn't eat much. We're all worried.

Because I was at home, I haven't been able to see Grace for a couple of Sundays. I lay awake at night and worry about what will happen. She's getting so big, and I'm afraid she won't want to come with me because she will have come to think of the people who took her in as her mama and daddy. Then what? I have met them both, and they are truly nice people, but she is not theirs.

I miss you and I miss getting mail from you. I don't have any idea what happened to those other two letters you wrote, why I never got them. Did you mail them here or to the house in the holler?

Do you yet know when you're getting out and coming home? Please be safe. I will let you know the minute I have Grace with me.

Love always, June

Invitation

BROTHER BREWER MADE THE ALTAR CALL AND MISS Regina launched the piano into the first verse of "Just as I Am." All service long, June had ached to be down in the nursery with Grace and Granny Letha, but she made herself stay upstairs that day because she was worried someone would figure out why she'd been coming there on her own and just going to the nursery.

She'd come early so she'd have time to spend a few minutes downstairs before the service. If Granny Letha heard her slip and call the baby Grace, she didn't let on. June told herself that it was a coincidence that Letha had stopped humming when it happened, as was her bringing up that Miss Regina had lost two babies before they fostered Grace. When she did, June had only been able to say, That's a real shame.

She'd had to introduce herself at the beginning of the service when they welcomed her as a visitor—had almost said she was June Akers from Myrtle Gap. Part of that would be true. All of it would be true someday, she hoped, but for some reason, there hadn't been a letter from Ellis since before Isom got sick. She tried to not think about what that could mean but worried over it anyway.

Grace had taken a few steps that morning, had walked

toward Letha with her arms out, grabbing at the air between them. Such a big girl, Letha said as she took Grace into her lap.

Thinking of it made June lonely and afraid—like she'd never get the opportunity to get Grace back. Like they would go on that way forever—her only seeing Grace at church and Ellis not answering her letters. She needed something to happen.

Before she knew what she was doing, she was standing, answering the altar call. She walked toward the sound of the preacher's voice.

Baptism

THEY GATHERED AT A SHALLOW SPOT IN LITTLE BLACKburn Creek where water had carved a slow arc in its course around the mountain. Wild cherry trees and willows threw curtains of shade on the summer-slow riffles. Cars and trucks sat on the red-dog edge of the road, and the people they brought mingled on the riverbank and the bridge above.

June worried the waistband of her double-knit skirt, regretted choosing it on such a warm day. She fretted that, when she was in the river, it would float up around her waist. She'd been careful to wear a T-shirt under her blouse, like Letha told her, so when it got wet, her bra wouldn't show.

Earlier, Letha had asked June if Bethel would come to her baptism. June had been glad that Bethel had to be home with Isom, for what if she saw Grace? She'd recognize her for sure.

Preacher Brewer stood waist-deep in the river, wrinkling its leaf-strewn surface, stirring up mineral-flecked mud that glinted in the sun. On the bank, Brother Workman read verses from the Bible, his voice reflecting off the ledges of stacked shale along the far side. June waited her turn to wade into the cloudy green water to be prayed over and baptized.

When she was twelve, she had gone to a tent revival over in Parsley Bottom with her mother's grandmother, Great-Granny

McCoy. During the altar call, she'd stepped into the aisle and walked across the uneven ground toward the bright lantern at the front of the tent, the chaos of the altar. When she reached it, it was her turn to have hands laid on her head. She'd felt an electric current running through her as the preacher prayed over her. Peopled touched her, clutched at her as she struggled to breathe. She thought she'd pass out from the odor of after-shave and the smell of sweet, bruised clover beneath her feet. After the service, Granny held her hand all the way home, but Isom had refused to let her be baptized, had said, No foreign preacher is going to lay his hands on my girl.

The Sunday before, things were different when she'd walked to the front of Blackburn Fork Freewill Baptist Church. There'd been no Granny, no heart-pounding feeling as she walked the aisle, and no conviction, only the selfish yearning to make something happen—to have a reason to belong where she could be close to Grace until she figured out what to do.

After altar call, people had encircled her, hugged her, shaken her hand and patted her back. Welcomed her. When the preacher and Regina asked June to come home with them for lunch, she was too wrung out to create an excuse.

Sure. It's awful nice of you, she said, wondering how many lies she would have to tell that day.

Brother Brewer said, Regina made a mess of fried chicken and biscuits this morning.

Regina slid onto the front seat, hefted Grace into the car chair beside her. She said, And I got green beans that I canned last summer and some new potatoes Sister Runyon brought me last week.

Regina is a fine cook, the preacher said as he sat down in

the driver's seat. He grunted, rummaged in his pants pocket for the car key.

I didn't have no choice, Regina said. I had to raise my younger brothers and sister.

She turned to look at June, said, My mama died when I was nine. Daddy had to work all the time over at Twenty-Two Mine.

She had to grow up fast, said the preacher.

June thought, *Me, too.*

Minutes after the car was in motion, Grace stopped wiggling and fell asleep. Regina picked her up and cradled her on her shoulder, swayed her upper body to soothe her.

June watched them from the back seat, sleepy and drunk on car-exhaust fumes and honeysuckle-scented air, grateful for the rush of wind that made conversation difficult. She hoped the Sunday dinner would pass quickly, longed to be alone in her apartment, dozing or reading Beauty's latest issue of *Cosmopolitan* magazine that Bethel had forbidden her to bring into the house. *Even better*, she thought, *would be for Grace to be there, too.*

She thought of those few moments back in the church nursery that day, when she could have picked up Grace and run. The mix of disappointment and relief made her lightheaded.

That too much air on you? Brother Brewer asked.

June startled, then shouted, No, sir. I'm fine.

If the preacher or Regina had turned to look at her, they would've seen her come awake enough to sift her fingers through the ends of her hair, trying to calm herself.

June thought of the Plymouth parked in the gravel parking lot back at the church. She said, I could've driven my own car. Followed you.

She met the preacher's eyes in the rearview mirror, knew he'd heard her over the rushing air. He said, Naw. I have to go back to the church this afternoon, anyways. I'll carry you back with me.

It occurred to her then that she had only enough gas left in her tank to get back to Myrtle Gap, and she was relieved she hadn't driven to the Brewer's after all. *It would be just like me,* she thought, *to get addled and forget about the last bit of gas I have until payday on Wednesday. I would just as soon die as ask for help from anyone.*

The Brewers' house was small, one story, its siding carefully placed roofing shingles. It sat on a hillside, its front porch elevated and supported by poles. She thought of the dogs under Ellis's porch, the swing on Bethel's front porch, the thud of Isom's boots against floorboards.

Regina said, Come on in. I apologize that I didn't pick up much before church. Laurel was grumpy this morning.

The front room was furnished with an orange Naugahyde couch, a small TV, end tables with hurricane lamps on them. Vinyl lace doilies covered most of the open surfaces.

It's new shag carpet, Regina said, then she swept her hand around the room, indicated the toys strewn about: plastic squeaky animals, a stuffed monkey holding a banana, and a pull toy shaped like a bumblebee. She said, Again, I'm sorry for not cleaning. I wasn't expecting company today.

June knelt, ran her hands over the nap of the brown rug. Its long fibers released a chemical smell. She said, My aunt has this kind, too, except hers is green.

She stood, followed Regina down the hall, waited while she lay the baby in her crib.

Back in the hall, Regina whispered, Let's go eat. I was afeared my stomach might growl all during church this morning.

She led June to the kitchen, opened the oven door. The scents of salt and lard, green beans and fried chicken, wafted out. June longed to be in the holler, sitting down at Beauty's table.

Smells really good, she said.

Throughout the meal, she tried to soothe herself, hoped no one would notice her right leg bouncing under the table. She willed it to stop but forgot herself and went back to it each time. She tried to not stare at the preacher, who now wore denim shorts and a Panama City T-shirt, and she answered their questions with half-truths, hoping to hide anything that might give away her true purpose for joining the church.

We're so excited to have you come into the flock, Brother Brewer said. Been prayin on it. Mind if I ask you which part of my sermon made the spirit move in you today?

June swallowed, rifled through the knotted ends of lies she'd told that day. She said, I'm not for sure.

Then she remembered in the many testimonies of saved people she'd heard in churches and revival tents. She pictured them standing among the congregation, palms turned upward, tears wetting their cheeks as they told how they'd gotten the Holy Ghost and were determined to get back onto the path of righteousness.

She spoke, attempted to sound genuine, echoed their words in a rush. She said, It was the whole thing—the sermon, the singing—like something or someone else was making my legs walk up that aisle. It was powerful mysterious.

Amen! The preacher slammed his hand on the table, jarring silverware and glass.

Shh! Regina said, pointing to the nursery. I'd like to finish my dinner before she wakes up!

Regina's exasperated tone surprised June. She'd never heard her speak like that. She found that she couldn't look at either of them then, so she fished a piece of salt pork out of the pile of green beans on her plate.

Brother Brewer tore at a chicken thigh with his fork, said, Gina hasn't been getting too much rest. Laurel is awful fussy nowadays. Must be cuttin teeth again.

June said, I'd be happy to babysit for you sometime.

Well, we don't much need a sitter, but we appreciate it, Regina said.

A quietness fell over them then, and they ate without speaking. June tried to ignore the chewing sounds the preacher made. Her head began to ache. She glanced at the kitchen clock.

Grace's wails cracked the silence. Regina slowly rose from her chair, and June put her hand on her arm, said, Let me go get her for you, Miss Regina. You just go ahead and eat.

Grace sat up in the crib, her legs tangled in a thin pink blanket, her face flushed with heat and confusion, cheeks glazed with tears. Wrinkles in the bedclothes had etched her face with lines and curves.

June moved toward Grace, checked her forehead for fever with her hand, found none. She cooed, It's OK. You're OK.

She picked up her daughter.

Can I take care of you for this little while? she whispered.

She unbuttoned Grace's little yellow dress and pulled it over her head.

That's better, June said. That itchy old thing would make me cranky, too.

She sat them down in a rocking chair that creaked when June began to rock it. Its corduroy pad and Grace's sweaty head made her skin burn, and she longed for her shorts and T-shirt. She looked around the room. Pink curtains and crib sheet, a mobile of pink and blue elephants over the crib, a yellow toy telephone under it.

She could smell the soaked diaper, feel it leaking onto her thighs, but didn't want to move, for Grace had stopped whimpering and leaned into her. June closed her eyes and began singing a song she'd been told Shag sang to Tom and her when they were babies.

Cheeks as red as a blooming rose and eyes are the prettiest brown,
She's the darling of my heart, sweetest girl in town.

Tears skimmed her face. Grace was still, and she sang on.

Shady Grove, my little love, Shady Grove I say,
Shady Grove, my little love, I'm bound to go away.

June whispered to Grace, I'm your real mama. I hope you already know that.

Grace wriggled away from her shoulder and searched June's face with wide eyes—Ellis's eyes. June felt the tears coming again, pulled Grace close once more, said, I'll come get you and make everything right. We'll be OK.

She wasn't sure she believed herself. There had once been a chance to reclaim her daughter, and she had been too afraid to take it.

•

When her name was called, June stepped out of her flats, gathered the seam of her skirt into her fist, and entered the dazzling water.

The water, warm and slow, still took her breath. Brother Brewer then took her hand, guided her over the moss-slick rocks back to the spot where he'd stood before. Murky water swirled around them, pulled the hem of her skirt between her thighs, brushed mysterious things against her legs.

Brother Brewer placed his right hand on the small of her back, raised his left above their heads, asked, Sister June, do you repent of your sins?

June nodded into the bright sun. The preacher placed a folded white hanky over her nose and mouth, lowered her backward toward the water, said, I baptize you in the name of the Father, the Son, and the Holy Ghost.

She let him push her under and the river closed over her, filled her ears with roaring. She held her breath. In that moment, pictures of Grace, Tom, and Ellis came into her vision. Garvin's work boots. Her own bare footprints in the bloody snowbank. She recalled the taste of dirt. Then, a wailing emptiness before she was urged back up into daylight by Brother Brewer's hands.

Praise Jesus! he shouted.

She slogged toward the riverbank, water-heavy, clumsy. Letha handed her a dry hanky to wipe her eyes. Others hugged her, patted her back, called her Sister June.

When she could see again, there was Miss Regina with a wall of sunlight behind her. She held Grace in one arm and a bath towel in her other.

She offered the towel, said, Here, June. I brought this for you.

June reached for Grace.

News

A SOFT KNOCKING ON JUNE'S APARTMENT DOOR, THEN Rena standing on the landing, holding Wyla in the crook of her arm like a football.

Where's Charlie? June asked.

Rena said, Mom wanted to keep him today.

Come on in here, June said, wiping matter away from her eyes. She closed the door after them, turned back to the room, realized that there was no place for them to sit. She yanked the quilts up over her bedsheets, patted the sleep-warmed spot where she had just been.

Here. Sit here, she said to Rena, then asked, What time is it?

Rena fussed with Wyla's receiving blanket.

June tried again. Is Mama alright? Did something happen to Isom?

Rena's eyes leapt around the room. She said, Mama's fine. I wanted to tell you, though, before somebody else does. Ellis . . .

June's chest caved in on itself. She grabbed the bed's footboard, remembered the day of notification of Tom's death, tried to stay upright.

Oh, God, she said.

He's missing, Rena said.

June turned the words over in her mind. She realized that

missing meant he could still be alive, if what Rena said was even true. She asked, Where did you hear it? in a voice louder than she'd intended. She hoped that Mrs. Mounts couldn't hear her.

Rena looked directly at her, said, Solomon came by the house last night.

She sat down on the bed beside Rena.

He wasn't lying, Rena said. I could tell he was all tore up.

Wyla put her fist into her mouth, began to suck it. Rena fumbled in the diaper bag, said, You got a pan for me to warm up a bottle?

June got up, tried to walk. The stove seemed miles away, like she might never get there. Halfway across the floor, she stopped and turned. She said, When? How long?

She had heard her mother ask the same question the day the army chaplain took her hands in his and told her that Tom was dead, after Bethel had been helped off the floor and placed in the rocker, spine straight and motionless, gazing into the middle distance. After she had shirked Isom's hands away from her shoulders. Later, June had wondered what exactly she, herself, had been doing the moment bullets split the air and shattered the breath out of Tom. Sleeping? Reading? She wondered what she had been doing in the moments between Ellis being in one place and then nowhere—before he just vanished. She couldn't allow herself to think him dead.

Rena was behind her now, handing her the bottle. She said, It's been several weeks. Solomon didn't believe it at first, so he didn't tell.

Relief flared in the back of June's mind—a reason for Ellis's not writing her. It didn't last. She was angry with Sol for not telling anyone sooner, and she knew there was something else—she heard it in Rena's voice. She waited.

Wyla began to fuss.

Sol's blaming you for this, too, Rena said. He's saying it's all your fault Ellis enlisted and now you will pay.

Granny Justice

SUFFER THE LITTLE CHILDREN IS THE VERSE I'M IN A mind of today. I don't know what all else June is goin to have to bear. Hit seems that the Lord has put a bushel full on her in the present time, and only he knows why. She is a fatherless girl who has also lost her brother and her child, and now her man is missin in a useless war.

I read that they was over seventy thousand never come home from World War II. Think of their mamas and daddies, not knowin where the bones of their children were. This war seems such a waste of life. I wish them men in Washington, DC, had to go over there and fight. Or put the women in charge! I'll allow that'd stop this killin.

June is a sturdy one. Has been since she was borned, but I'll keep watch over her and hope she can feel my love and be comforted. I'll pray for better times to come to her. The apostle Paul wrote down these words in Romans 8:18: *For I consider that the sufferings of this present time are not worth comparing with the glory that is to be revealed to us.* I don't mean to sound disrespectful, but I sure hope the Lord don't take his time to reveal the glory, for my girl cain't take much more sufferin.

Bethel

A EARLY HOARFROST WAS ON THE GROUND THE MORNING I heard about the Akers boy. Raw sunlight heated up the tin roof, caused it to make tickin noises—like the sound of time passin, if ever there was such a thing. Nearly a year gone since Grace was born. Over a year since Tom was killed, and now June has moved out. I woke up feelin sorry for myself.

Rena's the one brought word that Ellis has gone missin in action in Vietnam. She come over and told me that morning, said she was goin over to Myrtle Gap to tell June. I told her she could leave Charlie with me.

When his mommy was gone, me and Charlie had us a big time hullin the black walnuts I picked up out of Beauty's yard. Our hands was stained mahogany by the time we were through. Then, I filled up the washtub and dropped the nuts in, instructed Charlie to pick off all the floaters and throw them out in the yard for the squirrels, which he did, one at a time.

When Rena come back, she about had a fit over Charlie's hands. We have church tomorrow, she said.

I said, He ain't the first child to hull walnuts. It just shows he's a hard worker like his daddy.

Then I asked her how June was farin after the news. She

said, Hard to tell. She's all drawed up into herself. She takes that after you, Mama.

It like to shocked me when she said it.

After Rena had gathered up Charlie's things and zipped him into his coat, I handed her a sack of walnuts and said, You'll have to crack these yerself, but set them out to dry first. Let Charlie help you pick out the meats.

When they had gone, I set down in Isom's chair and studied my hands, all the stained-dark crevices runnin like a map a creeks over my palm. I closed my eyes and felt the tears spillin over onto my face. I hurt for my daughters, first for June who'll feel guilty, for she believes what Sol said—that Ellis wouldn't have enlisted if she hadn't rejected him. And Rena, who has lost a brother, although she don't let on that she knows it. Now this, added to ever thing else they've endured, the both of them. I hurt for myself and Merkey, too, both of our begotten sons lost. And for what? I'll tell you, I let myself taste them tears.

I come close to tellin Rena that Sol was her daddy that afternoon. A few years before, I promised myself I'd tell her after Sol was dead, if he went before I did, when he couldn't do her no more harm. That day, I knowed I had no choice. She needed to know it was her brother who'd gone missin in Vietnam, but I wasn't ready to say it.

Solomon

ANGEL IN MY POCKET WAS PLAYING, AND THE THEATER had been crowded for both showings. People, mostly families with kids, waited in line during intermission while June tried to keep up with the orders, handed out candy bars and cups of pop, took the sticky coins and folded dollar bills they handed across the counter.

She tried to keep her mind on her work but felt she was in a trance. The Sunday before, when June had asked, pretending it was a distant cousin who was missing, Mary Margaret had said that *missing in action* means that he could have been captured or may be injured and hiding. Or he could be dead and they haven't found his body.

Oh, June, she'd said. I'm so sorry about your cousin.

Everything June later read in newspapers and magazines at the library told her that this was true. She knew in her heart that Ellis would have to be hurt to be hiding. It wasn't like him to shirk, so he was likely taken prisoner or dead. And Solomon blamed her, and that frightened her.

And him knowing all that time before he told, she thought. *What if he finds out Ellis is dead and don't tell me?* It occurred to her then that, if Sol and Merkey got a notification of Ellis's death, she would be the first to know, for Sol wouldn't be able to control his fury.

After intermission, she swept up the spilled popcorn and flattened Junior Mints and Milk Duds from the lobby floor. She gagged as she swept the trash into the dustpan, for she was repulsed by the thought of food. She looked up to see Mrs. Mounts looking past her, toward the lobby window. She craned her head to see what it was that Mrs. Mounts saw—a man standing just outside the door, looking back at her, his stubbled face blank and frightening.

Oh no, June whispered.

You know him? Mrs. Mounts asked. Should I get Shep?

No, June said. She propped the broom against the counter, made her legs move toward the glass door. Laughter from inside the theater drifted into the lobby.

Solomon stepped back when she opened the door. He smelled like Isom used to after his shift—of Lava soap—and there was still a ridge of coal dust in the crease of his chin. His eyes were dark, deep tunnels that frightened her. He might have been drinking.

He didn't move to touch her, didn't raise a hand to her nor say anything at all. They stood silently under the buzzing marquee. June was paralyzed, could feel Mrs. Mounts and Shep watching them from inside the glaring lobby. June felt as if she were watching this scene in a movie, aware that the heroine was partly to blame that her man had gone to war. Had he come to tell her Ellis was dead?

Solomon cleared his throat, said, They tell me he's likely dead. Not much of a chance he survived that battle.

June shook her head, said, We don't know that.

Don't matter to me what you think. I know my son is dead. I know it.

She waited to hear him say it was her fault, but he didn't. He said instead, That baby girl is all's left of him. If you know where she is, I want you to tell me.

But you wouldn't take her when Isom brought her to you, June whispered.

His brows rose. He hadn't thought Rena would tell her that. He moved so close she could hear him breathe. He said, She's likely all Merkey and me will have of him. Do you know where she's at?

June stared into the dustpan she still held. He said, I just knowed that were why you moved over here.

I don't know where she is, June pleaded.

He glared at her for a long moment, said, Girl, you're lying, then turned to walk across the street toward Ellis's pickup. When he was gone, she stumbled past Mrs. Mounts and into the lobby bathroom. Vomited.

Rena

MRS. MOUNTS' WINDOWLESS OFFICE SMELLED OF BUG spray and cigar smoke. While June waited for Rena to answer her phone call, she scanned the wall above the green metal desk, gaped at a color photo of a Playboy Playmate, dressed in a sheer bed jacket, who pouted at her from a calendar advertising Mountain State Motors in Williamson. She was thinking that Bethel would never allow such a thing in her house when Rena finally picked up the phone. She sounded worn.

I really hate to call you so early, June said.

June, what's wrong? Where are you?

The movie house office.

Wyla whimpered in the background on Rena's end. Rena said, That's long distance! What's the matter?

Rena, listen. Solomon came here last night.

Wyla was closer to the phone then, making snuffling sounds. June pictured her in Rena's arms, suckling a bottle of formula.

What did he want? Rena asked. Is Ellis . . . Did they find him?

June's voice threatened to break. No, Reenie. He wants Grace. He wants to know where Grace is.

What? Why?

Said he knows Ellis is dead. Said Grace is all they've got left.

Oh, God, Rena said.

June heard the dread in Rena's voice and knew that Rena realized what she, too, might have lost.

What are you going to do? Did he hurt you? Rena asked. She had gained control.

The airless room tightened around June. No, she sobbed, relieved to have someone to tell this to. She twisted the greasy phone cord around her finger, said, He never hurt me. I cain't let him find out where Grace is. He cain't get her!

No, he cain't, Rena said. Are you going to church today?

June was crying harder by then. She said, I cain't. I'm afraid he'll follow me there.

She pictured him standing at the door of the theater last night, then on the church steps. She said, I don't know how he found me here, anyway.

Stay there, Rena said. I have the truck today. I'll get Watt's sister to watch Charlie and the baby. I'll be over directly.

June waited in her room for Rena to make the hour's drive, weighed what to do. She knew that Granny Letha would be wondering what became of her today. She was supposed to help her and Mary Margaret pick blackberries along the Copperas Mine Road to make a cobbler and vanilla ice cream to go with their Sunday supper.

June startled when Rena tapped on her door. She sat up, heart pounding, disoriented, realizing that it was already early afternoon.

Rena tapped again, louder, saying, June?

Hi, Rena said when June let her in.

June hugged Rena, said, I'm sorry for you, too, Reenie.

When they stepped away from each other, Rena was crying. She sat down on the bed, rummaged through her pocketbook.

June took the manilla envelope she offered, stared at it. Inside was a smaller envelope, and she recognized the stationery—her own handwriting on the postmarked envelope. It was her last letter to Ellis, and it had been opened.

Where'd you get this?

They sent all his mail home to Solomon and Merkey. June, Sol went to see Mama, gave this to her.

What? June asked. If Isom had been home, he would've whupped Sol!

Rena went on, He wasn't. Sol said that the letter proves you know where Grace is—that you've seen her—for you said so in the letter.

June slumped on the bed beside Rena, put her head in her hands, began to sob. She gripped the letter that had been halfway around the world and back. She tried to remember if she had written the Brewers' names in it, hoped that Ellis had received the letter and was able to read it before . . .

Rena said, Mama knows why you're here. Carrie told her about the newspaper. She knows you found Grace.

Why didn't she say something to me?

Rena took the letter from June, laid it on the nightstand. She said, I don't know. She wants you to come home, though.

June shook her head.

June, Rena said. I just now saw Sol parked down the street. I told him to leave you alone, but I don't think he's going to. Where's your suitcase?

Tom

EARLY SUN CAME UP OVER THE MOUNTAIN, LIFTED THE hem of mist high in the trees of the holler, lay down a wavering field of light over Bethel's withered garden. June stood at her bedroom window, reaching back into a dream from moments before, where something alive and warm grazed among winter-gray grasses, chuffed at frost-crusted leaves. From somewhere beyond that meadow, a remnant of Tom's voice saying, Keep walking, June. When people are freezing to death, they get fooled into thinking they're warm, so they lay down and die. Keep walking.

She couldn't understand what he meant to say.

The teapot whistled in the kitchen, broke off her thoughts. She was used to the sound effects and music from the theater below her apartment, but the sudden whistle was magnified in the otherwise-silent house. During her days at home, she'd noticed that the house held a deeper quiet than before she'd left home. That made the nights difficult and lonely, and mornings almost as unbearable, for the house made only small sounds then—the teakettle, the squeak of a closing screen door, the huff of Isom's oxygen machine.

Then, fully awake, she heard Tom's voice again. Keep walking, June, he said.

She slipped back into the dream, followed the tracks of winter birds stitched onto the frozen meadow, searched for the animal. She knew that if she could just touch it, the world would right itself. All that day, she would walk the thin line between waking and dreaming, trying to decipher Tom's warning.

Usually when she dreamed of Tom, he was lying in a forest somewhere. She came across him stretched out on a slab of rock or the damp, leafy floor of the woods—never in the frothing jungle where he died. He was always on his back, unable to move, always looking at her with widened, pleading eyes, never speaking but somehow telegraphing his pain. She could hear his thoughts—not in words, exactly, but a kind of roar, coming through him from someplace inside the earth. And always, always, she was unable to help him.

The first dream came in the quiet of the night after she had waited at the Charleston Armory with Bethel, Isom, Rena, and Watt for the plane that brought Tom's broken pieces gathered into a casket the color of the dimes they had plundered from Isom's truck when they were kids. June had awakened crying, and the dream followed her for days.

Weeks after he was in the ground, the dream came a second time, and again, she woke up whimpering, remembering the sound that came from Tom in the dream—by then the muted roar of a seashell held to her ear. It had been a howl from somewhere far away that reached into her sleep even before the black army car came slithering up the road, before she lost Grace and Ellis, before grief had swallowed her whole.

Years later, the dream would change. Tom would stand before her in a tuxedo at the edge of Laurel Lake. "Melissa," an Allman Brothers song he never heard but she knew he would've loved, would come to them from across the still water. He'd reach out and offer June his hand. Then they would dance, wordless, graceful until the song ended. He'd step back, smile, and turn to walk away. She would watch him go. It would be her last dream of him.

Rain

THE FIRST DROPS OF RAIN HIT THE PLYMOUTH ROOF before June got to the four-lane. An early shower. It was Sunday, and back home, Bethel would be getting ready for church. Beauty would pick up her and Charlie and take them around to Parsley Bottom.

June was driving to Rena's to watch Wyla while Rena went to a baby shower over at Gilbert. Afterward, she'd drive to the apartment in Myrtle Gap. It was time to go home.

She turned on the radio, tried to not think about Grace and Letha, Mary Margaret. She hadn't seen them since the Sunday before Bethel called her home. She had been desperate and took a chance on going to church one more time. As far as she knew, Solomon hadn't followed her.

That day, Letha had known something was wrong—had asked—but June was too terrified to tell her, had feared that, if the Brewers found out why June was there—what she wanted—and that Solomon wanted to take the baby, too, they would move away and she might never see Grace again. Instead, she only told Letha that she was needed at home to help with Isom, had written Beauty's phone number on the back of an offering envelope and promised to come to church the first chance she had. It had been her only choice. After that, she exhausted herself trying to figure out a way to get back to Blackburn Fork without Solomon finding out. He knew her Plymouth, Beauty's car, too, and she was sure he'd seen Watt and Rena's truck. She thought of walking to church but realized that it would be even easier for Sol to find her if she parked on the road, if he was still looking at all.

Grace had reached for June on that last Sunday and June lost her composure, had held her and kissed her dark curls until Letha took the baby out of her arms and said, June, you're going to cry yourself sick.

Something in Letha's face told June she might know something, but she hadn't pried.

June had left then, for she couldn't stand it any longer. Before she left, Letha snapped a picture of June and Grace with her new Instamatic. Later, when Mary Margaret gave June the picture—the only photo of Grace she had—June thought that she, herself, looked to be carrying the weight of a hundred years, like the older women she knew who had raised seven or eight kids and were just worn-out and too tired to fuss with their appearance. She hadn't bothered to hide the photo. She framed it and kept it on her dresser.

In a call from Beauty's phone, Letha confided that Mary Margaret had started seeing a man in Myrtle Gap. Even though she said she was glad for Mary Margaret, June sensed that Letha missed having both of them around. Letha had also passed on a little gossip about how people from the church were getting along, who was sick. June half listened, afraid to ask too much about Grace, but, at the end of the call, Letha told her that Brother Brewer was going to take some vacation time and that he and Regina were taking Laurel to see relatives in Harrisburg. Then, Letha said something that shook her: June, the law will take their side.

June was mortified, then relieved to no longer have to lie to Letha.

I'll not tell if you promise you won't take her, Letha said. It would break their hearts.

June had stayed home as long as she could stand it, had helped with the cooking and washing, helped Isom to the toilet when Bethel was out. She hated that. When her mother asked, she drove to Maynard's to get bread and other groceries. Then, one morning after breakfast, she announced she was returning to Myrtle Gap to get back to work. A half-truth. She told her mother that, since Sol hadn't bothered her lately, she was no longer afraid. An outright lie. Besides, she'd said, Mrs. Mounts isn't going to hold my job forever.

Still, Bethel begged her to not go.

In the car, driving back to Myrtle Gap, June realized that Letha was right. The law would favor the Brewers, if it came to that. Grace was their legal child. But what if she explained how Isom had stolen Grace against her will? That she hadn't known or given her up willingly?

Her mind and body were weary from worrying about Ellis and Grace, about Sol doing something that couldn't be undone. For the first time, she thought about giving up, leaving the Brewers alone, moving back home. Grace would be fine with them, and if she told them who she was, maybe they'd let her see Grace from time to time. Or maybe she could keep her job and stay in Myrtle Gap. She relished the independence of living on her own, away from Bethel and Isom's reach, and even though, by the calendar, she was still a teenager, she had never really belonged to them, anyway. She wondered how it could be that one person could *belong* to another.

The week before, June had met Viv at the new 7-Eleven. They'd sat on the hood of the Plymouth, sipped Icees, and talked. June told Viv about Grace and the Blackburn Fork church but left her baptism out of the story. Viv had heard that Ellis was missing and told June she was sorry. Their reunion turned sorrowful then, and Viv wondered aloud if someone was, at that moment, wearing a bracelet with Ellis's name on it. June said she hoped she'd never see one.

Viv was still babysitting for her sister and hated it. She said she felt trapped and wanted something more. Maybe that meant going to college or secretarial school. Maybe that meant getting married to Kenny Ray Bibb, whom she'd dated since her junior year of high school.

He has a good job in the mines, Viv said, but he don't want to take me nowhere when he's off work. I have to beg him.

They agreed that Viv should look for a job in Myrtle Gap, and they'd live together in a larger apartment that Mrs. Mounts might know about.

For a moment, June had stopped thinking about Grace. She said, We could save up for New York.

Hell yeah, Viv said. We're girls who finished high school. We can do anything.

•

It began to rain hard enough for June to turn on the wipers. At the mouth of the holler, she watched Solomon's truck pull off the strip road and fall in behind her. She eyed him in the rearview mirror. *Let him follow me*, she thought. *He'll not find anything but Rena, his own daughter, at the end of this road.*

Alarm

THE AIR IN THE APARTMENT WAS HEAVY AND SMELLED of the instant coffee June had spilled the night before. A man's agitated voice came from her clock radio, the morning announcer from WGUY just down the street. For a moment, June was back in her room at home, just waking for school, with little to worry about. She turned down the radio's volume and the voice softened to a haze. She snapped on the lamp and checked the clock. It was just after 6:00 a.m.

Dull light leaked around the edges of the curtains. June could sense the rain in it—a cold, river-deep smell that had seeped into the room, different from the warm, living rain of summer.

She turned off the light, pulled the quilts back over her, knew that she should get up and dress. There was a special kids' matinee that day, but the sound of rain on the roof lulled her. She drifted off as she thought of how to celebrate Grace's birthday, which was weeks away.

The next time she woke, Mrs. Mounts was pounding on her door, calling her name.

June? June! she said. Hurry!

June sat up and looked at the clock—7:41 a.m. She got up and opened the door to Mrs. Mounts' pallid face.

June! she said. The impound dam above Blackburn has give way. Ain't that where your church is at?

June searched the whirling room for clothes and shoes. The car keys.

Oh, honey, Mrs. Mounts said before she went back downstairs. They're finding people hurt and dead up there!

Keep Walking

SOL WAS WAITING FOR HER AT THE ENTRANCE TO THE on-ramp, but she didn't care. She hit the four-lane and sped ahead of him toward Blackburn. She thought of pulling over somewhere to hide and lose him, but she needed to get up that holler.

She prayed, Please, please, over and over again.

Squad cars and ambulances, fire trucks flashed past her in the left lane, streaked toward Blackburn. Each time one passed, June steered blindly through the sheets of water they flung across the windshield. When an ambulance passed her going the other direction, she prayed that Grace wasn't in it.

At the Copperas Mine exit, Mingo County Sheriff cars blocked the four-lane beyond. Canterbury sat in one of the open-door cars, his left leg out on the pavement, talking on the radio. He didn't see her, nor did she see Sol.

June backed the Plymouth into a turnout, threw the keys under the seat, and sprinted past the police cars, turning over horrific images in her mind. She had seen pictures from previous floods in the newspaper—had heard Granny describing their awful aftermaths.

She entered the woods and, no longer mindful of Sol, ran as parallel to the road as she could. She had to get to Grace. Her smooth-soled Keds skimmed and slipped over wet leaves until she was around the curve and out of sight of the law, and then she went back to the road. She wished she had thought to put on a raincoat.

The rain had lessened to a sprinkle, but low clouds scudded across the treetops, and June's clothes were wet. A cold wind had come up, and ice dulled the surfaces of puddles. She alternated between walking and running, still praying, Please, oh, please.

Later, she wouldn't remember much about how she got to Blackburn or even what had come before 7:41 a.m. that morning, and she would only tell the full story of that day twice in her lifetime.

At the mouth of the holler, a second roadblock. A National Guardsman in jungle fatigues waved an ambulance past the barrier. June's face and hands were numb, her sweatshirt soaked with rain. She left the road again, started up the side of the mountain, flanked the National Guard and emergency crews. Above her, helicopter rotors slashed the air.

Keep walking, she whispered.

Keep walking, Tom whispered back.

Granny Justice

HONEY, HIT SEEMS LIKE THEY'S A LOT MORE FLOODS now than they used to be. Just five year ago, they was a big un over on Cherry Creek, and now this un has struck Blackburn. They's catastrophic ones about every decade. When the 1908 one hit over at Mount Gay, I was still yet young. I heared talk of it for a long time but only seen it in pictures.

The one I recollect best is the 1916 flood up on Cabin Creek over in Kanawha County. Hit flooded on Paint Creek and the Little Coal at the same time, but it weren't near as bad as down on the Cabin. Hit was only showers predicted for that day in August. I heared they was six inches of rain fell in just five hour. I was twenty-three and been married for seven or eight year by then, and John had almost took a loggin job over there. Boy, we was relieved he didn't after hearin about that flood. Hit would've surely took us all, for they wasn't much warnin.

I got pictures of that flood somewhere, took with the Brownie camera Mommy bought us as a weddin present. They was still makin pictures in black and white at that time, but, honey, the dirty high-water mark on the sides of them coal-company houses showed up just the same, some of those greasy lines plumb up over the doors. I perish the thought of us tryin to get them young uns to higher ground. We'd a had to carry them, and I didn't weigh more than a minute at the time.

They was quite a few killed in that flood, near about eighty, not a countin the ones they never found. My Uncle O'Dell and his wife and baby daughter was among the dead. They was all found in different places. They're buried up on a hill overlookin where their house stood. I often wonder how many people survived that flood only to be killed by the Spanish flu that come two year later.

Floods can have long-livin consequences. After the 1916 flood, most of the miners on Cabin Creek moved their families outta there. Cain't say I fault them for that. A man and woman has got to pertect they family.

And now this flood on Blackburn. I know it's gonna hit June hard. I shouldn't have tempted the Lord afore this, wonderin if she could suffer much more. Lord, I hope and pray that her baby ain't lost. We'll soon enough find out.

The Tipple

A QUARTER OF A MILE INTO HER CLIMB, JUNE REACHED a clear-cut. She turned to look down into the holler for the first time. Cars and trucks lay jammed against the railroad trestle. Splintered trees and lumber jutted from the black, oily mud that covered everything to about six feet above the ground. *Oh, God*, she thought. *If it's this bad here, what am I going to find up the road?*

She walked back into the trees, calculated that she should be near the first bridge by then, blew warm air on her fingers. Snowflakes drifted out of the gray and sunless sky, fell through the bare branches above her. Down below, thrashing sounds in the brush, then a moment later, a muddy milk cow wandering onto her path, wild-eyed, teats engorged, a ridge of ice running the length of its backbone. It paid her little attention, lumbered farther up the mountain. She wanted to go down into the creek bottom, to get her bearings, but feared she'd be seen and told to go back. The gray sky gave her no grasp of the amount of time between that moment and when she left the apartment that morning, but she knew she'd need to get back out of the hills before a greater darkness began to fill the holler.

Shouts rose from the creek bottom. She dropped lower down the mountain, toward the voices, jabbed her heels into the mud, punched them through the rime of ice that had begun to form over the sopping earth, grabbed wet tree limbs to keep her balance. She smelled it before she saw it—an oily, shale-like odor rising off the bottom. The smell of a thing brought forth from the earth into daylight then burned until it changed into something else—slate. The tipple.

She squatted to peer through the trees. Across the creek, the tipple, dark for the first time that she knew, and the pulse of red ambulance lights reflected in standing water. A clump of men in hardhats stood at the mouth of the mine like they'd been roused from bottomless sleep.

Not much farther down the hillside, she met the high-water mark, stood at the edge of a sheet of black gob spread over the bottom like a glacier, saw what must've only taken an instant to play out. Coal cars pushed at angles with the mountain, train tracks twisted and curled like fiddlehead ferns. A dead calf floating in one of the overturned railcars, its front legs sheared off at the knees.

She traveled parallel to the black waterline, kept above it, passed a railroad tie jammed halfway into the hillside. In the next clearing, she stopped to gape at a jumble of wood and metal shoved against the railroad bridge, just below where Caney and Blackburn forks met. An upended VW bus sat atop the mess of refrigerators and cookstoves, cars and uprooted trees. As she walked on, something made her turn, look again at the pile. The tailgate and rusted cattle racks of Letha's truck were entangled in it. She began to run.

A Red Thermos

THE BRIDGE OVER BLACKBURN FORK WAS GONE. AS SHE gawked at the festering water between her and the pylon on the other side, a body floated by, a woman with long hair, face down, completely naked beneath the shroud of gob that coated her skin. June began to panic.

She backtracked, horrified, searched for a place to cross the road. It had stopped snowing and seemed colder then. She knew it wouldn't be long before dark, but she had to keep going.

A helicopter flew over, toward the head of the holler. After it was gone, she registered the silence that ran below the sound of the creek, the absence of birds. She realized it had been like that since she walked in.

A school bus lay on its side, trapped in a curve of the creek, wipers frozen midway across the windshield. She peered in, afraid of what she'd see. It was empty, save for weeds, branches, and a plaid thermos that thunked against the windshield. Trash and wreckage extended from the bus to within yards of the far bank.

June considered crossing over. Needles of rain jabbed at her skin. *When did that start again?* She climbed onto the bus's yellow hood, crawled across its slippery body. The wreckage was unstable, but she scaled it anyway, and even though she knew better, she waded the last few feet of swift water to the far bank. On the other side, she sat down in the black mud to rest and looked back across the water. Tom stood on the other side of the roiling creek, pointing upstream. Impossibly, she heard his voice above the whooshing water.

Go, he told her.

Goldie

NIGHT CAME. FIRES DOTTED THE HILLS ABOVE THE waterline, sparked by cigarette lighters and kitchen matches salvaged from shattered homes. One group had set fire to a rotten chestnut stump. Men and boys scurried in and out of the shadows carrying branches, going back for more. Farther down the constellation of firelight, a man tossed an oak table leg into the flames. June, nearly frozen, let the heat draw her to each one, where she stood until she could again feel her fingers and toes. Then she moved on.

Shadows hunched around the flames, featureless, silent as the birds, except for muffled weeping and coughing. At one gathering, June drew close enough to see their faces, and she realized she'd seen some of them in church, but they didn't seem to recognize her or even see her. *Have I, too, become a ghost?*

A woman she'd never seen held a limp baby that June knew was dead. The woman rocked it and wept, repeated its name. Macie, Macie, she said. A man sat beside her, his body drawn into itself, tiny fires shining in his dark eyes.

At each campfire, June wordlessly searched the faces, listened for Grace's cry, then moved farther up the holler, drawn toward the next ring of light. Every step took her closer to the broken impoundment, the beginning of chaos.

She fell more than once in the darkness, glad she couldn't see the bodies she knew would be caught in the jumble of trash, for Granny had told her of the floods she'd survived. She felt their dead eyes on her as she stumbled under the weight of her soaked-through sweatshirt and mud-heavy jeans. She had walked her wet socks all the way down into her shoes, felt the wadded fabric that pressed into the soles of her feet like stones.

At one fire, a man and three children in pajamas huddled under a mud-stained crocheted afghan. None of them wore shoes. June stepped into their light, stretched herself toward the fire's heat. The man startled, turned toward her. There was a brief deepening of his eyes, then he looked away. One of the kids, a boy of barely talking age, said, Mama?

The girls, both older than the boy, searched June's face, and as they did, there was a brief glint of hope before they began to cry.

June squatted to get closer to the flames. She longed to stretch out and sleep but took off her tennis shoes to fix her socks. The children stared at her, their faces weary, their eyes mirrors of raw light.

The man, who still wore his mining clothes, gazed past all of them into the darkness. He said, You lose your people?

I don't know, June said. She pushed her Keds closer to the fire.

Who are your people?

Brother Brewer and Regina. Granny Letha.

He looked directly at her then and said, The preacher lives just above me. I've not seen them today, but when I looked down the mountain this morning, after we run, the house was off its foundation. Looked like part of it was washed away.

The tallest girl blurted, We cain't find our mama. You see her?

I don't know, June said, watching the man. Tell me her name, and if I see her, I'll send her right here to you.

Goldie Muncy, the man said. She has strawberry hair.

Toy Piano

THROUGH THE DIMNESS OF THE NEXT MORNING, JUNE could see that Letha's house was gone, her yard and garden scoured away. Later, someone would tell her that Letha rode the flood all the way down to the next bend of the creek, standing on her front porch, screaming for help. They'd find her two days later, curled up in the roots of a standing sycamore.

She raced ahead to where she thought the Brewers' house should be. She strained to make out the roofline, ran downhill toward it, slipping and falling, gagging on the mud in her mouth.

Miss Regina! Regina! she yelled.

The roof was mostly gone, the back porch ripped away, but the house stood, its remaining cinderblock foundation broken and wet all the way up. She climbed over the ruins into the opening where the back door had been.

She stepped over a blue toy piano, yelled, Brother Brewer! Regina? Hello?

The house was funereal. She searched the stripped rooms, yelling until she was hoarse, found the small room that had been Grace's. The rocking chair was smashed, most of the books and toys gone. She knelt on the filthy, spongy carpet and let it all wash over her. Everything at once. The next sound she heard was her own fractured voice, wailing barely above a whisper.

Grace! she cried.

Birds

ROTOR BLADES THUMPED ABOVE HER. FROM THEM, A searchlight scoured the side of the mountain and creek bottom. June watched her breath pass into its beam as it hovered over the double-wide. She stopped breathing, huddled closer to Grace's bedroom wall, waited for the copter to fly away.

When she stood, her legs ached, although she could register little else. June knew she needed to get to a fire soon, regretted not waving the down the copter, whose blades whispered in the distance. She just wanted to lie down and sleep.

Keep walking. Keep walking.

She headed downstream in the dark, climbing down the mountain as she went, thinking only in pictures—dead woman, red thermos, clock face numbers reading 7:41. She crossed the waterline into the foothills. From the trees just up the mountain came the song of a mockingbird. She walked toward it.

The fallen beech must have camouflaged the car from the searchlight. When June opened the door, the dome light came on. Across the seat lay Brother Brewer, his skin the color of milk, his right leg, the seat, and the floorboard saturated with brick-red blood. The end of a femur jutted through his pajama leg. *He must have tried to drive them to higher ground and got marooned by the raging water*, she thought. How long had it taken him to die? She reached back in her memory, tried to measure the expanse of time since the flood. Later, she would picture him staring up into the canopy of the beech as he bled out.

The bird called again, this time from somewhere close by. June remembered herself, began searching the car, found Grace's bloody diaper bag on the front seat. *Oh, God!* she thought. She plunged her arm into the darkness of the back seat, searched for Grace, felt the heat of her before she even touched her. Grace startled from exhausted sleep. The birds began to cry.

The Smell of Antiseptic

JUNE TRIED TO START THE CAR BUT FOUND IT WAS OUT of gas. Brother Brewer must've run the engine as he bled to death until it, too, had died. She remembered the dome light, knew the car battery was still good. She turned on the headlights, and they shone out into the brush.

She lay Brother Brewer's body across the front seat so Grace couldn't see him, folded the seat down over him as far as she could, then wedged herself around him.

In the back seat, she took off her shirt and pants, hung them up to dry on the back of the driver's seat. Grace's diaper was soaked. June changed it and tucked the baby close to her own bare skin. She pulled Brother Brewer's wool coat around them. Grace, exhausted and hungry, went quiet again. June's breasts ached with the memory of the milk that had dripped from them for days after Grace's birth.

June dozed, too. She woke once and looked up. Granny Justice was standing in front of the car, just as if she were still alive. She stood there with her palms to the sky, a Saint Francis statue. She didn't speak, but June heard her say, *Do what you have to do to keep that baby.* Then the search light swept across the car and Granny was gone. June was disoriented again, heaved back from the boundless place where she had been lost in the thump of her daughter's heartbeat on her own skin—where her granny had been. She knew she had to get help, get food and shelter for them. She heard Granny say, Help's comin.

She whispered, Thank you, and waited for someone to come get them.

•

In the helicopter, she held her hands over Grace's ears to lessen the roar of the rotors and thought of Ellis, imagined him flying high over the South China Sea, safe, out of the reach of bullets and rocket launchers. In the weak sunlight, she noticed the gash crossing Grace's right eyebrow, the dried blood on her temple. She gazed up at June, lost in a world of strange and muffled noises, and in that moment, June remembered Regina for the first time that day. Her mind raced head-on into the possibility of what might happen if she was dead, too.

When they landed at the mouth of Blackburn, a man took Grace from June, wrapped her in a clean blanket, handed her over to a Red Cross nurse. June followed them past a row of sheet-covered bodies that lay on a tarp. Some of them, she could tell, were children. She remembered the dead baby at the campfire, could still hear the mother crying its name. Macie.

The tent was warm inside and smelled of antiseptic. The nurse who examined Grace said, I think it's too late to stitch up that cut on your baby's eye.

After June was examined and given a honey bun and a cup of coffee, she watched the nurse wipe Grace's face and hands. The nurse, not much older than Rena, fed Grace a warm bottle of milk. When she finally handed her over to June, she said, I'm sorry about your husband. They've gone back to get him.

June stared at her blankly, then said, Thank you.

The nurse pointed to a cot and said, Why don't you and her lie down for a while? After you've formally identified your man, there's a bus will take you to Myrtle Gap High School. I'll put you on the list so your people can find you.

She picked up an olive-green blanket from a stack on one of the empty beds, said, What's your name, hon?

Shelter

FOR THE REMAINDER OF HER LIFE, JUNE WOULD REmember the next part of the story like this: the silent bus ride to the school, Grace asleep in her arms, Mary Margaret waiting on the front steps, which seemed so much smaller than June remembered. When Mary Margaret saw them, she ran toward them, cried, I've waited here for every bus since they started coming in this morning. Is Letha with you?

June wouldn't remember exactly what she said to Mary Margaret, but she managed to convey that Letha could be dead. Then, they fell silent. After a while, Mary Margaret asked about the Brewers. June recalled the medic pulling back the sheet from Brother Brewer's face just before she and Grace boarded the bus. He had stood on the other side of the tarp, silent, waiting, avoiding her eyes. As June stared down at the preacher's expressionless face, she recalled a Bible verse she'd heard him recite several times, Proverbs 23:10: *Do not encroach on the fields of the fatherless.* As she nodded her confirmation, she realized that, likely, Grace was completely fatherless, that Ellis might be dead, too. She pushed the thought to a dim corner of her brain then wondered how she should hold her face so as to not give herself away to the medic.

June said, Brother Brewer is dead. I haven't yet seen Miss Regina.

In the gym, Mary Margaret waited in line with them to be assigned a cot on the shiny hardwood floor. They talked little until Mary Margaret said, I have to tell you something, June.

June thought she was already numb, but hearing Mary Margaret say the words aloud made her shiver.

She moved so close to June that she could feel Mary Margaret's fear-staled breath, then whispered, Letha and I figured out that you're Laurel's mother.

June didn't answer. She was too worn-out and couldn't think of what she might say that would make sense. She swayed her body to soothe Grace, keep her sleeping.

At last June said, Granny Letha is dead. I don't know how I know it, but I do. Rivulets of tears began to slide down their drawn faces, and all around them, from every corner in the gym, the sound of weeping.

Paul, Mary Margaret's boyfriend, elated to find her alive, rushed in, begged June to go back with them to Myrtle Gap. They offered to take her and Grace, but June, paralyzed, refused to go. Before they left June standing in line, Mary Margaret said, I won't tell anyone.

June thanked her and kissed her cheek. That would be the last time June ever saw her.

At the registration table, June gave her real name. A woman read notes from a clipboard, told her that Bethel had been waiting for word of her since the day before.

Your brother-in-law found your car parked on the side of the road, she said as she read her notes, and he drove it to his house. An older man, who wouldn't say how you're related, asked after you but didn't leave his name. Said he'd be back this afternoon.

June's mind lurched. She turned from the woman and started for the front door. The woman held the clipboard to the side of her mouth and called to her in an amplified voice, Your family is worried! You need to stay put!

The sun had come out while they were inside, but the afternoon was still as cold as the day before. June stopped on the steps and pulled the army blanket tighter around her and Grace, who still slept on her shoulder. As she walked down the steps, against a tide of people, she saw the woman from the campfire, now without her dead child, then after her, Regina, who hobbled off the bus, wrapped in an identical green army blanket.

This part she would remember clearly for the rest of her days: as the distance closed between them, June thought of pulling the blanket over Grace's head and walking past Regina, who hadn't lifted her eyes off the sidewalk. Then she thought of Solomon and what Grace's life might be if he took her to raise—how she'd never be able to prove that she, herself, hadn't been the one who left Grace at the filling station, how, even if Bethel and Beauty said differently, Solomon had too many friends in the courthouse and would likely win a custody battle.

The distance between them closed to a few feet. June called out Regina's name, then opened the blanket, enfolded her.

Regina wept, could hardly stand. She, too, was hoarse but managed to whisper, Thank you, thank you.

She stepped back, held her muddy arms out for Grace. Her right arm was gashed and bruised.

June motioned toward the first aid tent, said, You need to get your arm seen to.

Have you seen my husband? Regina whispered.

June felt like she might faint. She feared the intensity of her pulse would wake Grace. She shook her head, said, No, ma'am.

How did you get Laurel? Regina wailed, collapsed against them again.

Found her here, June said. She gestured toward the Red Cross tent, said, They'll doctor your arm in there. I can take care of the baby while you're treated.

As soon as Regina entered the medical tent, June slipped away with Grace. She wouldn't miss the chance again.

Macie

JUNE WAITED FOR SOLOMON TO PARK ELLIS'S TRUCK IN front of the main school building then went to meet him. It was all she could do to carry herself away from Grace, still asleep, stowed on the front seat of a nearby station wagon where Sol wouldn't see her. There had been loose change in the ashtray, and June had taken it. She prayed that Grace would sleep until the conversation was over.

Where is she? he asked.

Gone, June said, tears spilling down her face. *It could be true*, she told herself.

He stared at her for a long moment. For the first time, she saw something of Ellis around his eyes—the same pain as his son's that June Meeting day in the cemetery.

He asked, Is she dead?

Another bus pulled up in front of the school. People quietly walked off it. A woman screamed and ran down the school steps toward a small boy just off the bus. She fell to her knees, held on to him like he might evaporate, said, Praise Jesus! Thank you, Lord!

June remembered Sol's question. She's still missing, she lied.

Solomon flinched then. I'll keep looking, he said. I won't never give up.

He stared at the coal-black asphalt, then whispered, What's the name they call her?

She pictured the woman at the campfire last night, remembered her cries for the dead child she held. *Macie!* The name reverberated beneath June's breastbone, the imagined emptiness already taking hold. Macie's name would soon be added to the list of the dead. She knew she'd have to lie to make him believe that Grace was gone, and later, when he questioned her about a funeral for Grace, she would swear that the list was wrong and that her baby was still missing.

She worried the stolen coins in her pocket, answered Sol. Macie, she said.

Macie, Sol whispered.

Granny Justice

IT IS FINISHED. I'VE DONE WHAT I WAS LEFT HERE TO do. June has fount her baby and will not give her over ever again. Lord, bless her, for she's so young and has had to work so hard to achieve that and may still yet have a hard row to hoe.

I dearly hope that she'll teach Grace to love the land like we all do. Appreciate the very earth neath her feet that she can live with, not just on. Seems like people has forgotten how to shape their lives around land ruther than the other way around. Maybe Grace can change that.

I had a wonderful life, lived all of it in Mingo. Weren't always easy. I had my losses and regrets, but I seen the red curtain of the Borealis when it showed up here one September when I were a girl. I helped my mommy and sisters make suppers for the boys a-strikin over on Blair. We carried that food around there in Daddy's old hay wagon. Lord God, but it was cold by the time we got it there, but them men didn't care. Later, my daddy shook the hand of Mother Jones. They's a picture of it here somewheres.

I had me the best mommy and daddy, for shore, even though they was strict as could be. And wonderful sisters and brothers. We was poor, but it didn't matter. Although we fussed and fought, we all loved each other big.

Had a good husband and some fine children, John Henry a-doin for me ever what I asked. Took us all sleddin in the winters and molly-moochin ever spring. We'd have a contest—ever who fount the biggest one got a extry penny. We'd sell them mushrooms to a buyer parked down at the tipple.

John oncet took me to hear the Renfro Valley Boys over at Mount Vernon. Hit was a fine time. He were my one and only and I dearly loved workin alongside him in the garden—Lord, the taste of that Silver Queen corn—or just a-settin on the porch drinkin coffee of a mornin. Only fault I ever saw in him was that he was agin people who was differnt. I reckon he got that from his mommy and daddy, and I never knowed why. In my mind, there ain't ever a good reason to treat any folks bad. I weren't raised that away—at least by my mommy, who went to church three times a week. She raised me up to believe we are all equal in God's eyes. I told John I'd not allow him to infect our children with that meanness. But I loved him, anyway, right up to the end. Still do, but it's different now. A different kind of love.

When it was still a-runnin, I rode the doodlebug train over to the Tug for McCoy family reunions. We had us a big time a-playin Pretty Girl Station with all the cousins. *Well, get to work!* we'd all shout. We eat ourselfs silly, too. All the different foods the women would bring. My favorite was Aunt Esther's ambrosia. I'd save them marshino cherries that she put in it till the very last bites. Hit were the only time we got em to eat, cept in fruitcakes when we had the money to make one.

Grandmommy Jince taught me to plant by the signs and to put my beans and squash and corn in all together because they all get on with one another so well. She instructed me to only plant potatoes on Good Friday, regardless if it come in March or April. She also taught me how to stop someone's blood by sayin a scripture verse three times, among other things that for sure has come in handy. And, she helped me memorize my favorite poem, "The Lake Isle of Innisfree," by William Butler Yeats.

Mommy taught me the rest of what I needed to know. I passed on the healin and the old ways to the next generations of women in my family, but I am takin some knowledge with me. For instance, I know where John-John buried a jar of play pretties, marbles and such, in the garden and forgot about them, and I'm the only one knows that I stole them brass knuckles that Jupe brought home from the service and throwed them down the well where they still yet are. One thing I learnt, some secrets ain't ever meant to be revealed.

So I'm gonna just wait here awhile, until I must rise and go, content that I done my part, until someone comes back to get me. I'm hopin it's John Henry again, and them babies. Maybe my Tom.

No, honey, it's not been a entirely easy life, but it's been a good one just the same. Better than some. I am fulfilled in my time. I feel it in my deep heart's core.

Part III

Air

Abandoned

JUNE STOOD ON THE PORCH OF A VACANT YELLOW house in cold damp needles of air that pricked her face and watched the morning light break over the ridges. She longed to go back inside and lie on the mattress with Grace, join her in sleep, but she couldn't. She needed to find more food, more warmth and comfort for Grace, who cried out in the night then chanted, Mum, mum, mum, down to a whisper before she vanished into a haunted sleep. June didn't want to think of the images that followed Grace. *Did she watch Brother Brewer die?* As she tried to get Grace to sleep, June longed to console her, let herself hope Grace believed that it was Regina, just that once, who held her in the boundless, godforsaken dark.

Birds called from the trees in the yards of the feral houses that clustered, as usual, near the mouth of the holler. Kudzu vines snaked around and through some of them, covered their roofs, power poles, and smaller trees, claimed the outhouses. The broad green leaves served as markers of time that measured the lengths of their vacancies. Between birdcalls, the place was eerily quiet, the sounds of everyday living gone, except when a breeze wafted through it and dead leaves on the trees crackled like lit fuses.

She expected that the abandoned houses thinned out up toward the head of the holler, where home places had been settled by quieter, more private people, as in Twenty-Seven. Deeper in, the spaces between them were occupied new ground that had once been cleared for gardens and orchards.

There, at the mouth of the holler, though, where Viv had left June and Grace the night before, the abandoned buildings were a mixture of wood and mortar—cinderblock, logs, rough lumber, some with windows intact, some whose windows had long been shattered, still others boarded up beneath the vines, perhaps a sign the occupants had hoped to return.

Across the creek, a lone green clapboard building with a sign on the front, the top left corner sprung free of its nail. June could make out the word *Store* in a wash of red letters that time had bleached pink, over peeling white paint. Any slim chance of finding food, June wagered, would be there.

She studied the threadbare bridge crossing the creek to the old store, sized up the irregular gaps between timbers, measured them against her own stride, decided she'd have to wade through the freezing creek. If not for Grace, she'd have risked it then, leapt across those spaces between the boards, but a brief flash of finding Grace cold and alone in that car seat stopped her, for she knew Grace couldn't endure being left again. For the time being, she'd have to look elsewhere.

She began with the nearest house, mindful of Grace, alert as she walked up the slope of its yard, climbed its cement steps. Beneath the kudzu, the outside walls were bullet-pocked, most of the front windows broken. Later, she'd come across a constellation of spent shells left in the road, would guess that all the highway signs at the mouth of the holler would be shot up, too. Last night, she'd been too tired to notice them in the near dark when they drove in. *I'm not really sure where I am*, she thought.

It seemed to June that the time between hearing about the flood and that morning on the porch had been a lifetime. So much time had passed since she used the change she'd stolen from the station wagon to call Viv from a pay phone at the Gulf station and ask her to come get them. It seemed years since she had decided it wouldn't have been safe for her to go home or to the apartment, and that it would have been just as dangerous to drive the Plymouth anywhere. She had reasoned that Sol knew the car too well, and if he figured out she'd lied to him, he might find them, grab Grace, and do June harm, no matter that she was Bethel's daughter. Vivian had confirmed that Watt had found the car and taken it home with him, and that was too far to travel last night after what she and Grace had gone through.

When Viv had arrived at the gas station in her mother's VW Bug, she had rushed inside and bought snacks from the rack on the counter: peanuts, cheese crackers, two honey buns. She'd also bought two Cokes that she and June drank on the drive to Five-Mile. Viv had thought to bring along a loaf of white bread, a hunk of baloney, and, from the deep freeze, two half-gallon milk cartons of ice that would melt into drinking water—Viv's mother kept them for picnics—as well as two orange-juice bottles that they filled at the station spigot. It all rode to Five-Mile crammed onto the floorboard between June's feet.

Inside the one-story house they had chosen the evening before, morning light revealed a bowed living room ceiling and weather-ruined carpet. The smell of mildew and animal urine and feces, dried down to their essence, filled the empty rooms. The house had been stripped bare. No cans of food left in the kitchen. She found the others in a similar state—rapture-empty and vandalized, their walls holding vivid shapes on bright wood or wallpaper where pictures and whatnot shelves had once hung.

She ranged farther and farther from Grace until coming upon a trailer house tucked into a kudzu-blanketed hill behind a two-story cinderblock home. June couldn't tell if the two-toned mobile home was pink and white or whether the colored strips had once been red and then faded. Parched iris and tiger lily leaves scratched at its distorted and decaying plywood skirt, surely having bloomed during the past summer, and for a moment, June wondered how long it had been since someone was in there.

She had to find a way to keep Grace warm without electricity or chimney smoke that might give them away if anyone besides Viv came up the road. And she had to feed her something better than the food that Viv had frantically gathered the night before. Had Grace been weaned off the bottle when June last saw her at church? She had drunk all of the one offered to her by the nurse.

June considered the trailer, wondered whether its floors were rotted or if it was infested with mice and cockroaches, too. From what she could see, the front windows remained intact. Sun-bleached curtains slouched in their frames. Both doors remained on the front and seemed to sit straight enough in their sills, although the one toward the back of the trailer had no handle.

June knew she had to get inside the trailer to see if it could provide better shelter, but she couldn't make herself go in. She watched it until the birds went silent, then sprinted back toward the yellow house and the sound of her daughter's wailing.

A Pink-and-White Trailer

JUNE FED GRACE TWO OF THE SIX PEANUT BUTTER AND cheese crackers from the package and a pinch of honey bun as they sat in front of the coal stove where a low fire burned, then she tore off and handed her a wedge of baloney that just fit her small hand. *As long as she's eating*, June thought, *she cain't cry*. Between bites, June gave her sips of water from one of the paper cups they'd thought to bring. Grace's eyes followed her movement, and June was sure that Grace was confused and likely afraid. She said, I promise I'll take care of you now and for the rest of my life.

Her own stomach cramped at the smell of the food. She allowed herself a cracker and one bite of honey bun but took no more in case they ran short before Vivian got back. When Viv left the night before, she had said that she'd try to get back the next day. June hoped she would.

June wiped Grace's face with the hem of her shirt then tucked them both into the green blanket from the shelter. She held the baby tight against her body as she took her out into the late-morning sun that had burned through the October fog. Grace twisted her head, looking right then left, made a brief effort to whine, then rested her cheek against June's shoulder. By the time they reached the pink-and-white trailer, she was asleep again, still exhausted but sated and safe against June's chest.

June found the cinderblock house's coal shed. She pulled aside the vines and stood inside it, out of the wind as she watched the trailer again. Instinctively, she swayed her upper body to soothe Grace, hoped to keep her sleeping and quiet, for they both had cried a great deal in the last twenty-four hours. In the silence between gusts of wind, she heard the gurgle of her stomach through the layers of clothes and blanket. After a time, hunger drove her to move.

She climbed the wooden steps to the trailer door. The connected aluminum letters of the word *Englewood* were attached to the trailer near its doorframe. Thin mildew filled the valleys between the letters and the open spaces in the *o*'s. She rested her hand on Grace's back and listened. Around them, birdcalls and the sizzle of brittle leaves as they twisted in the wind, but no sound from the trailer. She turned the aluminum doorknob, half prepared to see someone standing there when she made a hesitant push at the peeling wood.

She poked her head inside. Light sieved through the thin curtains, streamed between their gaps, fell on fine rock dust that coated the countertops and linoleum floor, the arms of a blanched olive Naugahyde recliner to her right. She peered down the hall, noted that the trailer wasn't as large as Rena and Watt's.

She stepped inside, thought she might lay Grace down on the recliner but kept her inside the blanket instead. Although the trailer didn't smell of vermin like the yellow house, June thought, *God knows what could be living in that chair—things that leave no smell.*

She had to walk only a few steps to open the kitchen cupboards and scan them until she found a can of navy beans and a tin of potted meat shoved into a shadowy corner. As she flicked mouse turds off her hand, she whispered, Thank you, whoever left these. The words echoed back to her from the empty cabinets like dry wind.

Down the short hallway, she passed a bathroom with an iron-stained tub and sink, the scent of rusty water ingrained in its paneled walls. She searched its cabinets and drawers, found a hair roller from a home permanent kit and chalky stump of styptic pencil but nothing useful. In the closet of the single bedroom at the end of the hall, a moth-eaten bedsheet, and on a high shelf, a small bundle of green tissue paper, its faded layers bound by red curling ribbon and a plastic piece of greenery. She ripped the ribbon off the bundle. The tissue bloomed open to a can of talcum powder and a bar of soap. A faint scent of lily of the valley wafted out. A long-ago Christmas gift.

Back in the kitchen, June swayed Grace, who had hardly stirred since they entered the trailer. She surveyed the room a second time, noticed the imprint of someone's head worn into the back of the recliner. She pictured Isom's chair, wondered if he could still sit upright.

She found no toys or signs of children inside or out, no coal stove, as she'd hoped. She stared at the cans of food, then the tin of talcum powder and bar of soap she'd set on the counter. Her back had begun to ache, but she didn't dare disturb Grace or sit on the recliner.

June tried to imagine how her life would be then, since she had gotten Grace back. She allowed her mind to nibble at the edges of realization that what she had done had been impulsive and possibly a mistake. She worried that Grace would not adjust to living with her instead of the Brewers, and panic roiled through her. What would she do if Grace wouldn't stop crying?

After a time, she used the metal key that came with the potted meat to open the lid. She had hated the potted-meat sandwiches Bethel put in her school lunchbox, had complained until they were replaced by peanut butter and sugar on light bread. Now, she ate half of the mush by scooping it from the can with dirty fingers. The salty taste of it would stay on her tongue for hours.

As she made her way back to the trailer door, the floor went spongy under her foot, gave way. She clutched Grace, jerked her foot back through the jagged edges of the floorboards. When she looked down, tangled roots matted the ground below. *Cain't stay here*, she thought.

Bethel

I'VE NOT HEARD NARY A WORD FROM JUNE SINCE THE flood. I had Beauty call over to Myrtle Gap to speak to her landlady, Mrs. Mounts, and she told how June run off in a big hurry that mornin and she hasn't seen her since. Watt, who found Tom's car, might know something, but he hasn't said one way or the other. I can only speculate that June is safe, but I had them Red Cross people put her on the missing list as a precaution. If she ain't hurt, she ought to have more respect than to do us like this.

That preacher that baptized her up at Blackburn got killed in the flood. Somethin or the other about his leg gettin broke and him a-bleedin to death in his car. A compound fracture is a ugly thing, happened to my brother Custer once. Fell out a tree. Arm bone was stickin through his shirtsleeve. Mommy set the bone and sewed him up, kept the wound slathered in honey till it healed.

It's a cryin' shame about that preacher. His wife was hurt, too, but the newspaper said she'll get over it. She and the preacher somehow got separated from one another before he died that mornin. I'm not too sure of the whole story or which one of them it was that had their daughter with them at the time of the flood, but she's missing, too. Twice lost and not even yet talkin.

They're a-sayin it was June grabbed her and run off from the high school. That's when it dawned on me why June was goin to that church in the first place. Part of me cain't believe she'd steal that baby, but the other part of me wants to think they're together somewhere, and safe. Finally.

That girl's a Branham through and through—always bound and determined once she takes a notion. Shag's daddy was the worst, but I never knowed June to stoop low enough to break the law. Kidnappin! We taught her better than that. She cain't just take somebody's child and run off. Besides, how can she even be positive it's the same one she give birth to? I will allow that, from the picture they had in the paper, that baby looked like a Akers. Dark, curly hair. Still, they's lots of babies put up for adoption around here, and it might just be a coincidence that she looks how she does.

Isom said he don't want nothin to do with none of it. He said that if she comes around here, he'll run her off. I know he means it. He can be hardheaded, too, and isn't one to make idle threats. He says he's not gonna take part in a kidnappin or harborin a fugitive from the law. I cain't help but to wonder what Shag woulda done under these circumstances, but then I think he wouldn't have give that baby away in the first place. He was stubborn but a levelheaded and forgivin man.

Last week, the *Banner* printed the picture I seen of the little girl, Laurel, so people could be on the lookout for her. They was also a picture of June that looked like someone had snapped it down near a creek, probably over there on Blackburn Fork. She's smilin in it, like she's happy. I haven't seen her smile like that in a age.

Vivian

THE NEXT DAY, JUNE WOKE TO FOOTSTEPS ON THE front porch, then the screen door creaking on its hinges. She hadn't heard a car coming up the road. She covered Grace with the wool blanket and held her breath.

Vivian appeared, carrying more blankets, one of her old winter coats, and a grocery sack that held food, hand towels to use as diapers, a red plastic flashlight, extra batteries, and a pair of plastic pants for Grace.

June pulled the blanket off Grace's head, said, Lord God. You about scared me to death. I didn't hear you till you were on the porch.

I walked in, Viv said. Truck's parked around behind the scout camp.

June stood and stretched, her heart still pounding. She asked if there had been any word of Ellis.

Viv said, I haven't heard a thing, and I asked Rena when I called her this morning. When I've driven to work the past two mornings, Sol Akers has been parked along the four-lane somewhere, so I figure he don't know anything either.

Grace stirred then. June whispered, pointed at Grace, said, Sol must know then what I did.

Vivian said, Think so. That's why I haven't been back here until now.

She motioned toward the front porch, mimed lighting a cigarette. C'mon, she whispered.

Fog lay low along the creek bank and road, suspended between the near ridgetops like spiders' webs. June could barely make out the footbridge to the store. She felt as if she were trapped between two worlds.

Vivian took a drag off her Virginia Slim, blew the smoke out of the side of her mouth, said, It's been in the paper, June. They're lookin for you. They even printed your picture.

June couldn't speak. She slumped against the mossed-over porch rail and listened as Viv went on.

We cain't let him find you here, June. He'll overpower you for sure and take Grace.

She took another draw of her cigarette and kicked a dried cicada into the yard. Nearly weightless, it floated through the air and landed with a *tick* in the brittle weeds. She said, We have to move you farther up the holler and may have to move you yet again if he gets wind of you.

The night before, June had thought about the pink trailer, let herself imagine living in it with Grace, the floor beneath them sturdy and dependable. Ellis coming to find them. She fell asleep making plans on how she might fix the floor, spruce it up for them to live in. She could drag the mattress over there, and with the blankets Viv brought, she and Grace would be fine for a while. It was cleaner than the yellow house, nearly airtight, and would be easier to keep dry and warm if she could find a way to heat it, for it had no wood or coal stove.

Vents in the floor had told her it had been heated by forced air. She'd known that she would figure something out. But, at the moment, Vivian's news had disoriented her, and she couldn't keep up. She asked, They printed a picture of me? Where did they . . . ?

She knew that if her picture was in the paper, the police had it, too. She wondered whether her mother had given them the picture, then thought that Isom would have done it for sure.

What does the picture look like? she asked.

You're smiling and standin on a creek bank. It looks recent. You have the same haircut, only it's wet in the picture.

June remembered the day of her baptism. Brother Brewer had insisted that Regina take her picture, said, You're fairly glowin and I want you to remember the most important day of your life.

At the time, she had gone along with the idea, didn't dare tell him the real reason she was happy, that she'd been elated when Grace reached for her when she came out of the waters of Blackburn Fork.

It was Regina, June said. She realized then that she was being chased by three bogeymen—Sol, Regina, and the law. The awareness engulfed and paralyzed her. She began to cry.

Viv threw her cigarette into the yard then put her arms around June. She said, Sol's a hateful son of a bitch and just wants Grace out of spite. Grace is your blood, June, and she come from your body, so she's yours. Nobody else deserves her.

When June had cried herself out, Viv said, We have to move you deeper into this holler, and, honey, you need a bath.

Store

JUNE KEPT TO THE OUTSIDE EDGE OF THE FOOTBRIDGE, knew it would be easier to wade across the creek, but the water was still up from the heavy rain and it ran too cold for her to get her clothes wet from it. Just rinsing out Grace's diapers had left her chilled for hours yesterday. She looked forward to bathing in warm water.

Once across the bridge, she turned. Vivian held a crying Grace on her hip and watched her. June wished that, inside the house, there was a pot of bathwater warming on the stove.

She stepped up onto the loose doorsill of the store. The bloated door was open, slumped and straining its hinges. Its bottom dragged across the cement floor as she pushed it. She remembered easily opening the door of the pink trailer the day before.

The scratch of claw, the whisper of feather somewhere overhead startled her, but she stepped in anyway. She stood there, listening for more movement. There was none, but the smell of death was in the room.

She scanned the littered floor, found shreds of bread bags and an overturned potato chip rack. In the far corner, a mound of candy cartons, partially covered by a rotten tarp. In the near corner, a small coal stove, an abandoned rat's nest in its belly. She noted the half-full bucket of black chunks beside it, said the word *coal. Eternal*, she thought. *Made to outlast us all.* She lifted the coal bucket. Its paper-thin bottom gave out, and chunks of coal thunked to the floor. If she didn't find another way, she'd have to carry the coal to the house in the tarp or a gnawed-on candy box.

In the back room, shelves of empty gallon jugs sat inside cabinets whose hasps clung to their rotting doors. Long-dead flies lay trapped inside the jugs, covered the bottoms. June knew she'd need bleach to rinse them out before she could use them. A mouse carcass and a dented, rusted funnel lay amid them. Behind one of the jugs was a short piece of copper tubing. June knew that, were she to walk into the woods on the hillside, she'd find an old moonshine still.

Back in the main room, more piled boxes she hadn't noticed before. Something scrabbled among them. She turned, kicked at the pile, revealed a picked-clean dog skeleton. A large breed. Its faded green collar lay in a pile of neck bones just beneath the skull. She traced a chain from the collar to a bolt in the floor, looked away, shook her head, drew deep breaths to quiet the gag. After a few seconds, she spotted the brass shell cartridge that likely killed the dog lying a few feet away. She wanted to vomit.

When she was back on the other side of the creek, she used the lily of the valley soap to bathe herself with freezing water. She knelt on the bank and used her cupped hands to dip and pour it over her body like a frigid, repeated prayer. A baptism. She washed her hair, and when she finished, she ran to the yellow house, shivering, teeth chattering as the words *There will be weeping and gnashing* ran through her mind.

Later in the afternoon, June and Vivian moved June's things to a house the color of celery farther up the road. Like the yellow house, it, too, was drafty, but they had been able to close off all of the rooms whose windows were broken. The house had a coal stove in the main room, and June was relieved. Coal wouldn't make as much smoke as wood. She gathered tinder—dried leaves, pine cones, and the small twigs of a dead apple tree in the yard—so she could start a fire when it got dark enough. While outside, she found a small coal pile and was glad that she wouldn't yet have to go back across the creek for the coal she'd spilled.

They inventoried the day's plunder: one lidless cooking pot, a rusty butcher knife, a dented funnel, and a shorn and naked Barbie doll they'd found in the yard. June had rinsed the pitiful doll in the frigid creek for Grace, hoped it would console her. She knew she would have to watch her closely with the doll so that she didn't put it into her mouth.

There was other evidence that children had lived in the house—a flattened kickball, a filthy roll of kite string, matted-shut and rippled coloring books, and a copy of *Boy's Life* magazine. June had scoured the room they were camped in and gathered up anything small enough for Grace to put in her mouth and stowed it in one of the closed-off rooms.

She said, That was only four houses and the store. I'd wager I'll find more stuff when I explore farther on up.

Yeah, Viv said. Those folks were the last to give in and left in a big hurry, I figure. Mighta left some useful stuff behind.

Vivian began packing the food back into the grocery sack—two cans of Pringles, loose pudding packs, saltines, more bread and baloney, and a jar of peanut butter infused with swirls of grape jelly. Matches and plastic picnic utensils. The baloney and two gallons of milk Viv brought were in a box on the back porch, along with two new cartons of ice. She paused, said, I hope this will keep you until I can get back.

June finally spoke on what had been worrying her as they'd moved her things and searched the houses. She said, I wish I knew what to do next. How am I gonna get out of here and away from everybody, Viv?

I don't yet know, June. We'll figure something out, Viv said.

Late-afternoon light was falling over the holler—the hardest time of day for June since Tom died. She knew Viv would need to leave soon to get back to her truck before dark. A gray shroud of loneliness came down around her. She pictured the dog skeleton but didn't mention it to Viv. She wished she could just lie down and sleep, but she'd have to get Grace to sleep first. Tears stung the rims of her eyes, and her voice broke as she said, Thank you for everything, Vivie.

Vivian smiled, said, I'll bring some real food now that you've got somethin to cook it in. And be sure to boil that creek water if you have to drink any of it.

After Vivian started down the road, a whippoorwill called from the woods. Before she disappeared into the twilight, Viv looked back and waved. June lifted her hand, yelled, Hurry back!

You find a lid for that pot and clean that thing out good before you use it! Viv yelled back.

Rivulets of tears tracked down June's face as she turned back to Grace and the empty house. They both cried until they fell asleep.

Shots

THE FIRST GUNSHOT SHATTERED A FRONT WINDOW OF the house, ripped away the thin veil of June's sleep. June sat up until another shot came, then ducked. When the third bullet hit the house, she threw her body over Grace. Flashes of Tom and Ellis sliced through her awakening mind—people in the jungle shooting at them. In the space between the fourth and fifth shots, she began to pray that the bullets wouldn't come through the wall and that the wind had carried the smell of any coal smoke away from the road where the shots came from, that whoever was out there wouldn't see the piles of plunder on the porch.

Sol?

June stayed down, too frightened to move. She heard a voice speak—*A man's voice!* She waited to hear her name called from the road, but it didn't come.

Grace stirred beneath her, began to wail. She tried to quiet her, held her hand over Grace's mouth, hoped that whoever was outside couldn't hear her cries over the sound of the creek and the idling motor. Grace tried to squirm away, but June pulled her closer and whispered, Shh, shh. We'll be alright.

Finally, quiet filled the space between them and the gunshots, and moments later came the slam of a pickup door, then another—*Two people*, June thought—then the clatter of a diesel engine starting—*A truck!*—the shattering of a glass bottle on a creek rock. *Sol and one of Ellis's brothers?* she wondered.

June held Grace even tighter, said, I'm sorry, baby. I'm so sorry. She sat them up, wrapped the blanket around them, strained to hear over Grace's cries. More shots came from farther up the holler. *They'll have to come back by here to get out of the holler*, she thought.

June dampened the fire and carried Grace and the blanket up the hill into the woods to wait for the truck to drive past again. After a time, when the shivering had set in and Grace had stopped crying, began hiccupping gulps of air, June heard the diesel engine again, but in the new-moon darkness, she couldn't feature the make or the color of the truck. As it passed the house, she thought she smelled faint cigarette smoke. She sat still until she could no longer hear it.

Back inside the house, a trembling June gave Grace a cheese cracker and sips of milk, then they lay down again. In the silent darkness, June stroked Grace's tangled curls and began to whisper the only story she could think of just then.

Once upon a time, there was a girl named Snow White, and she lived in a castle.

For the first time since June had gotten her back, Grace sucked her grimy thumb, and with the other hand she twisted a strand of her hair as she listened to June's voice.

She must think I'm Regina in this dark, June thought. *I don't deserve her.* Tears fell as she continued. One day, Snow White went to live in the woods.

People and Things, Gone Before

ON THE FIFTH DAY, AS JUNE WAITED FOR VIV TO RE-turn, she and Grace roamed the houses like specters, tentatively testing doors before entering them. It felt to June a little like a crime. If the houses had been occupied, she never would've thought of entering without being invited, even if she'd known the people all her life. *I've been taught better,* she thought.

Some front doors were needlessly locked, as most of the windows had been shot out, others swollen into their rotting frames. June tried back and side doors or peeked through windows. A few doors stood open, which she told herself was a sign of welcome.

Once inside, June conjured the lives of the people that had lived in the rooms, and no matter whether they were dead or still living somewhere else, they, too, had become ghosts. She gathered items that she thought she and Grace might need. At the end of each search, she piled her plunder—chunks of coal, metal spoons, a mouse-nibbled copy of a novel, *The Moviegoer*—on the bedsheet from the trailer, coiled its ends, and hoisted it over her shoulder. Grace rode her other hip, and they'd start back to the house where the coal stove burned low, sticking to the road because June was not as wary during the daytime. She'd convinced herself that it wasn't Sol who shot into the house that night, that it had just been kids out for fun, for if it was Sol, he would've called her out. She studied the possibility that they might need to move again but decided it was safer to be in a house where all the front windows had already been shattered.

The next morning, Grace woke with a fever. She'd been agitated and fussy the night before, and June wondered whether she might be teething. By midday, she was still feverish and had begun to cough from some small, deep cave inside her. Each time she coughed, her face grew flushed and June could feel the phlegm rattling through her hand on Grace's chest. They fetched a pot of water from the creek, and June boiled it on the coal stove then used a blanket to make a steam tent. She wished for some yarrow or peppermint to add to the water. Even though June sat with Grace under the blanket, Grace didn't like having her face covered, had struggled to get free, but soon grew too weak to fight. Her cries became hoarser. June begged her to stop crying, to take sips of water, but she wasn't interested in water or food. June was terrified that she'd become dehydrated, for that had happened when Charlie was just a baby, and Rena had to take him to the hospital. June couldn't afford to do that.

Because of the cough, Grace didn't sleep much, nor did June. When Grace dozed, she dozed, too. When Grace was awake and whining from the frustration of trying to breathe, June wished desperately for catnip to make a sugar-tit to soothe her, and she let herself fantasize that she still had milk to feed her from her breasts. The only way June found to soothe Grace was to hold her close to try to keep her warm, to walk around the empty room in ever-winding circles, ripples on a pond. Half asleep herself, June hummed “In My Life” and “Blackbird” then all the other Beatles songs she knew.

The next day, Vivian returned with more food, milk, and an old sleeping bag that would be warmer than the pallet June had made with layers of folded blankets on the floor. She also brought more batteries and boxed matches and, this time, candles in case the flashlight’s extra batteries drained. To June, Viv’s bringing the candles was a sign that she wasn’t sure when she could get back.

Grace’s condition alarmed Viv. She said, June, two days is too long for her to have a fever, and you don’t even know how high it’s went.

I did the best I could, June said.

She felt judged, angry, delirious. She said, Her fever’s down now! I bathed her with cold rags. If I’d had to, I woulda dipped her in the creek to get it down.

I’m glad you didn’t, Viv said. She could get pneumonia.

June’s throat had begun to ache that morning, and her clothes chafed her body. The heat of Grace’s body had leached into her own skin, and she suspected that she, too, had a fever. When Vivian insisted on taking Grace home with her, June hadn’t argued much.

Viv said, My mom won’t mind, and you can trust her, but, June, if Grace gets any worse, I’ll have to take her to the doctor.

June knew that taking Grace into public might give them away.

I know, she said.

Before they left, she made Vivian promise to keep Grace away from Myrtle Gap—to take her to a doctor in Wayne

County if needed and to keep her away from Isom and all the others.

I'll bring her back as soon as she's better, Viv said.

They had waited for Grace to fall asleep before Vivian took her so she'd be lying in the seat and out of sight during the trip. June heard her own disconnected voice say, I hope the motion of the car keeps her asleep.

When they were gone, she lay her throbbing body on the pallet, and before she fell away from the world, she thought, *Grace is going to be so confused. She isn't going to know who her mother is.*

The next two days became an unraveling of time. June slept and woke just long enough to take sips of water and then fell back into the fevered jumble of hours. More than once, she woke and, disoriented and panicked, searched the blankets for Grace. A nebulous memory of diarrhea and trips to the outhouse, some by flashlight, that could have happened to someone else or in another lifetime came to her then, and when she finally sat up for more than a few minutes, she couldn't gauge the elapsed time since Viv had left with Grace.

When she finally was able to stand, she found her muscles stiff and weak, her head reeling, and she had to sit down again. She struggled to get her mind right. After a time, she realized she was ravenous, and she stood again and shuffled to the food box.

Seng

JUNE DUG INTO THE DIRT WITH A WINDFALLEN CHUNK of poplar branch. She'd finally felt enough strength to walk the margin of the hill behind the green house when she saw the wreath of tomato-red berries floating on rafts of leaves. Ginseng.

She had gone sengin with Granny, and sometimes Bethel, each fall since she could remember. Granny had liked digging roots in the late fall because she didn't have to beat the weeds for snakes. She admitted that waiting until late in the season was risky, for it started in September. Granny didn't worry too much that someone else might beat her to the plants, for she was considered an expert and knew the signs that most people might miss and that told her she was in a good patch.

Look for the sassyfrass and sugar trees, she'd say. Look for you a six-pronger!

After the roots were dried, June helped Granny sort them. They saved a few to make medicine and sold the rest. June loved going out of the holler with Granny, driven by Garvin or Beauty to find the seng man, who paid them good money for the roots. The tall, thin man whose age June couldn't guess was usually loafing at Maynard's store, waiting for sellers, and that meant candy and a cold pop for June, but he sometimes walked up the road and went house to house, calling, Got any seng here?

After Granny died, Bethel had taken up her sengin hoe, fashioned from an ancient pickax, the grain of its handle worn smooth, and led June to the hills to hunt for the prized root. June always enjoyed herself, but it wasn't the same as sengin with Granny, for Bethel was usually silent as they worked. Granny had told stories and instructed her in the collection and care of yarbs. Sometimes she'd held up a pearly, elongated root and said, Don't that look just like a human body, June?

Granny raised her eyebrows, watched June's face, said, A man?

The first time Granny referred to a man's private parts, June had been embarrassed and then amused, for she'd never heard a woman in her family speak of such things. After a time, when she'd realized Granny talked like that to shock her, she'd just laughed. It became their game.

June studied the root she'd just dug, flicked dirt from its seams with her index finger, then looked uphill. She knew there would be more plants above her, for Granny had said that when they threw their seeds, water and gravity carried them down the hills. The older, bigger ones were always closer to the top of a hill.

She considered climbing the steep, wild grade to hunt for more seng but felt too weak to do it just then. She'd have to wait. She pocketed the root, decided she would dry and keep it for medicine. If she found more later, she'd send it with Vivian to sell.

As she turned to go back to the house, she felt a shift. Something felt off—when had it begun? She climbed a bit farther up the hill into the trees, pulse thumping against her temples.

She grabbed a branch to steady herself, felt as if she would float away if she didn't, felt stupid for letting down her guard.

She heard a car coming up the road but couldn't see it. When it lumbered around the curve, it was not Viv's car but a black Buick that moved with purpose. June froze. Any movement she made, had she been able, might attract attention. The car stopped directly below her. Doors slammed, then came the sound of women's voices from the yard of the green house. June ran toward them.

Bethel shrieked at the sight of June, ran across the yard to embrace her. Both she and Beauty were crying, then all of them were.

We thought we'd lost you! Bethel sobbed.

Vivian stood apart from them, said, I'm so sorry, June. I had to tell them. I couldn't let em think that you was dead.

Is Grace OK? June asked.

Bethel had unwrapped the tinfoil from a biscuit she brought and offered it to June, said, She's got better now.

June took the biscuit, glanced at Beauty and Viv, who was looking at the ground. The air thickened.

Where is she? June asked.

Beauty said, June, we left her at Rena's. It's a good place for her to be right now.

No! June said. She felt an awakening panic, an echo of her recent fever. She said, Don't you know Sol will look there? The law will too?

It's just for this little while, Bethel said. I had to see you was alright, and now I see you're puny yerself.

June stared at her mother. Her throat was still raw. She realized that she hadn't talked in days. She whispered, Why?

Bethel winced, said, What do you mean, *why*? Because you're my daughter. Her voice rose.

It don't feel that way, June said.

Bethel measured her words, said, You wouldn't talk to me like that if Isom was here.

Well, he ain't here for you to hide behind, June said, the end of the sentence barely a whisper. She had never talked to her mother like that.

Beauty motioned to Viv, and they started for the house. When they had gone inside, Bethel looked smaller than before. *It would be easy to shove her to the ground*, June thought. She was stunned to think she might do it. Bethel buttoned her top coat button, said, It's too cold out here, June. Let's go in.

June yearned to wound her mother, to invoke any emotion in her besides anger. She said, You're not so tough when you don't have an audience.

Bethel's hand came up as if she might smack June, but June didn't flinch. Bethel said, How can you sass me after you put me through all you done? All I been through?

June felt the smoldering pile of coals that had been heaped in her belly over the past two years—*longer?*—flare. She felt it roar, felt the flames in her throat. She yelled, You ain't the only one that's lost things!

She felt her body ignite, as if the fever burned in her again. She said, You weren't the only one lost Tom. He died on me, too! Grace got taken from me, and you let it happen!

Bethel began crying then, which made June even angrier. Through the tears, Bethel repeated, I tried, I tried, I tried.

Tried what? June yelled. You never once tried to help us! Didn't protect us!

I did. I . . .

You chose Isom, June interrupted. You always chose him, and my daddy would be mad if he knew the way you let Isom do us, she said before she walked away, left her addled mother standing in the yard, body heaving puffs of breath into the cold air.

Beauty and Viv came back out of the house. Beauty said, Grace still has a little cough. We'll get her back around to Viv's right directly.

June still trembled. She managed to say, Thank you, Beauty.

Beauty put Bethel in the passenger seat of the car and closed the door. Before Viv got into the back seat, she whispered, I'm sorry, June. She made me bring her up here.

Kiss Grace for me, June said. I'm afraid she's gonna forget me.

June watched them drive away, Beauty steering the Buick they borrowed from Viv's mother, Bethel slumped in the passenger seat, a fistful of crushed tissue pressed against her mouth. For a moment, June thought she might run after them, ask them to take her home, but she didn't.

As she went to sleep that night, June replayed the fight with Bethel then called up the memory of the warmth of Grace's body, missed her stirring beneath the blanket when they were still together in the green house. Night brought loneliness into the room, and for the first time, June realized she hadn't felt Granny's presence in a while. She would have given anything to just feel her nearby.

The Green House

JUNE CAME AWAKE INSIDE A DEEP QUIET AND A QUALity of light that told her something had changed. Ridges of early snow stood on the sills and in the yard. She calculated it to be nearly two inches and filled the pot with it, melted and heated it on the stove. She bathed her face with the lily of the valley soap and brushed her teeth with the toothbrush and paste Vivian brought. As she carried out the familiar ritual in an unfamiliar place, she pictured Grace, safe and warm in Viv's house, where Viv's mother watched her while Viv worked, where Sol would not likely find her because he'd not look for her to be separated from June.

Had the snow not melted away by mid-morning, she would've kept to the woods to avoid leaving footprints out in the open. She walked up the road, moving against the current of the creek as it ran to meet another down near the tipple. The water had gone down more since she'd been there. Three or four inches of frozen mud coated the weeds along its margins. She longed for the shower in her apartment.

She homed toward the head of the holler, not sure of what she was looking for. She still had food and Viv's promise to bring more, along with clean clothes Viv laundered at home. If she had to stay long in the holler, she could use a teakettle and some kind of water dipper—knew she could ask for those, too—but took comfort in pretending that finding them was the day's purpose. In that way, she avoided the larger question of what came next.

She followed the sandy margin of the road to avoid further soaking her shoes, followed her plan to search only the houses on the right side that day. She passed a burned-out shell of a house where spongy, rust-colored hollyhocks slumped over a wire fence, itself sagging under the weight of a rotting frame.

Just beyond a bridge, where the road curved right, she came upon a house, its far end crushed beneath a car-sized boulder. It called to June, and she broke her plan, closed the distance between the road and the house. Her pulse picked up as she passed a child's sandbox beneath an elm, a mangled bunk bed frame and sodden mattresses tossed into the yard. She ran to the intact end of the house without understanding why she ran, for no one was there. She peeked through a window to find a kitchen, empty except for a doorless turquoise refrigerator.

She'd heard stories about this, knew that the boulder, hurled down the mountainside by a dynamite blast from the strip, had crushed the rooms at the other end. She willed it to have happened during daytime when those rooms were likely empty, especially of sleeping children.

Around back, she found a clothesline, still improbably propped on its pole. Strung along it, weatherworn washrags and tea towels, like captive spirits that had strained against their tethers until they fell to dust. A pile of mottled tomato stakes lay beneath the weeds at the edge of a garden, where rows of lifeless mildewed cornstalks leaned against each other.

She perched on the boulder, drew her knees to her chest, felt like an intruder on a family who now lived in another holler, like this one, but whole and safe, she hoped. She fished a Little Debbie cream pie from her coat pocket. The oatmeal cookie was balled up inside its cellophane, the cream softened by her body heat. She closed her eyes, took in the sweetness of it as she ate it.

She imagined herself in her apartment in Myrtle Gap, bathing Grace in the kitchen sink, swaddling her in a towel, dusting her with baby powder. She ached for the warmth of her small body, like pain in a phantom limb. She dozed, face to the sun, until the engine of a coal truck on the mountain woke her, disturbed a thought she reached for but couldn't quite retrieve.

That afternoon, back at the green house, June fetched fresh water, boiled it for a bath. The kettle was slow to boil, and while she waited, she went naked into the cold evening air, sat on the back steps, tried to pick up the thread of thought she'd reached toward earlier as she sat against the boulder. Something was unfinished, a lurking alarm that threatened her evening peace.

She stretched her legs, scanned her body from the ground up, noted the dirty toenails, the goose-bumped pale skin of her arms and legs, studied the deep bruises that covered them, yellowed like old paper. Something happened here, they claimed, though she couldn't exactly recall, but she remembered the yellow school bus, feeling things that knocked against her as she waded through the murky floodwaters.

She regarded the jagged stretch marks that blazed her thighs and belly, the mother-of-pearl lightning bolts that reached across her skin until they faded then disappeared. As she waited, she ached for Grace, then surrendered to the relief that Grace was warm, dry, and fed with Vivian. June acknowledged how lost they both were in the first days together. She tried to see an end to their running, being hunted, but couldn't. She couldn't imagine what would come next.

Then, the first flames of recognition began to lick her rib cage, became a fireball that reached up her throat, into her head. Her legs lost their heat as sweltering blood rushed toward her heart. The earlier dozing half memory returned, came in full: The night before, the sound of a pickup going up the road had passed into her sleep. She stumbled toward the roiling pot of water.

Later, June tried to read the Walker Percy novel before she lost the day's light and had to light a candle. She couldn't concentrate, for she had expected Viv to return before then, and her mind kept repeating the question, *What has happened?* She conjured scenarios of flat tires or Viv running off to get married and leaving Grace, and then she latched onto the possibility of Vivian being sick or hurt—or Grace's being sick again.

Or, *Has Sol got Grace?* She pushed away the thought, reasoned that Viv hadn't come because she had to work extra shifts at the drive-in.

She tried to steer her mind toward other thoughts, so she recounted her day. In a house up the right fork, she'd found a cellar dug into the hillside full of gnawed-at dried-up potatoes and turnips, a scythe like Grandaddy's, scarcely rusted, and an unbroken cane-back chair leaning against the earthen wall. She'd felt safe there, safe from bullets and crashing boulders, Sol. For a while, she'd stood in that womb of earth, imagined living there, then a desiccated snake skin in the corner reminded her that slithering things loved places like that, too, and they'd might not have yet gone to ground for the winter. She'd be out of there soon, anyway, she reasoned, and wouldn't have to hide forever. In the end, she carried the chair back to the house and placed it by the stove, thinking that, if she had to, she could use the cellar as temporary shelter.

When the last sunlight was gone, she made an open-faced sandwich of white bread and peanut butter by the light of the open stove door. She wished she had some sugar to sprinkle on it for sweetness. Like a starved person, she ate too fast, and the bread and peanut butter balled up in the back of her throat. Panic overpowered her, and she pictured herself choking to death alone, Viv finding her dead. After a few gulps of water, the painful, suffocating gob began to slide down her throat. Unable to eat any more, she slipped the rest of the sandwich back into the bread wrapper and took a few more gulps of water. She closed the stove door, listened for the sound of a car engine coming up the road.

Arlo

AN ICY DRAFT OF AIR FROM THE CREEK BRUSHED PAST June. In the handful of days since the flood, daylight seemed to grow shorter, the sun dropping below the rim of the mountain earlier each afternoon. Yet, even as dusk approached that day, a small patch of daylight hovered directly above. June knew she didn't have much time to get back to the green house.

It had been days since Viv, Beauty, and Bethel were there. June was listless, had done a great deal of worrying by then. To keep herself from losing her mind and even though she didn't need anything, she continued to plunder during the abbreviated daylight hours.

She had walked up the right fork again, used the scythe to hack the vines away from some of the houses that she hadn't been able to access before. She collected a faded rug to use as a wind block for a broken window, a cracked wooden ironing board to use as a shelf, and blanched photos that held the ghosts of people she'd probably never know. The day before, she'd found an old Sears and Roebuck *Wish Book* and carried it back to the house, useless as it was. She remembered Rena showing her how to fold the pages then fan them out to make a Christmas tree, then thought, *I won't need a Christmas tree. Won't be here.*

That day, as she gathered up her plunder, she thought she caught the scent of frying meat. She didn't trust her senses and told herself she had imagined it. Granny had always told her, Old Scratch uses all kinds of trickery to lure a body. Don't never whistle in the woods to call him, and never answer if you hear your name called. Hit's a devilish trick, and you'll not like what happens if you do.

She waited for the aroma of meat to disappear, to have been an illusion, but it didn't. She swiveled her head, looked for the source, realized that she was standing in the middle of the road and visible. She stepped into the weeds at the edge of the creek. When she had reached the opposite bank and turned to look around again, a dog was already there where she'd just stood, hackles raised and growling. *Did he not bark before?* she wondered.

At first, she feared that he was feral, abandoned, had walked in from the strip, but he appeared well nourished.

A shadow moved around the side of the darkened house, lit by the fire that she hadn't noticed before. *The meat must be cooking there*, she thought. She squatted, prayed that the dog wouldn't come for her.

A man yelled, Arlo, what in the hell?

The man moved toward her hiding place, yelled again, Arlo, come!

His voice was a mixture of anger and desperation, and the dog had escalated to barking a bark too large for its body. June flattened herself against the ground, turned her head away from the dog so he couldn't see her eyes. Next came a shrill squeal, then a gunshot, and then the sound of the man's heavy breath. He picked up the silent dog, carried it back toward the fire smoke rising from behind the house.

June pulled herself to her haunches, quivering, kept her head low. Her underpants and the seat of her jeans were soaked with the terror of waiting for the bullet. She knew she couldn't afford to remain there until full dark. She stood, hoping the man wouldn't see her. When she did, she saw the dead copperhead, the mangled arrow of its head, the blood bloom on the sand. Every hair on her body rose again. She thought of the cellar, then remembered the early snow, asked herself, *How could a snake still be crawling this time of year?*

The weeds around her prickled her skin. She got to her feet and ran down the far side of the creek, realizing she had likely stepped over the snake after she crossed earlier. When she was past the bend in the road, she ran harder and did not stop until she reached the green house.

Prayer

JUNE WOKE HUNGRY. THE NIGHT BEFORE, SHE LAY awake remembering the smell of meat cooking up at the head of the right fork. *Had it been rabbit?* She concentrated on remembering only that part but had gone to sleep and dreamed of barking dogs and snakes that crawled in the snow.

Even though she had rationed her food supply, it had shrunken to one can of tuna, a few stale graham crackers, and an inch of peanut butter in the jar.

What has happened? Why doesn't anybody come? she wondered.

She pushed away the anxiety and hunger that attempted to burrow into her belly, put on her shoes, walked out into the drizzling rain of a warmer fall day. She looked down the road—the direction that someone would come to her—then up the road, toward the man, the dog, the snake.

She stepped out of her shoes and carried them across the creek. On the other bank, she stopped to put them on again and moved up the holler.

The headless snake hung from a tree limb in the house's yard—a prayer that June recognized. When she was a girl, she had thought that hanging a snake on a fence or tree was a warning meant for other snakes: Don't come here or this is what'll happen—until Granddaddy told her that hanging a dead snake would make it rain. *Well, it worked for a minute or two*, she thought, knowing that when the sun came out later, that thing was going to start to stink to high heaven.

She watched the man's house until the clouds broke and mid-morning sun showered down. Gnats and flies had begun to bother the flayed meat of the snake's neck. Nothing else in or around the house moved. She thought she caught a whiff of death, and, but for the hum of flies and bees, the songs of oblivious birds, she would have thought she dreamed it all. *Were that true*, she wondered, *when did the dream begin?* Would she then wake to find a newly born Grace sleeping beside her? Would Tom and Ellis still be there?

Inside the house, the man sat on a cane-back chair, watched the wild girl in the weeds by the creek. On the floor around him, wood shavings, and on the upended box by the chair, a whetstone and knife. Because he had overloaded the stove to keep the wounded dog warm the night before, the room was hot in the mid-morning sun, and a rivulet of sweat trickled down his spine. He shivered from the heat of it, lifted the long hair off his neck, and fanned himself. The snakebitten dog at his feet whimpered and flinched in its sleep.

Hardy

JUNE WAS DRAWN TO THE STRANGE MAN UP THE HOLler but didn't understand why. She thought about him all day after she first saw him. He was an unopened letter that called to her. She had planned to stay away the day after he shot the snake, but she traced her way back up the creek toward his house and hid in the weeds. There was so much for her to study on. The night before, she'd thought she heard a truck go up the road, but there wasn't one parked anywhere that she could see.

The first time June came across the man, she hadn't taken a long look at him—had turned her face away from his dog as he walked toward her—but she'd featured him being tall and carrying no extra weight, his hair slicked back from his face. He'd walked like a younger man, had toted the gun with confidence, like one with little memory of missed shots.

She crossed the creek, then the road, and climbed up the incline of the mountain on a tangent that ended just above the man's house. She climbed like a blind person, arms up to catch tree limbs, swatted at barely visible gnats, tapped a stick against rock piles and the rotting mat of leaves underfoot because, after the evening on the creek bank, she didn't trust that they held no snakes.

She crouched behind a rotten chestnut stump alive with carpenter ants, recalled the blanched tree skeleton in the yard at Isom and Bethel's, left behind when the ink blight got it just before she was born. Shag had finally cut it down and chopped it up to use as last-resort firewood. She and Tom had often played on the stump. Then she thought of the tree that Ellis had carved their initials into, and she felt the full length of distance between there and home.

A thread of wood smoke rose from the man's chimney, but there was no sound other than the crows calling out to tell on June. She thought of the jungle in Southeast Asia, wondered about the last thing Tom thought about before he was shot. She hoped he hadn't known what was about to happen. Then she wondered whether he died right away like they said, or was he on his back, as he was in her dreams, looking up into a rainy gray sky or peering through the distant kapok limbs into the blinding sun? Had he heard the hoot owl calling him home?

One of Bethel's church hymns started up in June's head. It had carried new meaning since Tom's death. *Come home, come home, it's suppertime. The shadows lengthen fast.* She knew all the words because Bethel and Rena sometimes sang it in church, and she sometimes joined them, but that day it was Jim Reeves's voice she heard in her head. She pictured her mother's record album turning on the player. Bethel, somewhere in the house, was singing along in a high-lonesome voice. Then she remembered their recent fight.

An ant bite on her leg brought her back to herself. She flicked it away, then looked down at the house again. The man, even taller than she remembered, was standing in the daylit yard, watching her through a rifle scope. Just then, she knew he'd been waiting for her—had seen her that night. He could've shot her before she even knew he was there.

After half a minute, June decided to not run. She had to know. She stood, raised her hands in the air, started down the hill toward him. She moved on wobbly legs, remembered waiting for the bullet before, prayed that he wouldn't shoot her.

She kept her eyes on him, saw that his hair was not dark but shone red in the light of day. It was slicked back and broke atop his shoulders in waves. She judged that he wasn't much older than Tom.

He kept the rifle trained on her until she was a few yards away. When he lowered it, she saw that his eyes were green and framed by brushy eyebrows.

What do you want? he asked.

She tried to control her trembling legs and voice. She took in his size and decided that she needed to avoid riling him.

Don't want nothin, she said, trying to sound tougher than she felt.

She glanced around for a way of escape.

He shifted his weight, said, Who are you?

Even though his voice had become more forceful, June thought she heard the shadow of a tremor rippling beneath it as well.

Who are you? June shot back, trying to level her own voice, then added, Put down that gun and I might tell you.

Cain't, he said. You alone?

As she calculated whether to lie, a river of sweat coursed

down the back of her leg, aggravated the ant bite. She wished she'd had time to mud it but didn't allow herself to move again.

I'm by myself, she said. Then she blurted, I saw you shoot that dog last night.

The man winced, shifted the rifle to his left hand, pointed its barrel at the ground. He said, I never shot no dog.

He motioned over his shoulder and continued, It was snakebit. It's livin and layin right there in the house.

Something in his eyes told June that was true. Her nerves calmed some, but she was still primed to run. No way would she go into his house, but she was thirsty and her whole calf burned.

She rolled up her jeans, twisted her leg so he could see the bite, said, You got any water in that house? Any tobacco for this ant bite?

When he turned and started toward the open back door, she followed a few steps behind, noticed the dirty bare feet beneath the threadbare hems of his jeans. Before stepping in, he pointed to a canvas fishing chair by a sickly rose of Sharon bush and the firepit.

Set there, he said.

Inside the house, the man's voice went tender. She thought he was singing, until she realized he was using his words to soothe. She started to stand back up to run, then the dog whined and she froze.

When he returned with a scrap of rag that looked like something Granny would use for a gnat smoke, she thought, *That ain't gonna help my leg.*

She blurted, My name is June. Will you give me yours?

He hesitated, handed the rag to June, reached into his pocket and brought out a bottle of Bactine. June wiped the sweat off the welt on her leg. The rag was cool, rough from drying in the sun. As he squirted Bactine onto her skin, she caught her breath, stomped her other foot to distract her from the stinging wound.

He studied her, then said, Only my given name. Hardy.

He brought out the cane-back chair, and they sat together by the firepit, him with the chair rocked onto its back legs and leaned against the house, her still on alert, trying to guess where he'd stowed the gun. Each time Hardy stood to go inside to check on Arlo, he let his chair fall forward until its legs thumped on the hard-packed dirt.

He offered her food, and she accepted it, eating the oversalted ham, beans, and corn bread he'd cooked over the fire, swilling the cold soda he brought from the spring. As she ate, each of them told the parts of their stories they wanted known. Beneath their attention lay a deeper alertness, a listening for deception, for footsteps or the sound of a car engine—especially for June.

You're easy to talk to when you're not mad, she said, and, against her better judgment, she told him about everything except Tom's enlistment and death. Something told her to hold that part back.

They sat there together for a long while. Before she left, he said, Don't go hungry. If you need food, come up and get some, but just don't startle me again. He sent her back with the rest of the corn bread.

Hardy's Place

JUNE USED THE EXCUSE THAT SHE NEEDED TO RETURN the Bactine to Hardy. She longed for the company but didn't want to be a nuisance.

The weather had turned cooler, and she had awakened to another dusting of snow. She wrapped herself in a blanket and started up the road.

At the edge of his yard, she could smell the snake before she saw it. Tom had told her that copperheads smell like cucumbers. He said, If you smell a cucumber and you ain't in a garden, get the hell out of there quick.

That snake is well past smelling like a cucumber, she thought. She avoided walking near it, followed the road to the far end of the yard. She stopped and yelled out, Hello, the house! hoped he'd recognize her voice.

When he opened the door, she couldn't gauge whether he was glad to see her. He was cradling Arlo, who, in the light of day, looked to be a mutt with some terrier in him. The skin on his swollen foreleg shone through his fur, raw and angry-looking. She put out her hand to pet him, but Hardy pulled him back, growled, He's hurt and don't know you. He's liable to bite.

June jerked away her hand. Hardy said, I'm sorry. Didn't mean to be so coarse.

They went inside, passed through an empty kitchen into what had been a living room. Arlo dozed on a pile of rags in the corner. The fishing chair June had sat in the day before was folded up, propped in a corner. Hardy set it up for her again, said, I have to bring everything in of a night so it don't look like anyone is here. He motioned toward the back of the house, said, That's why I keep the firewood in the room back yonder.

He said, Be right back, and went outside again.

June scanned the room and wondered whether what she saw was everything he owned. There was a twin mattress, blankets, and a thin pillow inside a hand-embroidered pillowcase. By the front window was his cane-back chair and, around it, spirals of wood shavings. On the opposite side of the room stood a makeshift table. Newspapers, magazines, and warped papers littered its top. Above the table was a calendar from a car dealership in Williamson, some of the dates on it circled in red pencil.

Hardy returned with two Cokes. He opened one and offered it to June. He said, I keep these out in a spring that runs out of the back hill. Keeps things cold as a refrigerator would.

Hardy marveled at the copperhead's being out that late in the year. He said, They sometimes don't go into full hibernation at first. Sometimes they crawl back out to sun themselves, warm up.

But it was almost dark the other night, and cold, June said.

Yep, he said. I fear that means you were right on top of the den.

A picture of her sitting on a mound of writhing, poisonous snakes came into her mind then. She thought of the rattlesnake scene in *True Grit*, how it had terrified her. She made an exaggerated shiver, then laughed and said, God, you're about to give me a heart attack.

She told him about the movie scene.

Cain't imagine a whole nest of rattlers, Hardy said. But copperheads is mean sons of bitches. Aggressive. Chase you right down a road.

Not that one out there, she said, nodded toward the yard and laughed again, but thinking of the rotting snake or any snakes at all had caused bile to rise up in her throat. She took a generous drink of her Coke.

How long have you been here? Hardy asked.

I don't rightly know, she said. I was sick and lost track of the time. Maybe just over a week? Maybe two.

He pointed to the calendar, said, Me, about two and a half months.

June glanced at the calendar. The word *October* was printed on its top page.

The air in the room began to close in on her. Something prickled at her—anger? fear?—and she struggled to decipher it. Whatever it was reminded her of the way she felt as she walked toward Hardy the day he held a rifle on her.

I know I ain't been here that long, she said.

The day they met, Hardy told June he was hiding from the government, but he didn't give a reason. When he'd said, At least a few of us in these hills is allus hiding from the government, the way he had pronounced *always* reminded her of Granny.

Did you kill somebody? she'd blurted.

Aw, now, he said. It ain't like that.

June decided then that, considering that Hardy hadn't

murdered anyone, it probably wasn't wrong to keep his secret, whatever it was. Besides, he knew hers, as well.

Did you sell drugs or hurt anybody?

Nope, he said.

They drank their Cokes in silence. June tried to feature what Hardy was thinking. Finally, he said, Tell me another story. You ever been out of West Virginia?

No, she said, but I wanted to since I was in high school.

She conjured a memory from the near past, although she couldn't think how long ago it actually had been.

She began, I got a uncle in Oregon, and I was supposed to go to New York with my friend Viv.

She described a memory from her fifteenth year, nearly lost in a cavern of time: My Aunt Beauty was sitting in the corner of her couch, knees drawn up and under her quilted housecoat, the end of her cigarette pulsing each time she took a drag. Viv and me were sitting on sleeping bags on the shag rug, leaning against stacked-up pillows. I could see the reflection of the TV light in Viv's face.

On the TV, rain fell on an ocean of umbrellas in Times Square. People milled around, waving to the cameras, or tippin their faces up to the night sky, waiting for the giant shiny ball to begin its slow fall toward the roof of a skyscraper.

Beauty said something like, I'm ready for this year to be gone.

I lifted my bottle of orange Nehi from the coffee table and said, Me, too.

Vivian said, Preacher said it's the end times.

A shiver run through me then.

Bull! Beauty said.

Right then, a wild bottle rocket swirled over the crowd,

then tumbled earthward, like a used-up balloon, the air leaking out of a worn-out year. Viv and me counted down with the announcer until the glowing numbers appeared as the ball fell. Just then, we could not have imagined that in a couple of years, we'd be counting down again, watching a man land on the moon.

When Beauty turned off the TV and went to bed, she left only a hint of cigarette smoke that mingled with the smell of burned popcorn. We lay in the dark talking.

Vivian said, I wish I could go to New York.

Wouldn't that be something, I said. I'll go with you, but I figured we'd be goin to San Francisco on a Greyhound bus. Wear flowers in our hair. I sang that last part.

Viv said, I would, I reckon, but New York would be exciting, too. She sat up, took a sip of her drink, set the bottle down on the table a little too hard. From Beauty's room, the sound of bedsprings—Beauty turning over in her sleep.

Shoot! Viv whispered.

I put my finger to my lips, whispered, Shh, realized she couldn't see me. She went quiet, anyways, but I could feel her breathin beside me.

We lay there silent in the dark warmth of the living room, on Beauty's new green shag carpet. I was starting to feel let down after the noisy mess on TV. I sensed the change of Viv's mood, too.

She whispered, I've got to get out from under my family. I'm tired of taking care of my sisters' kids—of people telling me how to act and what to do all the time.

Viv talked about us graduating, savin up money to catch a bus to New York the day after. We'd be free. We schemed how we'd live in an apartment in Greenwich Village, right smack in the middle of things.

We'll walk everywhere. We'll hang out with hippies. Two years from now, we'll be in Times Square, waving at Beauty from the TV, Viv said.

Lord, I cain't wait, I replied.

See, a few months before, Beauty had taken me to Myrtle Gap to order a new washer from Montgomery Ward's. We ate at Morrison's Drive-In, then saw a movie: *Any Wednesday* with Jane Fonda in it. Mama would have hated that movie and would've killed Beauty if she knew I saw it, but we never told. For days, I savored the glamour, replayed the city sounds in my mind, saw the colors, the things I imagined we would see. Now that Viv had planted the seed in my brain, I could picture myself working in a café or even a theater, buying bagels, pastries, reading fashion magazines bought off the sidewalk, wandering through bookstores. I pictured ridin the Staten Island Ferry, lookin across the harbor to see the Statue of Liberty—to be on my own with Viv, far away from home in a place impossibly alive.

When June had finished, Hardy smiled at her, said, You're a good storyteller.

Thank you. I bet you can tell I have a big imagination. No TV at home, so hearin stories is what I'm used to.

She took a sip of Coke, said, I loved writin them in school.

She remembered Miss Cline then, and her dreams for June, but didn't mention it.

Hardy rocked back the stool, bare feet hardly touching the floor. He caught her staring at them, said, I come nigh unto choppin off a few toes or puttin a bullet through my foot, he said, picking at his thumbnail. He sighed, said, I run out on the draft.

He told her that eight and a half months before, his daddy took him to the station in Logan, thought he was putting him on a bus to the induction center, and even though Hardy meant to go, in the end, he panicked.

My mind and body just wouldn't allow it, he said.

He'd lied to his father, told him the bus was running late and to go on home, had even shaken his father's hand.

Soon as the old man drove away, he said, I picked up my bag and ducked out the back door. Eventually, after nearly starving to death, I found somebody willin to help me.

He described how he'd been dropped off in the holler, and how once every few weeks, the same man brought supplies.

Hardy fetched June a bowl of cold macaroni and stewed tomatoes and a fresh grape Nehi from the spring. She tried to remember her manners and not eat too fast. Although Hardy's explanation for why he was there sent her mind racing, she hadn't pressed him further. Later, he said, I cain't tell you who it is because I need to protect both him and you. If I get picked up by the law, you won't know nothin.

Hardy whistled toward Arlo, who lifted his head and looked around, said, It gets cold up here without no electric. When I first got up here, I like to have froze my hind end off, and I had to find wood ruther than scrounging about the houses. Had to burn furniture and shit.

Arlo hobbled to Hardy, sat down on a bare foot. Hardy said, Must've been late winter when people left up outta here, for there weren't too much wood already cut for the next year. They must've knowed.

He scratched Arlo's ear, said, Now I got a bucksaw, so I can get my own wood if I'm still yet here in a month or two.

He picked up his knife and pointed it at the wooden bird he was carving, then to the shavings on the floor, said, I like to whittle some. It passes the time.

Then he motioned to a box of paints on a makeshift table, an old door set upon cinderblocks, said, I make art for anti-war posters and write petitions for protestors to pass around over at the college in Huntington.

On the table, among piles of scattered paintings, a picture that he'd sketched out on heavy paper. It was good paper and it reminded her of the thick pages in Granny's copy of *River of Earth*. In the sketch was a human skull with a vining flower growing through a vacant eye socket.

These are really good, she whispered.

He said, I never did have no use for fighting anybody atall, especially people I don't have a quarrel with or maybe cain't even see.

I wish I'd known that before, she said. I wouldn't have been scared of you.

Truth is, I was more scared of you, he said. Didn't know what you wanted.

It was then that she began to tell him about Tom, and he'd listened like it was the most important story he'd ever heard. When she said goodbye and began her walk to the green house, she remembered Hardy's calendar and realized that she'd forgotten Grace's birthday. She cried the rest of the way home.

Tarpins

JUNE WAS SICK OF EMPTY ROOMS, NO LONGER FELT LIKE exploring. She stayed close to the green house unless she went to see Hardy. The last time, he'd asked her to move up near him so they could keep each other company, look out for one another, but she was afraid Vivian would come back and not be able to find her. And she didn't want Hardy to get the idea about her that JT had.

Hardy often left food on her porch, things he cooked over the fire: fried chicken, hamburger, or a limp paper plate of cold, peppery fried potatoes and onions. Sometimes he left an open can of peaches or fruit cocktail.

Even though she longed for the comfort of another book, she didn't want to bother Hardy or ask too much of him. The food was plenty, and this day, she would tend to herself, go for a walk, try to find something that interested her.

At the edge of the property, she came upon the upturned shell of a box turtle—*tarpins*, Tom had called them—atop the layer of rotting leaves, her eye drawn to it by the sunlight reflecting off the pool of water inside. No ribs or backbones left, not even the shell bottom, but she knew it was likely nearby, had been moved by the racoon or bird that ate the flesh.

She and Tom often came across tarpins crawling through the woods or yard, in the garden where they'd nibbled halves of low-hanging tomatoes. Some, they carried home, kept them as pets, fed them lettuce and tomatoes for a few days, but eventually ended up tipping the cardboard boxes they'd kept them in, letting them crawl away.

June picked up the shell from its bed of leaves, emptied and studied it. Familiar yellow patterns, narrow streaks of orange against a green-gray shell. Tarpin, she said aloud.

Tom had thought some of the shells looked like human brains, imagined the secrets hidden in their folds. A few times, he'd held one to his ear and listened as if it were a seashell, then told June the secret he heard. Once he'd remarked, Ooh. That one is too good to tell!

He'd carried several tarpin shells home, put them on his bookshelf, and Bethel complained about the stink, faint as it was. He liked to tease their mother about having plenty of spare brains as long as the shells were around.

A cold caul came down on June as she stood there remembering Tom. It wound around her as she thought of Bethel and the fight. She looked around for another sign, lifted the shell to her ear, asked it if Ellis was alive. Nothing came.

She laid the empty shell back into its bowl of leaves, stood, felt her bones humming. She recognized the same agitation she felt from the morning the army chaplain drove up the holler. She spoke aloud to herself again, said, Something's wrong.

Hardy had left a *Myrtle Banner* in front of her door. It was two weeks old and folded open to a story about Grace—how she'd been rescued from the gas station, put up for adoption, then went missing in the flood. *Tragedy*, the headline read.

There was a picture of Grace, younger, taken at the church, embedded in the article.

Hot blood rushed to June's head, pounded her skull, sent sparks through her field of vision. She sat down on the steps and read the story in the glaring light of the sun.

The article stated that some authorities believed Grace hadn't drowned in the flood at all, and since her body hadn't been found, she was likely alive and had been picked up by *person or persons unknown* who had failed to return her. At the bottom of the page, a picture June had never seen. In it, the beaming preacher and Regina, who held a newborn Grace.

June's eyes ached from the harshness of the light. *I should've just given her back to Regina*, she thought. *I cain't take care of her proper.* She sat frozen to the concrete, tried to make sense of the article, arrange her thoughts. *This article is from two weeks ago. The law may have found Grace by now and took her away. Or worse, Sol.*

Tears welling, unsteady in her limbs, she wadded up the newspaper and threw it on the embers in the stove. *I cain't do this no more*, she thought. When the fire settled again, June tossed a canful of water onto the coals, stuffed her coat pockets with some of Hardy's ham and biscuits, decided that she couldn't risk leaving a note. On the living room wall, she used a damp, dead coal to draw an arrow toward the mouth of the holler. Under it, she scrawled, *New York*. If it was Viv who finally came looking first, she'd know what that meant. If it was Hardy, she hoped he'd remember her New Year's Eve story, recognize the meaning of *New York*.

She stepped out onto the porch, determined to go, but she hesitated, rooted by the memory of the dream she woke with that morning. She had been a child again, not more than three or four, sitting on the floor of the house they lived in when Shag was alive. She was looking at a page in the Sears *Wish Book*, yearning for a pink ballerina outfit she saw there, imagining how wearing the leotard and tutu, the tiny buff-colored shoes, would make her feel special and new. Then, Bethel entered the room and sat down in Shag's rocking chair. She pulled June into her lap, and June could smell the butter and cinnamon from the kitchen in her clothes. She leaned in, whispered into June's ear, I love you, Junie, and I loved your daddy Shag. Rena and Tom just as much. I'm sorry. I truly am.

Until she found the newspaper article, June had wondered all morning at the meaning of the dream that had left her longing for home, wondered if Bethel was truly sorry for what she'd done or failed to do.

Up on the strip, the muffled growl of machinery overpowered the songs of birds, the enormous, holy silence of the tipple down the road. A haze hung over the holler, the fall-morning air so unusually warm and thick that she thought that should she catch it in her fist, squeeze it, she could make rain. She closed her eyes, angled her face to the sun, said aloud, I don't know what to do.

She needed to find Grace, to find out why no one had come back to her, but she also longed for the safety of Hardy. When she opened her eyes again, she saw the black Buick coming up the road.

Bethel

I ALWAYS KNOWED I HAD THE GIFT, BUT I DECIDED early to put it mostly out of my mind. I had too much other things to concern myself with. It sometimes woulda come in handy if I hadn't ignored it so. After Tom's funeral was all over and we come back to the house, it dawned on me that bird had warned me of his death, but I just wasn't payin attention to my gift.

I learned them roots and the ways of a granny woman from my mommy and grandmommy, just like they did from theirs, but after I got saved, I used my knowin only in the most desperate of situations. I've seen my share of haints and things that goes unexplained, but I had to put my faith in Jesus to keep us safe, and I tried to do his will, but I'll tell you, honey, I did question my faith a few times after Tom was killed. But I just couldn't study on it too long, for I would've been more bitter than I am.

Mommy come to me last night in a dream. She spoke on signs and wonders and how beautiful it is where she is now, then she told me in her stern voice that it was time to let June come home, no matter what Isom might say. He ain't in much position to be orderin folks around right now, she said.

Before I woke, she pulled me in close and whispered in my

ear, Bethel, you got to find it in your heart to forgive so you can be at peace when your time comes. That girl needs you, and Gracie does, too.

Then she smiled and was gone. I woke with a start, thinkin the kids was all still yet little and I had been sleepin aside Shag again, and I tell you, right then a rush a love come through me so big I didn't think I could keep ahold of it all. Honey, it cut a deep V in the mess of anger and fear I've been packin around with me for so long, specially since the fight with June. I've gone around all day feelin a lightness I hardly recognize, and I'm gonna ask Beauty to take me around to see June again so we can break through this miserable thing atween us.

I don't know if I loved Sol or even Isom in the way I've loved Shag and my babies. I don't think so, but it don't matter now as long as I have the memory of that dream. Tonight, I'll lay myself down once more, alone in this bed without Isom, who sleeps on the hospital bed in the front room, say my prayers, and wish I could dream of Mommy again.

Bathing the Dead

THERE IS NO ONE ELSE TO DO THIS, JUNE THOUGHT. RENA and Beauty had gone to the funeral home over in Belfry to make arrangements, and Watt was up on the cemetery opening a grave next to Tom's. Isom, propped up in bed in the front room, stared out a window at intermittent showers of rain-battered leaves that fell on the yard. June didn't even try to guess what he might have been thinking.

She poured a ribbon of warm water from the teakettle, caught it in the cup of her left hand, watched it spill over into the wash pan, a habit from dishwashing. It occurred to her that the temperature of the water wouldn't much matter to Bethel, that it might as well have been cold.

Isom insisted that they bring Bethel home for a wake, for she always said she wanted that, and after the men from the funeral home picked her up from the hospital, they drove her body directly up the holler and transferred it gently from the velvet-covered gurney to a cooling board on the bed. She had not been embalmed, nor would she be. She'd always said she didn't want "no long drawn-out affair. And don't let them cut on me."

Now, there wasn't much time. They had to get Bethel in the ground. People would have heard the news and would soon come knocking with food and homemade bouquets, and it had been left to June to bathe and dress Bethel before she, herself, had to hide again. *I'll come back and sit with her after they're all gone*, she thought.

She picked up the folded washrag, dropped it into the water. In the bedroom, she set the wash pan on the rug by the bed, where, just then, a puddle of yellow evening light was forming. She wrung the rag then rubbed it across the bar of Ivory soap Bethel kept in the kitchen. She plucked a long red hair—Bethel's—from the dried-out bar. White flecks of soap clung to the ends of her fingers.

June lifted Bethel's left hand and wiped the rag across the palm in the direction of its thin fingers. A warm medicinal smell rose from the dampened skin. She turned the hand over, rubbed a widening circle on its thin parchment, then finished with more slow sweeps toward the fingertips.

That morning, when Beauty had come to her with the news, June thought it would be about Isom's death. They had expected that, and Beauty's shocking words sent a blade through June: June, your mama died early this morning.

As she worked, she thought of last night's dream and made a note to ask Rena what time Bethel dropped to the kitchen floor before Watt loaded her into the truck, her heartbeat already waning. June could not allow herself to acknowledge that they had not spoken since their fight, although it felt as if they had, for there, in her mother's bedroom, she felt an inexplicable peace coming upon her. *It must be why she came to me in the dream*, she thought.

She rewet the rag and wrung it again, wiped the coal tattoo from the day of Grace's birth, closed it over her mother's fingers, let the water soak into the deep creases of the knuckles, the whorled tips and ridged nails where inky shadows had begun to form. She wiped away the ridges of dirt, still there from digging potatoes and carrots yesterday, wondered where Bethel had put her wedding ring when it no longer fit. She pictured Bethel on her knees in the garden the spring before Grace was born, praying.

June pitched the cloudy water out the back door, went to the kitchen for more to wash the rest of her mother: neck, both arms, bruised by emergency room needles, and her stubbled, paper-white legs. She bathed the slack skin of her belly, its diminished stretchmarks echoing her own. Before she turned her on her side to wash her back, she laid her hand on that place in the hollow of her mother's bosom that shielded her broken, worn-out heart.

The pool of light moved farther across the bedroom floor as she worked, and June listened for Beauty's car, back aching from bending and turning the dead weight of her mother's body. Earlier, when they got home from the emergency room, Rena had covered the mirror and stopped the clocks, and then, as June worked in the evening quiet, there was only the sound of water licking the sides of the pan, a fly jarring the window screen, the whisper of the threadbare washrag against skin.

June draped Bethel's body with an ironed sheet, then went back for more clean water to wash her face a second time. A swipe across the forehead, each eyelid, each shallow cheek and its blanched freckles. The porous nose. Behind her right ear, a tiny star-shaped scar she'd never noticed before. When she asked Rena about it later, she'd say that Garvin caused it, had poked her there with a splintered stick when they were kids.

She rolled up a towel and placed it under Bethel's chin to hold her mouth closed, and just like Granny had shown her, she mashed several aspirin and dumped them into a glass of water, then poured it over a clean rag to make a poultice to lay over her face. It would keep the dark color from rising there.

A tube of Isom's Brylcreem lay curled up on the dresser, next to Bethel's hairbrush. June applied some to the wiry ends of Bethel's faded red hair, brushed it, then swiped a bit across her mother's wild eyebrows.

She lifted the sheet off a pair of feet as pale as the legs and as burled and tortured as the beech trees by the creek. She remembered the high heels Bethel wore when she was younger, the faint stink of her blue quilted house shoes, the damp smell of them when she had worn them all day. Unlike her children, she never liked to go barefoot, had walked on her toes to retrieve her shoes if they were out of reach. Thinking of this made June smile.

June bathed her mother's feet, recalled foot washings at church, how odd it had seemed to her at first for people to be so intimately cleaning each other in a church. She rummaged further in the dresser drawer, found a pair of nail clippers, and trimmed the corrugated toenails that indented Bethel's skin, cracked under the steel jaws. While she concentrated, her own loose hair fell from its clasp, trailed across her work, became dampened at the ends as she leaned so close she could see the fine red hairs on the toes.

She rifled through the chifforobe for a blouse that wasn't too stained from Bethel often neglecting to wear an apron when she cooked. Having found a long-sleeved one that would cover the bruises on her arms, June chose a navy wool skirt that

Bethel wore on special occasions. The scent of mothballs rose out of the clothes, and, for a moment, she wondered whether the skirt would be too warm, shook her head to regain her bearings. *The hour is growing late*, she thought.

In the skirt pockets, she found a folded hanky, a cough drop, and a Mercury dime. She tucked the hanky and dime back into the pocket and put the clothes flat on the bed beside Bethel, where they waited like cutout paper doll clothes.

In the bottom of Bethel's dresser drawer, she found, beneath neatly stacked stockings, a newspaper article about the Brewers fostering Grace, exactly the same one that Carrie had mailed to her, and, beneath that, the article about Grace being left at the Esso station. The room began to swim, but there was no time to think on the meaning of what she had found.

Before she put on Bethel's hose, rolled them up just past the skirt hem, she brushed the cold skin of her foot with her palm, then enfolded it as if to warm it. She bent over her mother's feet, lay her forehead against them. Granny's voice came to her just as it had that morning at the bridge: Forgive those who trespass against us.

June thought of Mary then, using her hair to dry Jesus's feet. She let go, wept.

I forgive you, she said to Bethel through her sobs. I forgive you.

Up on Five-Mile

JUNE SAT ON THE FRONT PORCH OF THE GREEN HOUSE. She hadn't wanted to return after the funeral. Rena had doubted that Sol yet knew that Bethel had died, so June risked going to the service.

She had cried a little when Beauty dropped her off, but there was no other choice. Likewise, she'd not seen Grace while she was home on the creek, had thought it better to not confuse her again, but Beauty promised to bring her soon. Together, they had vowed to find a way out of the mess they were in.

Shag and Garvin would know what to do, Beauty said.

June lost herself in the warm autumn sun, the cool wind that stirred the brittle leaves on the barren yard. She thought of her mother, how she had come to June in the dream to let her know that she was alright, and she let herself be grateful, knew she couldn't have lived with her guilt if Bethel hadn't come to her in the way that she had.

In truth, June had been gone only a few hours longer than a full day, and she wondered if Hardy had noticed. *Probably not*, she thought. There was no food on the porch when she'd arrived.

Again, she heard a car coming, slipped back into the house, peeked from the corner of the window. She prayed it was Beauty or Viv, but it was not. The car glided toward the house, a silver minnow flashing in the upstream current, moving with a purpose. June saw the set of red lights on its roof. Black bile rose up into her throat. She crouched on the floor and waited for Canterbury's knock. Time slowed, expanded by her terror. Nothing happened, so she risked raising her head to look through the window. The car had completely passed the house, turned up the right fork. *Hardy!* she thought. June opened the door again, leapt off the porch, ran through the woods toward him.

She kept to the shelter of trees, ran until her throat burned and she couldn't draw breath enough to fill her lungs. Branches raked her face, scratched at her legs and arms. Sweat scalded the newly opened wounds. Just then, she had no thought or fear of snakes or anything else besides Canterbury. She simply ran on a current of adrenaline.

Keep running. Cain't stop. Cain't stop. Cain't stop, she repeated in her thoughts.

She came to the little clearing behind Hardy's house where she'd stood the day he pulled the gun on her. She squatted, peered downhill through the tree trunks.

The back end of the sheriff's cruiser was just visible from where it was parked in front of the house. Its fender glinted in the mid-morning sun.

Canterbury was banging on Hardy's front door.

Be gone, be gone, Hardy, she prayed.

The banging stopped. Canterbury came around the house, shielded his eyes, peeked into windows. He stared into the living room window, backed up, looked again. *The drawings.*

At the back door, he yelled, Hardy Webb, I know you're in this house! Come on out!

Silence.

Hardy, come on! FBI's looking for you. I'll not cuff you if you behave.

More silence.

Communist faggot, he muttered to himself, then he kicked in the door.

After a time, he emerged, carrying Arlo in the crook of his arm like a football. He looked around the yard, then up the hill. June stopped breathing.

Arlo squirmed and barked, struggling against Canterbury's hold. June made herself smaller, feared Arlo or the man would see her. She heard him mutter, To hell with it.

When he had taken Arlo and driven away, she moved a few feet up the hill and waited to hear the car engine coming back up the road, wondered if it was a trap, listened for the sounds of Canterbury's thick body moving through the brush. She squirmed against the razor-sharp stitch in her side, counted, tried to slow her breath.

Where is Hardy? June featured him waiting, too, somewhere above her in the thick trees of the mountain. Finally, she stood and stretched, hoped to hear him coming down the hill behind her.

She knew exactly where she, herself, was, could have found it in the dark, but she was lost, just the same, without Hardy.

The first time Tom ran away from home was when he was ten, after Isom had beaten him for talking back. Tom had left the coal shovel down in the branch where he and June had spent a day trying to make a dam. Tom had remembered it a week later, and when he brought it back home, it had rusted. He tried to clean it with a Brillo pad, then hid it behind the coal stove where it might not be found until cold weather. Bethel had found it, asked about it, and, that evening, when Isom woke up, he took it up and beat Tom's back and shoulders with it. This, after Tom had smarted off and said, It's just a old shovel. It still works.

Tom had been gone for days and later told June he had camped out at the rock shelter. Granny had slipped him food when he came to her door. When he did go home, he didn't speak to Isom for weeks, and Isom hadn't seemed to care, went about his business like nothing had happened.

The next time Isom beat Tom was when he was fourteen and had gotten caught with a *Playboy* magazine that one of the boarders had given him. Bethel found it that time, too, and, once again, gave Tom up to Isom. Isom had taken off his belt and whaled on Tom, who cried, My daddy was a big man, and, you mark my words, someday I'm gonna be bigger than you!

His prophecy was realized. When he left home for the army, he was a full five inches taller than Isom. June had been so proud about that. The next time it happened, Tom wouldn't say where he'd been, but June suspected he was staying in town, for it was winter and he hadn't missed a day of school.

Now, he was lost to her for good. And Ellis was lost, and now Hardy.

Light drifted between the trees. June edged down the hill toward the house. The back door hung cockeyed on its hinges; a half-empty Nehi bottle sat sweating on the cookstove. In the front room, she found empty pop bottles, pencils, Hardy's drawings littering the floor. His open New Testament and the copy of *Desert Solitaire*, by Edward Abbey, sat atop a Missouri Star quilt on the mattress. She gathered the drawings and put them back on the work table then looked around for a note, saw that the rifle was gone from its place in the corner.

Back outside, June climbed the bank to the spring and pulled out the cold drinks, stuffed them into a grocery bag she'd found in the house. She left an orange Nehi for Hardy, so he'd know it was she who had last been there and was waiting for him. Years from that day, a lineman tending lines would spot the encrusted neck of the bottle in the muck and pick it up. He'd lift the bottle to the sun and marvel at its murky, swirling sediment.

June went back into the house for Hardy's bottle opener. She studied on whether he'd likely return right away, and her mind told her no. She grabbed the Bible and the Abbey book and shoved them into the grocery sack, opened a soda, then climbed the hill again, started back through the woods.

In the green house, June made a supper of cold beans and the last grape Nehi. Her stomach began to ache even before she'd finished. She lay on the pallet, fretting, too distracted to read, studying on all that had happened, how her life had shifted in the scant days since the flood.

The loneliness that set in at the ends of those days enfolded her. The next day, when there had been no word from Hardy, she feared that, while she waited in the woods that day, he was caught—or worse—and she hadn't been able to save him. Her belly churned. She could hardly bear it.

In the last natural light, she picked up *Desert Solitaire* and opened it. An endpaper fell out. On it, Hardy's precise lettering:

> *June, I knew you'd soon open this book. Can't help yourself. Phillip has taken me to Canada. You can have*

everything in the house. Keep my drawings and take care of Arlo. I just couldn't bring him. Love and peace, Hardy.

June considered moving up to Hardy's, wanted to feel safe, be among his things, but even though no one had come up the holler since that day, she feared Canterbury would eventually come back and find her there.

She made several trips to carry his belongings back to the green house. She took the drawings, including one of her she'd never seen. She studied it, realized she hadn't often seen her own reflection since the flood, but it seemed he got her about right, captured the way she saw herself—maybe even made her prettier than she actually was.

Hardy's cabinets still held cans and boxes that she packed in the paper bag that had, by then, traveled up and down the road a few times. It had been crisp and fresh from the store when she used it to haul the Nehi. It now looked like a wrinkled, empty tick. She grabbed small, useless things she knew she didn't need, but she couldn't bear to leave Hardy's things behind. When she was done, nothing of him was left there, save a few sticks of firewood.

Even though it was a hot day, she put on Hardy's miner's jacket, tucked the New Testament into the front pocket, pulled on his too-big boots and wore them back to the house, hoped she wouldn't be there long enough to need them.

Inside the green house, June worked to hide her presence. She stashed the food under an old washtub out back, slid the drawings under the mattress, all but the one of her, which she impaled on a tiny nail on the bedroom wall, decided that anyone might think it had belonged to the house's owner. *It won't be long before spiders drape it with webs to make it look that way, anyway.*

She folded the jacket and threw it and the boots onto a high, warped shelf in the closet. When the shoes landed, made thumps, they called up a memory of Isom's boots on Garvin's porch boards.

When she finished, she decided to make one last trip to search for the gun. Surely Hardy couldn't have taken it with him, and Canterbury hadn't found it. She just needed to think where Hardy could have left it.

The night before, after she'd crossed the threshold of dusk, she lay down to sleep, thinking of Grace, as she always did. She thought of Tom and Ellis, of Garvin, and began to picture a scene from *The Wizard of Oz* where Dorothy finds her family gathered around her as she wakes from the dream. But then, June's room was full of ghosts who watched her sleep. After a time, she began to drift, heard herself say to no one, Tomorrow, I'll hunt for that gun. An electric hum started up in her forehead, and just then, she knew she'd never see Hardy again.

She found the gun behind the kicked-in back door and snickered at the picture in her mind: Canterbury blasting that door so hard it drove the doorknob through the wall. Then she imagined him searching the house high and low for it.

June's food store was getting low. She had a gun but didn't dare hunt. The miners on the strip, or worse, someone else, might hear the gunfire. She couldn't risk it, needed to ration her food while she tried to figure how long she could hold out.

Her belly was flat, her jeans threatening to slip off her hips. She wondered if there were fish in the holding pond. *Doubtful,* she thought, *and if there were, they'd probably be poisoned and belly-up, anyway.*

She rifled Hardy's cupboards again, found a Zero candy bar that she'd missed. One end of it had been nibbled away, but she pocketed it anyway and kept looking. Thinking of breaking the ruined end off the bar and eating the rest made her mouth water.

June took to the hillside, scoured the woods for edible plants. She'd run through the undergrowth several times, unmindful of them. Before long, she'd collected fireweed, nettles, and three dried-out morels. Farther in, she came across serviceberries. As she started for the house, she was already building a cooking fire in her mind and realizing she missed her mother, that help wasn't coming. She couldn't go on much longer, and she'd have to make something happen.

Sol

JUNE FELT HIM COMING BEFORE SHE HEARD HIS Blazer. She rifled her memory. How could Sol have known where to find her? Neither Beauty nor Bethel or Viv would have given her up, and she'd been so careful when she was home a few days ago. She had even lain down in the car seat as Beauty drove her out of the holler.

She turned the pot of greens over on the burning coals, and the room filled with acidic smoke. She slammed the stove door closed and waited, a motionless rabbit enraptured by a black snake.

Solomon parked in front of the house, slammed his truck door. June scrambled, took to the woods. He called, I know you're here. Seen your smoke.

June froze again, listened to him yell, heard the front door open and him say to the echoing rooms, Miss Branham? You been give up by your stepdaddy. I had to threaten to whoop his sorry ass to get him to tell.

Something in the ground beneath June's crouched body cracked and shifted. Fury enveloped her like a blanket. Sol yelled again, Isom, that sorry thing, weren't in much shape to argue with me.

He walked back out of the house. She heard him hesitate

before he descended the porch steps. She realized she was weary of running and hiding. She wanted to kill him, to get it over with.

The last thing she heard him say before he climbed into the truck was, I will find you. You're the only one can sign that baby over to me, and I'll whoop you, too, if I have to.

She came to her full height, filled her lungs with air, and ran toward the sky.

She hid in the night-saturated woods until she could no longer stand the chill. A full moon showed her the way back to the green house and Hardy's quilt. And the gun she knew she was going to need. She marveled that she would need that miner's coat so soon.

She didn't sleep, didn't dare start a fire, sat wrapped in the quilt and watched the door. At dawn, she gathered up the candy bar and morels, told herself there would be more food, knew she'd eat it raw from the ground if she had to. The coat and boots in the closet were out of her reach, so she rolled the box of .22 shells up in the quilt but kept out a handful that she shoved into her right pocket. The already-loose jeans sagged under their weight.

Outside, she lifted the rifle from the well, where she had suspended it, barrel down, from a length of old clothesline threaded through the trigger guard and attached to the lid hinge. When she pulled it up, there was moisture on it, and she knew that Tom would have scolded her for that.

The strip above her was quiet. *Must've been a breakdown or holiday*, she thought. She headed toward it, thinking she'd have a good vantage point and that Sol wouldn't expect her to be there.

Three-quarters of the way up, she rested on a stump she found in a stand of black locusts, used the quilt as a pad to sit on and pulled its edges around her. Now that she had the rifle, she was a little less afraid. She dozed then started when her body tumbled off the stump. In her panic, she came full awake, realized the full weight of her fear returning, scolded herself for being careless. She rose and started for the strip, carrying the rifle the way Isom taught her. He'd tapped the stock and said, This ain't a toy. Never point it at anyone unless you aim to use it.

The rest of the way up the mountain, June wondered if she could actually kill a person, even Sol. Up until Tom died, the worst thing that had happened was her own doing. She'd put that stray dog down, just like she knew Isom had done with their pets when they were kids.

As she stepped out into the light, she heard the quarreling voices of half-wild dogs. *More strays, and they're fighting over an open lunch bucket.* A plastic bag hung from the mouth of a large cur that looked for all the world to be a purebred English bulldog. The others lunged and snarled at him.

June reached into her pocket then chambered a bullet into the rifle. It was then that she realized she'd left the box of ammunition and quilt in the locust trees. She pulled the bullets from her pocket and counted them. They didn't add up to the number of dogs she could see, but she wouldn't shoot unless she absolutely had to. *That goes for Solomon, too*, she thought then realized how exhausted she was, how desperate to have everything be right again.

She shoved the extra bullets into her pocket, tiptoed back into the brush, and moved parallel to the service road, came out near the sludge pond. The dogs had gone quiet. She leaned against a house-sized coal truck, scanned downhill for the celery-colored house. She didn't find it, but, after a time, made out the word *Store* on the building on the other side of the creek. Once she'd gotten her bearings, she climbed up the high ladder to the cab of the truck, winced at the sound of the rifle barrel clanging on its metal rungs. The ascent was difficult and dangerous. A man Isom had known had been killed when he fell off a similar platform headfirst.

The cab sweltered, magnified the late-day sun. June cracked a window and lay down on the seat, prayed that she didn't fall asleep and suffocate. *I'll be warm enough tonight*, she thought, *but I'll have to leave before daybreak—before the next shift starts.* She knew that she'd long for the quilt, and she did.

The moon rose and illuminated bulldozer blades, the crowns of the trees below. June looked for the grocery sign but couldn't see it. She'd had to pee for some time, willed herself to stay put in the safety of the truck. Then, she could no longer wait. She left the loaded rifle on the seat and the door open behind her, minced down the ladder. When she'd climbed up, she hadn't looked back, hadn't realized how high the cab was. At the bottom of the ladder, she got her jeans down just in time to squat by the tire and pee, listened to the steam as it hit the dirt, then stood to see a flash of color in the brush. *Dog*, she thought and started back up the ladder, quick and careless.

Halfway up, she heard his voice.

These yours? he asked as he rattled the box of .22 shells.

Shit.

She turned to find Sol standing at the edge of the road. She scrambled up into the truck, slammed the door, fumbled for the door lock.

June was scrabbling toward the other door to lock it when she heard his voice again, this time wafting through the open space between the glass and doorframe. She froze, listened to him climbing the ladder, his voice coming nearer. She leaned back against the passenger door and aimed the gun.

When he reached the platform, his breath condensed on the glass.

Can he see the gun? she wondered.

In a quiet voice she'd never known him to use, he contorted his lips, over-enunciated through the crack in the window, Gun won't do you any good without the bullets.

Did I lock that door? she wondered so forcefully he might have heard her thinking it.

That door's locked, she said, the tremor in her voice giving her away. And this gun is loaded.

The rifle nearly rattled the bones of her hand. She steadied her elbow on her outstretched leg. The world fell so quiet that she knew he likely heard her disengage the safety. She tried to settle herself, tried to say the next thing evenly.

One shot to the head is all I'm wont to do.

She didn't know if she believed that, herself. Sol yanked on the door but it stayed put. Locked. June angled her legs, the barrel of the gun to the floor, and moved across the seat toward him.

Sol swiped his hand across the glass, peered more intently. His face was inches from hers, and she imagined she could feel his hot breath. She spoke, hoping he couldn't hear her pulling up the door lock. She said, We've got to get quit of this, Solomon.

I'm agreed, he said. Give up, girl.

He leaned back a little and yanked the door handle again. The truck door swung open and their eyes locked. He gave only a grunt as his body came back and knocked against the truck, then he vanished.

Later, she wouldn't remember how long she sat there before she moved to climb down the ladder, how long the daylight was in coming. She had thought to relock the door before she closed it behind her, slung the rifle over her shoulder, and descended the ladder on wobbly legs. Maybe the company would think Sol had been trying to steal the truck. Canterbury wouldn't even bother to look for fingerprints.

June was emptied out, quivering from hunger, weightless. Halfway down, she turned to look at the ground for the first time. Her eyes fell on Sol's tortured legs, his splayed arms, the sheen of black gob that leaked from his head into the clay and sand. At the bottom of the ladder, she took the box of shells from where he had dropped them on the ground and swiped away her footprints with a tree branch. If she'd looked closely, she would have noticed his open, surprised eyes. By the time she got to the bottom of the mountain, carrying the rifle and Hardy's quilt, the sun was up.

Part IV

Fire

Grace

I STAND IN FRONT OF THE BATHROOM MIRROR AND wipe off my makeup. The awards dinner ran late, and now I feel myself drifting toward the comforting country of sleep. Tomorrow is Sunday, and I'll have the whole day to lounge.

I lean in, study the crow's feet around my eyes, then wipe away the brow pencil I used to bridge the gap in the hairs made by the scar. My scar, my story. I suppose I'm vain for disguising it.

My mother always said people should wear their scars proudly, that they are evidence of survival, especially mine, and, over her life, she taught me the geography of her own wounds.

You sometimes have to hear the story before you can really see the scar, she told me.

And in that yearslong cartography, I suppose she told me as much as she could bear.

All of the people of her stories are gone now, some like ellipses that paused the unraveling—Ellis, my father, and Hardy, even though she said she knew it in her bones that they were both dead. The others lie in the cemetery at the mouth of the holler where she grew up: her father, Tom, Beauty, Isom and Bethel, Granny Justice, and Carrie Vance. Even Solomon

Akers, my grandfather. All of them resting there, among their people, except Mom and Lovell, who lives in a nursing home over in Baker.

We owe everything to Lovell. It was he who wired Mom the money to drive me to Oregon in her Plymouth after she walked out of that abandoned coal camp and came to get me—her with no driver's license, crossing state lines, and me in the back seat, aware that we were flying. He found us a place to stay with a widow who lived on the ranch he ran for her, a little bunkhouse that I grew up in.

My mother told me all she could of my father, and I have no doubt she loved him wildly. I love him, too, and she saw to it that I did, but I have known and loved Lovell all my life, and I tell him every time I visit him. For all practical reasons, he has been my father, and he taught me many things, and for that, I'm ever grateful. On the evenings he came to sit with Mom on the front porch of the ranch cabin, I'd stand in the darkness of the living room, hypnotized by the stories they told, the glow of Lovell's cigarette. Sometimes the stories were hilarious, but often they were full of longing. I once heard Mom ask him, Do you think I might've nudged that truck door a little? Lovell had reassured her she couldn't possibly have done that.

Evenings were often hard for Mom, the gloaming, she called the time between day and night. Her melancholy was worse when it rained and especially near the end of her life. Even in my childhood, I was aware of her staring off, gone to some other place like she was waiting for something. I felt her sadness seeping into me at times, learned to expect it. Then, after it was fully dark, she always came back to me.

We never went back to West Virginia but once. It was when

Beauty died of lung cancer. We flew, both of us for the first time, out of the airport in Portland, where I've come to live in my adulthood. I had to. My practice and life are here. Rena picked us up when we landed in Charleston.

I remember the heavy silence of the empty house, the untended garden, the pink peonies and scrawling dog roses blooming in spite of its disordered and terrible beauty. I felt it would smother me. A few years ago, Rena called to say that the empty house had burned completely in the middle of a winter night. Mom always blamed the coal company. After that, she sold her share of the property to Rena and Watt for half its worth and used that money to put me through school. For years, Rena kept a garden there until they sold it and moved to Florida when Charlie and Wyla left home.

My mother was a tough and stubborn woman—quite stoic—but she loved me with all of her soul. Between her and Lovell, I never wanted for a thing. She could be over-protective at times, but I can't fault her for it. Until she got sick and moved in with me, she called me every evening to say good night and that she loved me.

Mom never married, and I never questioned her about it. She said that I was enough. After I finished my master's degree in child psychology, Mom moved off the ranch into Fletcher, then went back to school and became a licensed nurse midwife. It suited her nurturing spirit, I think.

Mom was content in her little house with central heating and air and the garden out back. Between birthing calls, she puttered there in the warm months, planting pole beans, squash, and Hickory King corn on a mound the way Great-Granny did. She tried to raise coal-camp beans from seeds that Rena sent her in the mail, but they wouldn't grow in the high-desert climate. She gave up and planted seeds she got at the co-op that were simply labeled *Green Beans*. She'd string them up on the back porch to dry then take down the strands and we'd shell the pods. Eating her tomatoes was a spiritual experience, and I'd give anything for one right now.

Her kitchen cupboards and sills were filled with jars of herbs and potions teased from them. Granny Carrie's niece mailed boxes of sassafras and other herbs from West Virginia right up until Mom died.

Mom quilted until she was too weak to push and pull the thread for very long. I'll have to finish the last one she worked on, a flying-geese pattern, someday.

When Mom finally had to move in with me, I brought along her altar and laid it out on her dresser so she could see it from the bed. On it, I kept fresh flowers that I bought from the grocery. Now those things lie on my own bookshelf altar. Sometimes I pick up the objects, a ritual I saw her perform many times: a small jar of dirt from Granny's garden she scooped up before she left, a faded rabbit's foot, once the color of blue cotton candy, a POW bracelet with the name of a man lost to the jungle, and the statue of Saint Joan that she bought when I took her to Santa Fe. When I do this, I swear I can hear her voice.

There is a picture on my bedroom wall that Hardy drew when Mom was just eighteen. He must've drawn her as he, himself, saw her: beautiful, her close-set eyes already tired.

I am thirty-eight years old now, and it gives me pause to think that I am only seventeen years younger than Mom was and that soon, I'll catch up the years and pass her. She died at forty-seven of lung cancer.

Mom wanted to be cremated, her ashes spread over our favorite huckleberry patch in the Wallowa Mountains. She took me there every summer, some seasons lean and some abundant, and we'd pick enough berries to make a fresh cobbler and preserve the rest. She went alone after I went to college, and Lovell and I worried about bears. He urged her to get a gun, but she refused.

She said, I'll not own one. Had one once and threw it down a well.

When the time came, Lovell and I rode in on horseback, with Mom's urn lashed to my saddle horn.

It isn't right that I outlived her, Lovell said as we watched her fine ashes fall over the huckleberry bushes, and that was pretty much all he said the rest of the day.

I carried home an urnful of huckleberries that day. At home, I laid them out to dry then put them back in, placed the copper urn on the sill of the window over my kitchen sink. I think of her, am with her, when I stand there.

I am childless, a conscious choice. That is not to say I haven't been in love or thought of having a family. I just didn't. I work my practice and see my friends, go out to plays and to hear live music. Sometimes I swim or play tennis at the YMCA.

I often go to the movies alone. I prefer it that way because no one else can distract me from the feeling that Mom is with me. She loved films, especially old ones and particularly *True Grit* and any Jane Fonda movie. If possible, I'd take her to afternoon showings that lasted until full dark. I hid her from the melancholy that haunted her. When she got too sick to go to the theater and too weak to sit on the couch, I bought a VHS player and put it in her room. We'd lie there together in her bed, under Hardy's quilt, and watch movies while she dozed in and out.

Mom knew things. When I was old enough to grasp that, I was frightened, but I gradually came to accept it as her nature. She knew Bethel was dying before Beauty even came to get her.

The last few days that Mom was lucid, she told me that Tom had come to see her. And Granny. As she drifted off, she carried on a conversation with them. This is how I learned the story about Mom shooting the stray dog. Aside from that, she often smiled and sometimes giggled. Although that didn't surprise me, it did unnerve me a little, but eventually, I came to believe I could feel them in the room, too.

He's going to prepare a place, she said of Tom.

After that, *her rally*, the hospice nurse told me, she slept more and finally began to drift away. In the few minutes before she surrendered into the final two-hour coma, I held her skeletal, translucent hand in my olive one and counted her erratic breaths. At some point, she tenderly released her grip and stretched her arms into the air above her, reached for something I couldn't see. I held my own breath. Then, in a voice so clear I might have thought she was speaking to someone on the other end of a phone, she called out, Ellis!

Joy flooded the room then, swirled into all its empty spaces. I'd like to think my father walked her home.

Acknowledgments

Thank you, thank you, to Jane Vandenburgh, my friend and spirit guide as I rode the steep learning curve of writing a first, and now a second, novel. You have been a patient and loving mentor and visionary. I love you wildly.

Thank you, Jack Shoemaker, my editor and friend, who "publishes writers, not books," and whose encouragement helped quell my impostor syndrome—mostly. Your infinite grasp of all things literary kept me on the right path after I sent you an earlier "final" draft and you returned it with a recommendation to make it a larger story. You, as always, were right.

Thank you to Yukiko Tominaga and the rest of the crew at Counterpoint Press. You made this process completely seamless and delightful.

Thank you, Rich Wandschneider, who convinced this poet with a fresh MFA to enroll in Jane's yearlong novel workshop. Meeting you has enriched my life in myriad ways. Thanks for being such a good friend and listener.

Thank you, Erin Keane, my *anam cara*. Your careful reading of my drafts and our talks over coffee and toast made the book so much richer.

Thank you to Glenn Taylor, who believed in this book from

the beginning and introduced me to *The Milkweed Ladies.* Your own work continues to sustain me.

Thank you, Brad McClung, cherished brother and my *person*, and Mickey McClung, beloved uncle, for answering my questions on everything from gathering ginseng to treating mange. Thanks for paying so much attention when we were kids.

Thank you to the Hindman Settlement School and the Oak Ledge Writing Residency for the time in Mr. Still's cabin to rein in this manuscript. It was a privilege and a wonder to work at his desk, surrounded by his books, and I swear I felt him there every time I sat down to work.

Thank you, Djerassi Arts, for the time and space to begin the manuscript while hosting me on the foggy, magnificent California coast.

Thank you, Robert Stubblefield, my longtime friend. You gave me the initial exercise that became this book and advised me to break the reader's heart and then make her whole again. I hope I did.

Thank you, Colleen Anderson. You graciously educated me on the experience of being a VISTA volunteer in Appalachia in the 1960s. West Virginia is so lucky that you stayed.

Thank you, Amy Zahm, for allowing me to use your little cabin on Chief Joseph Mountain when I was desperate for a week of wood fire, snow, and enough silence to smooth out the rough edges of the story. And thanks to Henry and Charlee, too.

My deepest gratitude to Wendell Berry for the words that gave me encouragement and a purpose to keep writing this story.

And finally, thank you, Dana, for supporting me through

this miraculous process. You were new to living with a writer, but you championed me, loved me, and gave me the time and space to stay in my head while the story told itself. Thanks for building my studio. I love you big.

PAMELA STEELE is the author of *Paper Bird: Poems* and *Greasewood Creek*. She has been awarded residencies and fellowships by the Djerassi Resident Artists Program in Woodside, California; the Oak Ledge Writing Residency from the Hindman Settlement School in Knott County, Kentucky; the Jentel Artist Residency in Banner, Wyoming; and Fishtrap's Gathering of Writers in Joseph, Oregon. Steele lives on a ranch in the high desert of Eastern Oregon.